THE ROAD TO

KALAZAD

THE ROAD TO
KALAZAD

K.L. MITCHELL

Desert Palm Press

The Road to Kalazad
(Kalazad – Book 1)

By K.L. Mitchell

©2021 K.L. Mitchell

ISBN: (book) 9781954213067
ISBN (epub): 9781954213074
ISBN (pdf): 9781954213081

Desert Palm Press
1961 Main Street, Suite 220
Watsonville, California 95076
www.desertpalmpress.com

Editor: CK King
Cover Design: Rachel George

Printed in the United States of America
First Edition May 2021

Dedication

The author gratefully acknowledges Desert Palm Press, her editor CK King, a lifetime of great English teachers who showed her the way, and the marvellous Wendy T.

This book is dedicated to the memory of Kassidy Diane Luck."

Chapter One

"WELL," SAID THE MARE, "That could have gone better."

The clearing stood a little way off the main path, a quiet haven of grass and sunlight. The trees were thick around, this being the old style of forest you just don't get these days, and quite hard to find except by accident. For a long moment, mount and rider held still, ears pricked for sounds of pursuit, but there were only the faint background noises of nature going about its business. After a few tense minutes, it was clear that they were no longer being pursued, and the centaur – for that is what she was – allowed herself a word.

Her rider dismounted and stretched, twisting her back this way and that. "Well, how was I meant to see that coming?" she asked. "You see a screaming lady being chased by a bunch of nasty looking types, you don't immediately think, 'Oh, look. A sorceress being chased out of town because she cursed everybody's pigs.' I mean, do you? It's sure not the first thing that comes to my mind." She flopped down on a nearby fallen tree, wincing at the sudden tenderness.

"You might at least have asked." The centaur lowered herself to the ground, grabbing a handful of grass and chewing thoughtfully. "Instead of just galloping us in all helter-skelter and attacking everyone. And that 'Fear not, fair maiden' stuff, where on earth did you get *that*?" She scrunched her face up. "Ugh."

"Hero talk." The rider was busy unlacing her boots, which was proving to be unusually hard going. Perhaps the best way to describe her is to imagine the sort of barbarian warrior woman you get on the cover of certain fantasy novels, then drop her in the woods for about a week and a half without so much as a wet comb to keep her company. "Anyway, I didn't hear you making any suggestions."

The centauress shrugged. She was tall and sturdily built, with the telltale muscular build of a Percheron. Her chestnut pelt blended so smoothly into her dark skin that it was rather difficult to tell where one ended and the other began, if you weren't looking closely. She watched her companion with the mildly amused indulgence which only comes from having someone ride around on your back all the time. "I thought you were supposed to be the brains of the outfit, Revka, remember?"

She looked around the clearing, frowning. "I wish there were apple trees around here. Or some berries, at least."

Revka snorted. "I don't know what you're complaining about, Iyarra. At least you don't have to go hunt your food."

Iyarra tugged up another handful of grass. "Sure, but have you tried the grass here? It's got no flavor."

"Well, that's not—" she blinked. "Wait, what do you mean it's got no flavor? It's grass. It's grass flavor. Er, isn't it?"

Iyarra shook her head. "Not really, no. I mean, there's grass and there's *grass*. Remember when we were going through the Eyre Plains? Now *that* was some grass. I wish I'd brought some with me. I'd almost kill for a patch of it right now." She munched another despondent mouthful, looking around.

"Not even any clover or anything," she muttered.

Revka finished tugging off the other boot and stretched out her legs. "All right," she said. "I'm going to hunt something up. Should be a fair few rabbits and such around here." She moved over to Iyarra's saddlebags and pulled out a small crossbow. "That patch over there would make a good firepit when you're done eating." She selected a few bolts and headed for a break in the trees.

"Look, if you find any apples..." Iyarra called out, but Revka was already gone.

***

Later that evening, Revka slowly turned a rabbit's carcass on a spit over the fire. She leaned in and inhaled. "Oh, that's just perfect, right there." She carved off a hunk with her knife and tasted, eyes closing in bliss.

"Beats me how you can eat that stuff." Iyarra was munching some wild strawberries that Revka had brought back with her. Around their makeshift camp, the woods were busy with the chirrups and hoots of the night creatures.

"Aw, what do you know? You got a horse stomach. You can't appreciate the finer things in life." Revka sliced another chunk of meat away. "Anyway, admit it. We've never had it so good."

Iyarra shrugged. "Well, I wouldn't go that far. At least back on the farm I knew where my next meal was coming from." She looked down at the bounty in front of her. "Mind you, these *are* good strawberries. We should grab some before we leave tomorrow."

Revka grinned. "See? I never said it would be more comfortable, but you have to admit life is a lot more interesting these days. I'm sure it beats hauling a plow all day, right?"

"Oh, yes. Hardly anyone tried to kill me back then." Iyarra ducked as a rabbit bone flew rapidly past her cheek. "Okay, okay. Yes, it's nice. Not quite what I expected, but it's definitely been an experience."

"You, uhm...you glad you came?"

Iyarra moved behind Revka and gave her a firm hug from behind. "Yes. Yes, I am."

Revka laid an uncertain hand over Iyarra's. "Even when things are...not so good?"

Iyarra took Revka's knife and set it aside. She tilted the woman's head back toward her and touched soft lips with her own for just a moment. "Even then."

Revka sagged a little, leaning back against the horsewoman. "I'm glad," she whispered. "I worry about it, you know. Taking you away from your home and your job, off to make our living on the road and all that...I wouldn't blame you if you were upset, you know. Wanted to go back, and..."

"Hey, hey." Iyarra cupped Revka's face in her hands and smiled down at her. "I wouldn't have come with you if I didn't think it was worth it. Every little bit of discomfort is still better than spending my days sitting on a farm and being worried sick about you out here in the middle of nowhere."

Revka leaned her cheek against Iyarra's. "You're too good for me."

They held each other a quiet moment, then...

"Iyarra?"

"Mm?"

"Is that your hand?"

There was a muffled thump as Revka's leather breastplate slipped to the ground.

Afterward, Revka nestled against Iyarra, resting her head on her withers and staring up at the sky. The stars were just visible through the gap in the trees. If she concentrated, she could hear the centauress's heartbeat. She stretched like a cat, took a deep whiff of the musky scent, and watched the fire until she drifted off to sleep.

***

3

It was a little after dawn when Revka, in response to Iyarra's persistent nudging, stirred. She grunted, rolled onto her back, and batted away the business end of a spear that was brushing against her face. There was a moment of stillness, and Revka woke up really, really quickly.

There were about nine of them, all told, centaurs and men on horseback. They were dressed in uniform leather and mail, and each held a very nasty looking spear. Revka noted at least three spears were hovering about an inch from various parts of her body, so she kept absolutely still. Beside her, Iyarra, arms bound behind her, glowered at their captors.

One of the men on horseback slid to the ground. He peered at the two for a long, almost calculating moment, then he nodded. "Right, this is them. Let's go."

"Excuse me."

The senior officer turned and brought his gaze down on Revka. "You had something to say?"

"Well, *yes*." She managed to sit up. The spears moved just enough to let her do so. "Just who are you, anyway? What is this about?"

"We serve our employer, who has requested your presence. That is all you need to know right now. We have been advised to bring you in, whole if possible, but you would be amazed what can heal with time. Now, was there anything else?"

Revka looked at Iyarra, then down at herself, then back up to the commander. "Actually...do you think we could be allowed to put our clothes back on, first?"

***

"I hate clever soldiers," Revka muttered to herself. They sat in a drafty, stone corridor surrounded by guards. They had been about two hours traveling over the main forest road, with Revka tied hand and foot and slung over the back of the leader's horse. She had offered to ride on Iyarra, but this suggestion had been politely declined (so much for *that* plan). Iyarra herself had been secured between two guards, also centaurs, her legs hobbled against anything above a walking pace (and so much for *that* plan). Feigning illness hadn't worked, and neither had asking for a rest stop. Neither had bribery, nor seduction, nor trying to grab the guard's knife out of its sheath with her teeth. In fact, the guards seemed to have no idea about how guards ought to behave.

They just carted them along, hardly saying a word and keeping them quite secure all the way up to the stone castle in which they now found themselves. It made you cry; it really did.

It was about twenty minutes by the hourglass, when the two were finally ushered into a surprisingly small room. A middle-aged man sat behind a desk. Thin and dapper, he had a clerical look about him; certainly, nature had seen fit to give him a natural tonsure and the sort of beaked nose that practically begged for pince-nez. His mustache and beard were small and neatly trimmed. Overall, he gave an impression of the sort of person who goes to bed at night tired but wreathed in the certain knowledge that the place would fall apart without him. He continued to read from a paper in silence, only occasionally glancing at them. When he finally spoke, his slightly nasal voice matched his other features.

"Revka of the Three Wolves clan. A bit far south, aren't you? Well, probably the milder winters. I quite understand. Iyarra Brings Plenty, out of Toth Fairmane of the Greatfoot. I believe they hail from the red plains, don't they? Ah, yes. It says here. Now then, it seems about a year ago, you both departed the Stonewall area in a bit of a hurry, not even a note. Since then, you have hired yourselves out as bodyguards and security escorts. I see some busking here and a few accusations of petty larceny. Ah, and one rather novel wrestling act that I understand was quite the talk of the Amber Ridge harvest festival, before the sheriff intervened. All in all, quite a busy year for you both."

Iyarra blushed, not answering. Beside her, Revka glowered. "Yeah, but nothing that would justify being dragged here at spearpoint, or is that just how you do things around here, Mister, uh…"

The clerk's facial expression didn't change. "You may call me Mister Treadwell. In point of fact," he said, "we brought you here to offer you an exciting opportunity. Well, two exciting opportunities. Granted, one of them involves being hanged for horse thievery, but I suppose that could be considered exciting. Briefly anyway."

Revka snorted. "Look, I don't know who's been telling you all this, but if they don't have any proo—" She stopped. Her face slipped from rage to puzzlement and back to rage with commendable speed. "Hang on. *Horse thieves?* You think we were… But we… I mean come on! Why would we even do that? For pity's sake, Iyarra is…is…"

Beside her, Iyarra had started scraping her right front hoof in a rough circle on the stone floor. Revka squinted at Iyarra and leaned over to catch her eye, but the centaur bit her lip and looked away.

Revka sighed. "All right," she said. "What is he talking about? And don't say nothing. I know you. What's this about horse thieving?"

Iyarra shuffled some more and gulped. "Well," she whispered. "You remember when we met? The job I had at the farm?"

"Yeah?"

"It wasn't just a job, Revka. I was...well, I was..." The rest of the sentence trailed off into mumbles.

"You were what?"

Treadwell leaned forward. "Indentured. She was indentured. Only had two months left, too. If only she had waited she could have gone, free and clear, and with a small separation purse to boot. But to break an indenture is, in the eyes of the law, the same as stealing. Since Miss Iyarra here was brought on as a farm horse, well I'm afraid the law is very clear in the matter. There have been precedents, you know. Most unfortunate, but you really must look on it from the poor farmer's point of view. Have you ever seen gallows fitted for a centaur? Quite unusual. They have this remarkable—"

"Now, just wait." Revka turned to Iyarra. "How did you wind up indentured?"

Iyarra shrugged. "It was my first time away from the herd. I didn't know much of the world, and frankly, by the time I got to Stonewall, I was in pretty bad shape. I was desperate for work. Farmer Green said he'd take me on, but as I was unskilled, it would have to be under contract. I pretty much would have agreed to anything at that point. Anyway, it was only for three years, and I did learn a lot. Then one day, he had me hauling goods into town, and you were there, and well, you know."

"Well, sure. But you couldn't have told me? I would have waited."

"I was afraid you wouldn't have. I'm sorry, I really should have told you, I know."

"Quite," Treadwell cut in. "But the fact of the matter is she didn't, and now here you are. I believe Stonewall is only a few days' journey west. We can have you there in a matter of—"

"All right, all right." Revka sighed and leaned back in her chair. "How about you tell us about the other exciting opportunity."

The clerk smiled. "What an excellent idea."

***

The three of them stood around the clerk's desk, which had been more or less covered by a map of the kingdom. "Now then, we are here at Castle Lonngren of the Duke of Gainsburgh, whom I serve. Over here are the Icarine Mountains." His finger traced from the middle of the map rightward, almost to the very edge. "At the base lies the village of Tam. Tam primarily exists to serve the needs of the Kalazad, a cluster of monastic orders that are spread through the various mountains. We are particularly interested in the order Kalazad-Faan.

"Now, this order is there for the usual reasons: meditation, study, holiness, and so on. It has recently come to light that they have possession of a certain artifact, a stone jar." He lay a piece of paper down over the map. The watercolor depicted an old jar, etched with age and carved from a single chunk of bluish-gray stone. The lid, also stone, was sealed to the jar by a band of metal. "To the order, this jar is simply a curiosity of bygone days, nothing more. We have reason to believe that it is, in fact, very dangerous indeed. If the contents were ever released they, that is to say the monks, would suffer greatly."

"We cannot alert them to the fact, as they will no doubt see it as their holy duty to guard the wretched thing themselves. And we cannot buy it off of them, as they are notoriously reticent about letting go of even their most trivial relics. Therefore, and entirely for their own sake, we must remove it from their care."

"You are to proceed to Tam. Take the mountain trail up with the weekly supply carts, whereupon you will scout out the place, find a way in, and remove the item with as little fuss as possible. This being a monastery, I cannot imagine it is a bastion of security. You should be able to get in and out quickly, and above all, quietly. You will return here and relinquish the artifact to me. At which point, His Lordship, the duke, will be more than happy to pay the remainder owed on your indenture, as well as some nice financial remuneration for you both. You will travel on the duke's warrant, so your reasonable food and lodging costs will be taken care of. Any questions?"

"Yeah, I got one." Revka looked up from the map and glared at the clerk. "Why us? I mean, you've got no shortage of guards and soldiers and so on running around here. Why not send a few of them?"

Treadwell shook his head. "That would never do. The guards and soldiers are...well, straightforward. They are rough, headstrong types. They know fighting, and they know guarding. What we need are experts. People with finesse. People with a very specific set of skills that can be counted upon to perform a delicate job with alchemical precision."

Revka blinked. "R-really?"

The clerk looked them over for a long minute. "No," he deadpanned.

"In point of fact, you are here for exactly three reasons. One, you have just enough ability to pull the thing off without mucking it up completely. Two, you really have no choice. If you value your lives and freedom, you will do exactly as we say. And three, not to put too fine a point on it, you are expendable. The actual job is quite simple, but the journey there and back is long. There are areas which are not safe, road patrols or no. We would really prefer not to risk some of our highly trained and well-equipped guards when we've got you two handy. Oh, don't worry, we have some extra armor in our stores for you and a few weapons that can be returned to serviceable condition in no time at all."

"I see," said Iyarra, "Thank you. I think that takes care of everything."

"Actually..."

Iyarra froze. "Oh, no."

"Just speaking hypothetically, what would happen if we were to, y'know, take your nice weapons and armor and gallop away in the opposite direction, never to be seen again?" Revka asked. Beside her, Iyarra slapped a hand over her eyes and muttered something unpronounceable in Low Equine.

"Ah." Mister Treadwell smiled mirthlessly. "Very conscientious of you to mention the possibility. You will be pleased to hear we have taken that into account. Gentlemen?"

***

There was movement behind them. Revka and Iyarra felt a sensation of hot and cold all at once that spread out from their left shoulders. Two men in red robes stepped back into the shadows, as Revka and Iyarra looked down at their arms. A blue and silver sigil adorned each left shoulder like particularly sinister tattoos. Iyarra gasped.

The clerk smiled. "I suppose I should not be surprised that a Greatfoot would recognize a curse-mark. The one you are wearing now is quite a good one, developed by our court sorcerers and sealed with the sigil of Milord's house. It will lie dormant for two months before it begins to eat away at the flesh. I suggest you get back here before that happens. We estimate that, even with poor traveling conditions and a week at the monastery, you should return with several days to spare.

"Not that I would take that for granted. Sometimes the curse tends to leak in a bit early. No one knows why. I wish they'd fix it but alas, your best bet is to conclude your business and return here as soon as possible.

"Now then, I believe that is all for now. You will be fitted for your armor later this afternoon and will depart in the morning. I wish you the best of luck on your journey. The guards will see you to your room."

After they had been marched out, the clerk turned back to the map, studying it over. Well, well. The field people had certainly done their job thoroughly; the two were exactly as advertised. *This should go well.* He allowed himself a brief smile, then reached for the small bell on his desk.

In answer to the ring, a guard put his head around the door. "Yes, sir?"

"Kindly tell His Grace that they will do nicely. They leave tomorrow."

"Yes, sir. And the others?"

"All in good time. Now, off you go."

***

Revka leaned back against the wall in their room. "I said I was sorry," she muttered.

Iyarra looked up. "I didn't say anything."

"You didn't have to." Revka fidgeted with the corner of her new breastplate. They had been given complete sets of used—but still quite good—armor of leather and chain, with insignia in the ducal colors. It was much better than the makeshift armaments they had been using, but they did take some getting used to. The tunic itched.

Iyarra sighed. "Look, they almost certainly would have curse marked us, regardless. These are not nice people, and they clearly thought this whole thing through pretty thoroughly."

Revka nodded. "True. I can't imagine how they knew all of that about us."

Iyarra shrugged. "So, what do we do?"

"What can we do? We just go there and try to get this thingamabob and get back before our skin falls off. I don't like it any more than you, but I don't really see that we have a choice."

"Well, they could have gone about it nicer, you know? All that talk about us being expendable. I mean, I was having a bad day already. They didn't have to say that."

"Yarra?"

"Mm?"

"Do you believe what they told us? About the jar?"

"What, that it's dangerous and they want to have it here out of the goodness of their hearts? Shouldn't think so. These are not altruistic people we're dealing with here. It's probably full of gold or gems or something. Or maybe it has some sort of old magic in it. You mark my words: as soon as we get it back here, they'll probably smash it right open."

"Suppose you're right."

"I mean...we are going to make it, aren't we?"

"Oh, sure. That's only a couple of weeks either way. We should be able to do it. I don't know about you, but I don't intend to let grass grow under my feet."

"Well, that's all right then." Iyarra lay out on the straw that served as a bed. "Anyway, we should get some sleep. They're probably going to want us out of here first thing in the morning."

Revka stretched out on the floor next to her. "All right," she said. "Blow out the candle, will you?"

For a long time, Revka lay in the dark, listening to Iyarra's gentle snores. *That's always the way with Yarra. Always the sensible one.* Revka liked to think of herself as a cool customer. Deep down, she knew that, compared to Iyarra, she was an impulsive fool. She sometimes wondered what Iyarra saw in her. It was a mystery.

She pulled a blanket over herself and curled up in a bundle, waiting for sleep to come.

***

Dawn broke early, too early. Iyarra stamped her hooves on the courtyard paving stones, willing herself awake. There had been a rushed breakfast. Now, as the sun was just pushing its way over the horizon, she was being loaded down with necessities for the trip. At least they had thought to reshoe her, so there was that. Revka had been corralled by Treadwell, who was giving her last-minute instructions.

"You follow the coach road all the way to Peccaray. That will take you to the lake district. Take a water ferry across and head east. At Dundin, the road curves south around the plains. Follow it past Kenning and east through to Port South and the River Ataqua. Follow the river upstream, northeast to Port Mill. From there, follow the pilgrims' path to Tam. On the way back, just follow the same route in reverse. Do you understand? It's all marked out on the map."

"Yeah, yeah, got it." Revka gazed uncertainly at the route. Now that she looked at the map, it was quite a trip. It was going to take a pretty good pace for them to get there and back in time. She glanced over at Iyarra. She was standing in the middle of the courtyard, loaded up and ready to go. The morning sun caught her silhouette in that particular way it sometimes did, and Revka sighed. Iyarra's people were gentle and wise and steadfast in even the worst circumstances, but they tended more toward strength and endurance than speed. Well, she could get them there, no problem.

Probably.

"It would appear your, er, partner has been prepped and loaded. I suggest you depart at once. Here are your letters of transit and travel warrants. Just show these at any inn, and they should take care of your dinner and lodging. Do not lose them. Here is a small purse for incidental expenses. Now then, any questions?"

Revka shook her head. She crossed the courtyard to Iyarra, gave her a pat on the flank and boosted herself up. "All right, we'll be back with your jar before you know it. Just make sure your magic guys are ready to get these curse things off of us."

The clerk nodded. "Just make sure you return with the jar. Now, off you go."

The clerk and a half dozen guards watched as the two rode out of the gates and into the morning sun. He looked up at a certain window in the main keep. A shape moved within. He bowed his head slightly and headed inside.

About an hour later, and with rather less fanfare, there was another departure from the castle by way of a hidden exit farther south than the usual gate. That was all right: they were moving very quickly indeed.

Chapter Two

THE MORNING PASSED QUICKLY. The pace helped along by the prospect of a new adventure. Even if they hadn't exactly volunteered, it felt nice to have a goal in mind. Revka even seemed fairly upbeat, as they made their way through a thickly wooded area. The road carved wide through the forest and made a nice, easy trail to follow. Iyarra took it as quietly as she took most things, but even she seemed to be trotting a bit more than usual.

"You know what I think it is?" Revka chewed on a blade of grass she had plucked a few minutes before. "I bet it's some super holy relic with powers or something. Like maybe it's a mummified hand, and if you hold it and make a wish it comes true, right? Something like that."

"I suppose it could be," Iyarra shrugged in a noncommittal way. She was never one to engage in idle speculation at the best of times, but something in her voice caught Revka's attention.

She leaned forward. "You okay?"

Iyarra kept going, not bothering to look back at her rider. "Revka, what do you think is going to happen if we succeed?"

Revka blinked. "Well, assuming we give 'em their magic trinket, they'll take these stupid curse-marks off of us and we can get out of there. Or, maybe they'll even have some more jobs for us, once we've proven ourselves. I grant you, they're not the ideal employers, but better them than nothing."

"You think so? I don't think those people are the kind to keep people like us around. We're probably loose ends, in their opinion. We're expendable, remember? It would be just like them to, I don't know, knife us on the spot. Or maybe they'll give us a 'congratulatory feast' and it'll be poisoned. Or maybe they'll just save the expense and toss us in a dungeon and let the curse-marks do the job for them."

"Ugh. You think so?"

"Could be."

Revka sighed, leaning back in the saddle. "Hunh. I may have to think about that a little."

They rode on in silence.

A junction joined their road to another. As they passed the junction, there was the sudden din of a coach coming from the other road at speed. Iyarra hurried to the side, just in time to see a beat-up coach-and-four rocket past them onto the main road. The driver was standing up in his seat, whipping the horses to full speed. "Bandits!" he cried, as the coach shot by.

Revka did a double take. "Did he just say ban—" But Iyarra was already galloping after the coach. Revka groaned and tucked herself down, cinching her arms in a tight hold around Iyarra's waist.

Pumping her arms seemed to help her get up to speed. Iyarra turned and looked back at Revka. "I don't know if I can outrun a pack of bandits. They tend to have very fast mounts."

"Never mind!" Revka shouted, "You just have to outrun that coach!"

"Why's that?"

"Better them than us!"

"Oh. Right." Iyarra leaned forward a little more, picking up the pace.

They pulled up level with the coach, just as they were coming to a smaller side trail that left the main road. The coach headed down the smaller trail. The driver shouted, "This way!" and beckoned them to follow. Iyarra galloped behind, striding easily now that she was up to speed. Behind her, Revka poked at her shoulder. "Uh, Iyarra…"

"Not now. Running."

"Iyarra…? I think you should know something."

"Tell me when we've stopped. I'm kind of busy right now."

"Yeah, but…"

"*Running!*"

After a minute, the coach began to slow down. The horses came to rest in a small clearing, well away from the road. Iyarra stopped and stood still for a moment, catching her breath. The two looked around, ears pricked for the sounds of pursuit. There was only the coachman settling his horses.

"Well, we seem to have given them the slip." Iyarra looked around. "Funny though, you would think we could hear them from here. I wonder how far back they were."

Revka sat up. "Well, see, that's what I was trying to tell you. I glanced back to see how they were coming, and there wasn't anyone there."

"What, not anyone?"

Revka shook her head. Iyarra glared up at the coachman.

"Hey, you up there! What's the idea getting us all spooked about bandits? Where are these bandits of yours, anyway?"

The coachman whistled one sharp note through his teeth. From around the clearing, several hooded figures emerged. The doors and windows of the coach shot open. Suddenly, there were a *lot* of crossbows.

The coachman doffed his cap. "Right here, my lady."

***

"Is it just me," asked Revka, as they sat in the stone hut that served as a holding cell for the bandits' prisoners, "or is this sort of thing happening way too often lately?"

Iyarra stretched herself and gave the door a test rattle. At least they hadn't hobbled her this time, but it wasn't like she was going anywhere. Iyarra had a kick on her that could go through timber, but the walls were stone and the door was iron. All she could do was pace and fret and pace.

"First day out," Revka muttered. "Almost a year we've been on the road roughing it, never had any trouble with bandits. Suddenly we get some decent armor and weapons, and a job with a nonnegotiable time limit, boom. First day. This has got to be some kind of record."

Iyarra leaned against the wall, watching the comings and goings of the camp through the small, barred hole in the door. From time to time, a bandit would glance in and make sure they were still there, then go back to standing guard.

Revka picked a piece of straw off the floor and idly toyed with it.

So, what do you think will happen?" Iyarra finally sat down.

"Oh, sell us for slaves, most likely." Revka shrugged. "You'll probably wind up on another farm. Me, they'll probably send off somewhere to be a house slave or something."

"You think so?"

"Yeah. Though, if it's any help, I'm sure we won't be slaves for very long."

"Really? That's good." She noticed Revka's meaningful glance at her arm.

"Oh, sure. No more than a couple months. Maybe less."

"Oh. Yeah."

"Can't believe we fell for that." Revka sat back and sulked.

"My fault. I get running and that's it. Mom always said I couldn't think and run at the same time. Guess she was right."

"Sounds like a wise woman."

"Oh, she is."

Revka hauled herself to her feet. Above her, a modicum of sunlight came through the bars of the window. She grabbed two of the bars and hauled herself up. She swung herself around, bracing herself and tugging as hard as she could. Nothing. The bars didn't so much as budge. Great.

She dropped back down again. "Any ideas?"

"Not a one, sorry."

"You know what we could do? We could wait for the bandits to bring us our dinner, then overpower them. I bet you could buck any one of those guys into next Tuesday."

Above them, a small hatch opened. Two large chunks of stale bread and a sack of water were thrown in. The hatch snapped shut again.

"Oh."

Iyarra tossed one piece of bread to Revka and started munching on the other. The waterskin was passed, and the two ate in silence.

"Okay," said Revka, "Here's my plan. We'll probably be too closely guarded to do anything until we are sold. But with any luck, we can escape from wherever we're sent and head back to the duke's castle and explain. Whoever gets there first waits for the other, then we can try again. What do you think?"

"It's a good plan, dear."

Iyarra sat in a soft spot in the hay. After a while, Revka scooted over to her side. They sat for a long time, gazing up at the tiny window above, watching the sky outside grow dark, and listening to the voices grow faint.

"Yarra?"

"Mm?"

"Why didn't you tell me about the indenture?"

The horsewoman sighed and fidgeted for a moment. "Well, I didn't want to worry you, if I'm honest. I kind of hoped nothing would come of it. Or he'd just be mad and that was it."

"Well yeah, but running away like that! It was sweet, but I just don't understand you doing something like that." She half grinned. "I thought I was supposed to be the reckless one."

"Well, you said you were getting ready to leave town, and I was afraid that maybe I was never going to see you again."

Revka sat up, and hugged Iyarra from behind. "Oh, for pity's sake," Revka said. "I'd have come back. Hell, I woulda stayed if you'd wanted me to. Get some short-term work, you know."

Iyarra leaned back into the embrace, letting her eyes close. "I'm sorry. I'm just...well, I'm new at this stuff and wasn't sure of what to do. And my people? We...well, we tend to follow our hearts. So I did."

Revka, for once, didn't say anything. She just gave the centaur an extra squeeze. They stayed together in the quiet for a long time and gradually drifted off to sleep.

In the camp, torches were put out, one by one. A few sentries were stationed, and the bandits went off to sleep. The camp fell silent and dark. Just outside the camp, a patch of that darkness swore quietly to itself and got to work.

* * *

Iyarra stirred, throwing an arm in front of her face to block out the morning sun. She stretched herself out, blinked a couple of times, and looked around in mild confusion. Revka was next to her, curled up and snoring lightly. Iyarra carefully brought herself to her hooves and peered at the cell door in half-awake bemusement.

It was open.

Cautiously, she peered outside. The camp seemed awfully quiet for this time of morning. By now people should be stirring, shouldn't they? She tried to nudge the door the rest of the way open, but it was blocked by the inert form of a bandit who was standing guard. Had been anyway. This was apparently no longer the case.

A minute later, she was shaking Revka awake. "Get up, get *up!*"

Revka groaned and hauled herself up. "What? What is it?"

"It's the camp! Someone's been here in the night! Revka, everyone's dead!"

Revka rubbed her eyes, stumbled to the door, and peeked outside. After a moment or two, she leaned against the door jamb and muttered "Damn, we're *good.*"

A brief inspection showed the camp was now indeed devoid of life. They moved from hut to tent to firepit, checking for survivors. Everywhere the result was the same. Every one of the bandits was dead.

"You see this?" Iyarra nudged one with her hoof. "The ones who were asleep got their throats cut. The ones who weren't were strangled. Look, you can see the marks around the neck."

"And always far away from a torch," Revka noted. "They got 'em in the dark, every single one." She reached down to a body, drawing a knife from its sheath. "Not one of them had their weapons out, either." She seemed to be speaking to herself. She eyed the weapon, turning it over in her hand.

"What are you doing?" Iyarra said. "We need to get out of here!"

"Not just yet, not just yet. Those bandits have our armor and supplies around here somewhere. I'm not going back on the road in my underwear, thank you very much. Besides, there might be some extra stuff. This is a good knife. You want one?"

Iyarra trotted after Revka, who started checking each hut in turn. "But Revka! What if...whoever did this...what if they come back? And we're still here? What if they kill us?" She pawed at the ground, glancing over her shoulder.

Revka sighed. She put down the knife and reached for Iyarra's hand. "Iyarra? Iyarra. Look at me. Listen. They're not coming back. Whoever they were, they're done here. Even if they did, there's no reason to believe they mean us any harm. They opened the door, right? If they wanted to kill us, they could have done it then. But they didn't, did they? Did they?"

Iyarra sniffed. "N-no?"

"That's right. Probably they were from one of the coach companies. They send people out after bandits, you know. I expect they didn't want to deal with dragging us back with them and everything, so they just set us free and left it at that. Now, help me find our armor."

In the end, they found it in the largest hut, in a chest at the foot of a surprisingly large bed. The coach driver was there, or at least, most of him was. Presumably, the head had gotten misplaced somewhere.

Chapter Three

THE SUN WAS HIGH, and the morning chill had burned off by the time the two were back on the road. Revka was sulking.

"I can't believe they didn't even have a decent hoard. I mean, they're bandits."

"*Were* bandits."

"Were bandits. Yeah. Obviously, they were organized. I know we couldn't have been their first victims. There should be, like, lots of bags of gold and armor and jewels and a mystical sword that goes *ting* when you hold it up to the light. I mean, if you're not gonna have a big, giant hoard, then what on earth is the point of being a bandit in the first place?"

Iyarra navigated her way around a small convoy on the road. This consisted of several grath, large insects, horse like in size and general shape. Their carapaces shone rainbow hues against the black, as their hooded mahouts guided them along. "I'm sure they had one somewhere, Revka dear. Probably stored away from the camp in a hidden location. I understand caves are quite popular."

"What caves? We're on clay."

"Well, somewhere else then. I don't know. Anyway, once this is over, we can go back and look. Would you like that?"

"S'pose."

"All right then." She nabbed a couple of apples from an overhanging tree and tossed one back to Revka. "Anyway, we didn't make out too badly. We've got some nice provisions; my saddlebags are definitely heavier."

"Yeah, that's true." They proceeded down the road in silence for a while, then Revka blurted out, "Wouldn't it be great if we did find their hoard? Can you imagine how much gold and treasure they must have squirreled away by now?"

"It would be nice, yes. Wouldn't have to work on a farm anymore, that's for certain."

"Yeah, we'd have to move into town, get a nice house together, maybe a travelers' inn. Buy some fine clothes. Hey." she gave Iyarra a playful nudge. "I'd have to learn how to ride you sidesaddle, you know?"

"Would you?"

"Oh yeah, without a doubt. Ladies of quality never straddle each other, well-known fact."

Iyarra coughed and sputtered. She stood thumping her chest.

"Are you all right?"

When Iyarra had recovered, she cleared her throat. "Sorry, sorry. I just, er, choked a little on my apple for some reason. I'm all right now."

"Oh. Good."

***

That night they stopped at an inn where, buoyed by the day's adventure and in accordance with tradition among people suddenly in possession of a *per diem*, they proceeded to eat and drink rather more than was strictly necessary.

"Nah, honest to gods. There had to be about a hundred of 'em." Revka helped herself to another hunk of bread, dipping it in her stew. "They took us back to the camp and were going to sell us off. It was terrible."

"What did you do?" asked one of the pilgrims, who was seated opposite her at the long table. There were three such tables in the dining area, each filled end to end with travelers.

Revka gestured airily. "Oh well, I don't want to get into too much detail. But they won't be a problem anymore."

Iyarra rolled her eyes. Revka never could resist telling stories, especially if she could embellish them along the way. Of course there was no use calling her on it, because she would only put on that innocent face of hers and insist that she hadn't actually said anything untrue, had she? How was it her fault if people chose to make assumptions? They'd go back and forth about it, and Revka would talk Iyarra around in circles until she got all muddled. No, best to just let her have her fun. She mentally shrugged and tucked back into her salad. It was rather good.

"Good evening, ladies." The owner of the tavern appeared behind them with an obsequious grin on his face; the travel warrants had apparently made an impression. "I just wanted you to know I have set aside one of my finest rooms for you. Very nice, complete privacy. Anything for the esteemed representatives of the duke."

Revka took it graciously. "Very glad to hear it, my man. I believe we'll be retiring shortly."

He bowed and turned to Iyarra. "And for you, miss, one of our *deluxe* stables has been cleaned and fresh straw laid down. I'm certain you shall find it to your liking."

Revka blinked, nearly dropping a handful of bread into her stew. Iyarra just smiled. "Thank you," she said. "I'm sure I will."

***

Later, in the stable, Revka helped Iyarra take off her tack. "I'm sorry," she murmured, "I forgot about that."

"It's all right." Iyarra neatly folded her saddle blanket. "At least we're indoors tonight. I think I smell rain."

"I know, I know, it's just... Well, we've been sleeping rough for so long now that I kind of got used to you being there."

Iyarra grinned and ruffled her girlfriend's hair. "Well, I suppose I *could* climb up those steps and try to squeeze into a human bed with you. I'm sure the innkeeper wouldn't mind."

"Ha, ha."

Iyarra turned Revka around. "Hey. It's all right. You know we have to be careful when we're around other people. After all, we are still, technically, illegal in most places."

Revka lifted away Iyarra's mail shirt, leaving behind the simple cotton garment that was a must for anyone who didn't want tiny links of cold metal against their skin all day. "It's just...stupid, is all."

Iyarra leaned down and nuzzled. "Well, if they ever change things, I'll let you ride me right up the aisle. How does that sound?"

A half smile pushed its way onto Revka's lips. "All right. Deal."

"Good." Iyarra stretched and settled into the straw. "All right, you. I will see you in the morning, bright and early for breakfast. Then off we go, right? We've got to make up for lost time."

"All right." Revka bent down and gave her a good-night kiss.

Iyarra sat alone in her stall, listening to the sounds of the night. A few stalls over, another centaur was snoring. She stretched out in the darkness and let her mind wander. Well, they shouldn't be too far behind schedule, all things considered. *If we can keep going at a good strong pace tomorrow, we should be just fine.* She thought about the bandit camp and the odd fate that had come in the night. Those sorts of things didn't just happen, in her admittedly limited experience. She wished she could think it through like Revka. She was really quite clever, provided you got her to stay on topic for more than a minute. Iyarra stretched herself out and flicked her tail a couple of times.

Maybe she was wrong. Perhaps Revka was right, and it was the coach companies. They were known to take a very dim view of people who waylaid their coaches or made the roads unsafe. Yes, that seemed likely.

Upstairs in the inn proper, Revka was fast asleep. She had managed to get rolled up in the blankets until they were a complete jumble, and was currently half curled up within them. Her sleeping form would scoot forward a bit, unconsciously searching for the warm body that was usually there. Around about two-ish, she scooted forward one time too many and went over the edge of the bed to land in a heap on the floor.

It took her a good five minutes to get untangled.

***

The next morning they hit the road again. Neither had slept well, and it took them a while to get up to speed. Later, they caught up with and joined a group of pilgrims who were headed in the same general direction. The next few days passed quickly, with the group riding by day and swapping stories by night. All in all, it was a perfectly uneventful trip to Peccaray. There, things immediately went wrong.

"What do you mean they won't take us across?" Iyarra paced back and forth, snorting. The wharf area was crowded with pilgrims, merchants, and travelers of all sorts. Lake Peccaray was only about a mile wide, but over ten in either direction around. You either took a ferry across or added a day or two to your journey. The ferrymen of Peccaray, in their waterproof leggings and broadbrims, knew it was so, and consequently felt free to charge whatever they liked. Cash.

"You showed them the warrants?"

Revka shrugged. "Of course. Every last one of 'em told me the same thing. A warrant covers food and lodging, not transportation. If we want to ride, we've got to pony up. Er, crap. Sorry. You know what I mean."

Iyarra ran her hands through her mane. "All right, all right. So do we have enough?"

"Well, we have enough for two people. Three even, but..."

"Yes?"

"Well, you know how centaurs weigh about as much as horses?"

"Yes?"

"And horses weigh about four times as much as people?"

Iyarra sighed. "No, don't tell me. Let me guess. It costs four times as much for me to ride as it does you."

Revka sagged. "It's the weight, you see. They can only haul so much across. If they charged the same, they'd be losing money."

"Right, right." Iyarra sighed. "So. What are we going to do for money?"

Revka shrugged. "Beats me. But we've got to think of something. I'm not about to turn around and head back to beg the duke for money. Anyway, we're supposed to have finesse and surgical precision and whatever else it was he said."

"Expendable."

"Yeah. No! Stop that. Look, we're good at improvising, aren't we? We just gotta come up with a clever idea to raise some quick cash. Preferably without breaking any major laws." She looked around the busy wharf at the crowds. Merchants and porters were running back and forth, loading carts full of goods onto the ferries, nonstop. At the corner of the tavern, a juggler was practicing his craft in front of a half dozen or so spectators. Occasionally, one would throw a coin or two into his cap.

"Okay," said Revka, "Here's my plan..."

***

Half an hour later, in a small alley just off the village square, the usual quiet was broken by a muffled curse and the cacophony of a dropped tambourine.

"Take it easy. That's the only one we've got." Revka glanced in a darkened window, checking her reflection. There had been a frantic rummaging through saddlebags, and rather more improvisation in the wardrobe department than she would have liked. It would do for now. A wrist load of bangles clanked up and down her arm as she primped.

"I still can't believe you saved all of this stuff." Iyarra tugged at the red silken top that only just about covered her chest. She was not, by nature, the outgoing type. Dressing like a showgirl, even if only from the waist up, was not doing her mood any favors. She scooped the tambourine back up and gave a desultory shake.

"Thought it might come in handy." Revka nodded at her reflection, then patted Iyarra's shoulder. "Hey, it's just to get enough to get us across the lake, right? Lots of tourists here, people with loose change. I'll keep an eye on the take. If we play our cards right, we'll be over the lake in no time. What do you say?"

"I just hate doing this. It's so...*corny*. And they never like the jokes, you know."

Revka arched an eyebrow. "You would prefer something else, maybe? A novelty wrestling act, perhaps?"

Iyarra shuddered. "No. Not that. Not that ever again."

"All right then, are we going to do this?"

"I suppose."

"You suppose? Come on. I think we can do better than that." Revka lay a finger on the tip of Iyarra's nose. "Come on now...who's my pony? Who's my pretty pony?"

Iyarra's ears went pink. She mumbled a reply.

Revka cupped a hand over her ear. "Sorry? What was that?"

"...I am..."

Revka grinned. "That's right. Now get out there and let's show 'em."

***

It was midafternoon, and the square was in full swing. Farmers in from the surrounding areas cried their wares beside the fisherman who worked the lake. Merchants who traveled the coach road from end to end set up stalls full of cloth, dyes, and spices. The continuous hubbub of voices in discussion and debate rang around the square as business chugged along.

Cymbals crashed from one of the more distant corners, and two figures emerged from an alley. It was a woman and a centauress, dressed gaily in red and yellow foolery. The woman twirled into the middle of the empty space that formed around them, tweaked the bustline of her outfit just a little bit, dropped a battered old hat on the ground, and threw her arms out in greeting.

"Ladies and Gentlemen!
Four legs and two!
We've come here today to entertain you!"

"Ladies and Gentlemen!
Two legs and four!
By the time we are done, you'll be calling encore!"

"Thank you, thank you ladies and gentlemen! I am The Amazing Revka, and here, all the way from the red plains, please give a warm hand to Iyarra, the Wonder Mare!"

The centaur, who had been hanging back a bit from her partner, seemed to hesitate. Then she threw a fairly convincing smile on her face and trotted forward. She arrived next to Revka and dipped slightly as she brought her right legs behind her left ones. Revka swept an arm toward her.

"There you are folks! Two curtseys for the price of one! But not only that, I want you to know that she is absolutely brilliant! We will now give a demonstration of her formidable powers of cognition! First, Iyarra the Wonder Mare, can you tell us please: What is the opposite of Yea?"

The centauress stepped forward. "Neiiiigh!" she whinnied.

There was a crash of noise, as Revka slapped the tambourine against her hip. "Brilliant! And now, anatomy! What do we call the back of the neck?"

"Neiiiighpe!"

"Marvelous! Now, what would you call a dishonest man?"

"Neiiiighve!"

"Genius! Genius! All right, last one. What would you use to attach two pieces of wood?"

The centaur tilted her head and looked puzzled. The woman danced around the audience, coaxing out their cheers. "Come on now! No hints! No hints! She can get it if you cheer her on! Louder! Louder!"

"AHA!" Iyarra the Wonder Mare threw her hands in the air, an exultant joy suffusing her face.

"Oh, I think she's got it! Go ahead, girl, attaching two pieces of wood, you use a...?"

"Rope!" proclaimed the Wonder Mare proudly.

Revka staggered back against Iyarra, clutching her chest. "Well, they can't all be gems." The crowd laughed. Coins started to tinkle into the hat.

"We thank you! No, no, keep applauding. It'll keep your hands warm! Seriously, make all the noise you want! We love your laughter, we love your cheers, we even love your boos. In fact, we'll be drinking it

25

after the show!" Another *slap* of the tambourine. "And now, ladies and gentlemen—I think that takes in most of you—Iyarra will sing for you a mournful little ditty called, 'She Was Only a Minotaur's Daughter, But She Knew How to Sling the Bull!' Take it away please!"

Iyarra clutched her hands together under her chin and assumed a pathetic attitude. "Ohhhhhhh..."

Revka stormed over. "Wait, wait, wait! What are you doing?"

Iyarra put her hands on her hips and snorted. "I am *trying* to entertain these nice ladies and gentlemen!"

"Like that? You'll never make it! Now listen! Tell me if you can: Why do unicorns have only one horn?"

"Why do unicorns only have one horn? I don't know! Why *do* unicorns only have one horn?"

"Because if they had two, they'd be rhinoceroses!"

Iyarra groaned and gave Revka a backhanded swat. The woman tumbled into a backwards somersault, landing with a very convincing splat. The crowd roared with laughter. Well, maybe the joke never got a laugh, but the splat? You could *rely* on the splat. She staggered back up to her feet, making sure not to step on the place where the hat had been.

Where the hat had been...

There was a gap in the crowd, and the jingle of coins ran with the footsteps.

"Oh, *hell* no," Revka growled and took off.

The thief dodged and weaved through the crowd, using the confusion of the mob to his advantage. Revka barreled after him, ducking here, leaping there, diving between someone's legs and tumbling back to her feet somewhere else. The little so-and-so was nimble, she had to admit. Only let them get out in a clear stretch, and she'd catch the bastard in no time.

The thief ducked into an alley, followed by Revka in hot pursuit. He easily navigated an obstacle course of crates and barrels that had been left there for no other reason than to make life difficult for pursuers. Up ahead, the alley crossed another. The thief darted through the crossing just as a cart appeared and began making its way across. Revka swore between her teeth, put on an extra burst of speed, and threw herself under the cart just as the front wheels passed. Fortunately, the alley was slick with the slimy mud of the lakeshore, so she was able to slide quickly across on pure momentum before scrambling to her feet in time to avoid the rear wheels.

The thief was further ahead now, moving fast. They were on a straight shot, with no crossings for a good hundred meters and no hiding places. If she could just put on a burst of speed...

The thief grabbed a rope in passing, yanking it hard as he ran. Behind him, several barrels tumbled to the street, just large enough that she wouldn't be able to vault over them. Revka swore again. It would have to be a scramble. She ducked her head down and charged. If she got a good leap up, she should be able to pull herself right over the middle one and leap off the other side without too much of a slowdown. Only about fifty meters away...she kept her pace swift but even, saving a little energy for the big burst.

A hand came out of nowhere and yanked her off her feet. She landed with a heavy thud across the back of a very strong, not to mention tough, horse. Below her, the mud and loose cobbles of the alley zipped past. A familiar voice called back, "Hang on!"

Revka fumbled a grip around the—now that she thought of it— very familiar waist. She lifted her head just in time to see Iyarra clear the barrels with one mighty leap. A moment of near weightlessness followed another, then the landing knocked the wind out of her. She scrambled to get herself upright.

The thief had reached the end of the alley and was running fast. Clearly, he hadn't counted on being chased this far. They'd reached the wharf, and suddenly the going was very difficult indeed. The thief dodged and weaved through the crowd, but Iyarra kept right behind. He tried knocking down men and beasts laden with cargo as he went. Iyarra vaulted over one and all. He tried getting lost in the crowd. The centauress followed his scent and wouldn't be deterred. Plus, Revka kept pointing at him and shouting "Stop! Thief!" which was starting to attract some serious attention. Finally, in an act of desperation, he ducked off one path onto another only to realize he was on one of the piers going out to the boats. There were no boats, or at least none big enough to hide in. He'd reached a dead end, and Iyarra was close behind.

The thief reached a small fishing sloop tied up against the pier, and desperately grabbed at the boom, swinging it after him so the path was blocked by the mainsail. Iyarra groaned and skidded to a halt before she collided with the sail.

Revka dropped from Iyarra's back, letting the momentum tumble her forward and under the boom. She rolled to her feet and took off after the thief. He was only a handful of paces away and getting near the edge. Revka's footsteps pounded on the wooden pier. The thief whipped his head around, looking surprised, and tripped over a loose coil of rope.

He stumbled, nearly fell, just regained his feet, staggered, tripped over himself, and finally sailed face first, the hat slipping out of his grip and arcing gently through the air.

"No,no,no,no,no,no. *NO!*" Revka cleared the last few steps, vaulted over the luckless thief, and made a leaping dive for the coins just as they sailed over the edge of the pier.

For a moment, time seemed to stand still. There was the hat in front of her, arcing lazily away. A few coins danced in slow motion, as the hat left them behind. Below her, the lake waited. Oh, well. Dreamily, she reached out to the hat and grabbed it with both hands.

Time came back. The coins that had been arcing out of the hat landed back in the crown with a resounding *ching*. She let out a breath she hadn't realized she was holding and sagged with relief.

It was about this moment when she realized that, for some reason, she still appeared to be hanging in midair. She looked down. Yes, there was the lake below her. Her feet were definitely not standing on anything. She could feel gravity's pull again, but somehow it just wasn't happening.

There was a grunt behind her, and her view swung around to the pier. She felt herself lowered down to the wooden planks just as whatever force it was finally gave out.

Behind her, Iyarra groaned and rubbed her arms, glaring at Revka. "I think somebody's gaining weight," she muttered.

As the two staggered mud-stained and disheveled back to the shore, they were greeted by a crowd of onlookers, even some of the audience members from the show. A couple of watchmen politely pushed their way past, en route to the thief. Revka and Iyarra looked at the crowd. The crowd looked back. Revka felt something was expected of them. She held up the hat, now quite worse for wear but still, somehow, intact.

The crowd roared. Suddenly there was a tidal wave of applause and cheering. Coins showered them from all directions. Revka was the first to recover. She dropped to one knee, swinging her arms wide. "Thank you, ladies and gentlemen! Thank you very much indeed! You're a wonderful audience! Next show in twenty minutes!"

"Oh, *like hell*," snorted Iyarra, who got to work scooping up the coins.

***

Just over two hours later, the performers, cleaned up and back in their traveling gear, stood at the foredeck of one of the lake ferries, watching the opposite shore fade into view. Revka was in full preen mode.

"Enough for the fare *and* the return trip," she gloated. "See? What'd I tell you? Worked like a charm."

Arms leaned against the railing, Iyarra tested the air for new scents. "Oh? So someone stealing our money and chasing them halfway through the village while getting covered in bruises and mud was all part of the plan, was it?"

Revka was undeterred. "Sugar, when a plan works, for pity's sake, don't question it!" She leaned closer. "We would have gotten the money either way. They were really going for the Wonder Mare routine; did you notice that? Really, that thief did us a favor, let us put on a real show." She grinned sheepishly. "Er, your arms okay?"

"I'll be fine." Iyarra shrugged. "Just don't ask me to do any heavy lifting."

They watched the lake for a while.

"Revka?"

"Yes?"

"We are going to make it, aren't we?"

"Oh, sure. We've only lost a day. We're making good time right now. I wouldn't be surprised if we made it back with a month to spare."

"You think so?"

"Trust me."

They fell silent again, watching the distant shore. Iyarra almost fancied she could see the distant blue haze of the Icarines, just above the horizon. She didn't have her partner's gift for working things out, but it seemed to her to be one hell of a long run.

K.L. Mitchell

Chapter Four

THE ODD COLLECTION OF inns on the opposite shore could hardly be called a town. Mostly it was there to handle the ferry traffic before travelers dispersed to parts unknown. They stashed their goods in the slightly less derelict inn and headed out to the single tavern.

The place was full as they elbowed their way in. Some glared, but mostly the patrons stayed their distance. Only a reckless or extremely drunk person messed with a centaur, let alone one in uniform.

Revka's gaze swept the room. The tavern was such as you often got in these parts. Shadowy figures scurried about on the straw covered floor. Not-quite-human types hunched over their drinks in the dimly lit room. A few child sized patrons scuttled around, dodging and weaving between the other patrons' legs and trying not to get kicked. At one table, a group of richly dressed, rail thin characters with long ears and light gray skin sat drinking their mineral water and viewing the rest of the bar with distaste. A gaily dressed bard occupied a makeshift stage, strumming a lute and singing something about espying a maiden all on a summer's day and what he proposed to do about it. The air was blue with the smoke of pipe weed, ditch weed, dill weed, skunk weed, and weed-weed. In the darkest corner, a mysterious hooded figure lurked ominously over his pint. In short, throw in a couple of dragons and a magic sword and you'd have just about every cliché in the book.

Iyarra snorted. "Tourist trap. I hate these places."

Revka nodded. "Tell me about it. They always overcharge, and the drinks are watered down. Hey, speaking of which?"

"Just a water for me, please. But see if they have any oatcakes."

When Revka returned with the drinks and a plateful of buns, she saw that Iyarra had been joined by two men. A wizened old coot dressed in threadbare robes leaned back in his chair, puffing a thin pipe. Tangled, gray locks tumbled down and mingled with his rat's nest of a beard. He'd probably spent ages in front of a mirror perfecting that expression of crinkly beneficent wisdom. Revka sighed inwardly. On the table before him was a battered, old conical cap with a wide brim and the last, straggling threads of what might have been embroidered moons and stars.

The other man, oh dear. The other one was a seven foot tall lump of meat with a face attached. He wore a simple cotton tunic, which showed off his beefy arms and some definitely worse for wear breeches. His thick neck tapered slightly as it came to his head. Tousled, brown hair tumbled almost to his shoulders, and his face had the look of a twelve-year-old on a field trip to a fireworks factory. Everything about him screamed *hero*. Also, *twit*.

Iyarra smiled. "Oh good, you're back! I was just telling them about you."

The old codger raised his pipe in salute. "Alaman the Wise, at your service, my lady." He turned to his companion. "Go on, introduce yourself."

"Hi," he said. "M'name's Porter. It's just Porter."

Revka put the food and drinks down and took her seat. "I see. Well, I'm Revka, and I guess you already know Iyarra." She gave them a quick grin and slugged back a bit of her ale.

"We were just discussing the possibility of traveling together, since we're heading the same way," Iyarra explained.

"Only as far as the river," Alaman added. "Our business takes us away from the mountains, I'm afraid. We will, of course, handle all our own traveling expenses, and should there be difficulties along the way, we will gladly lend what aid we can."

"Alaman's training me to be a hero," Porter explained. "He says I'm the Chosen One."

Revka's grin stayed frozen to her face. "You don't say? Chosen for what, if I may ask?"

"I've got to fulfill my destiny." He leaned forward eagerly, like a three hundred pound puppy. "Alaman says my destiny is scribed in ancient prophecies in hidden temples far beyond the wit of man."

Revka allowed herself just the barest flicker of the eyes toward the old man, who had, at least, the grace to look somewhat embarrassed. "Really? That ancient, huh?"

"I don't think we need to trouble these young ladies with the details," the wizard interjected. "Suffice to say, the road east has been particularly active with bandits and wild animals and such lately. It is always wise to travel in numbers."

"Yeah. And Alaman says a good hero should always travel with a...what was it?"

"A clean change of pants?"

"No, no, that's not it. Good idea, though. I should remember to – *entourage!* That's it. I need an entourage. A party of adventurers thrown together by, uh…"

"Circumstance," Alaman prodded.

"Circumstance, yeah, to explore the furthest reaches of the world and fulfill our destiny. Well, my destiny. But you help." He turned to Iyarra. "You can be the funny sidekick," he offered.

Revka decided this was her cue. "Er, if you'll excuse us, I need to talk this over with my, uh, funny sidekick." She stood quickly, nudging Iyarra to her hooves. "Don't go away."

"Okay," said Revka, hands on her hips after they had moved to a quieter corner of the tavern. "You want to tell me where you dug up those two clowns?"

"I didn't mean to." Iyarra shrugged. The old man just came up and we fell to talking, then he had the other one join us and, uh, that was pretty much it, basically."

"Iyarra hon, when are you going to learn?" Revka shook her head. "Just because they follow you home doesn't mean you have to keep them. I mean, look at them!" From their vantage point, the two could just be seen. The old man sat sucking contentedly on his pipe, while the would-be hero swished an imaginary sword and made *kssh* noises. "I'm telling you, those two are trouble magnets. I can feel it."

"I just thought it would be nice to have help." Iyarra wore her best meek expression. "You know, in case something like the bandits happens again. It would be nice to have backup, especially in rough territory. I remembered what you said about safety in numbers."

"Well yeah, but Dirk Chinbutt? Does he even know how to work a sword properly?" Back at the table, Porter executed a particularly brutal crosscut and managed to knock a tray of drinks out of the hands of a barmaid. The abuse she heaped on him provided a few minutes' entertainment.

"Chosen one," Revka snorted. "As pickup lines go, I've heard better."

Iyarra looked shocked. "Oh Revka, you can't really think?"

"Oh, I could tell you stories, sugar." Revka grinned. "Old guys like that like 'em pretty and dumb. Anyway, that's about the least-worst possibility of what's going on between those two. He's gotta be using Golden Boy for something. He sure ain't a hero."

33

"All right, so the boy is clearly a bit new to all of this, but all that muscle has to come from somewhere, right? And they are paying their own way. Besides, the old man is a wizard. I thought maybe he could help with the curse-marks. Maybe we could get rid of them?"

Revka pursed her lips. "Well, that is a possibility, I suppose. I can't say the guy exactly fills me with confidence, but it wouldn't hurt to ask. Why not? We might actually be able to get the curse lifted and get scarce. I suppose it's worth a try."

Iyarra beamed. "That's right. Even if he can't, he might be able to give us some advice or something. After all, what do we have to lose?"

Revka sighed and rubbed her temples. "Iyarra hon, I'm just worried they're going to slow us down. I mean, what happens if we get attacked on the road, eh?"

"Well, the way I see it, they'll go for the most obvious target."

Revka's eyes narrowed. "You mean Studs Meatbucket over there?"

"Mm-hm."

"Giving us time to attack or sneak away?"

"Mm-hm."

Revka looked thoughtfully at her partner. "You know," she said, "I think I'm starting to rub off on you."

Iyarra only smiled.

"All right," Revka said, as the two sat back down at the table. "Here's the deal. You handle all your own traveling expenses, including any tolls or other miscellaneous costs, til we get to the river. You don't slow us down. Hero Boy takes point, and nobody rides Iyarra but me. Got it?"

The old man's face broke into a wide, genial smile. "Absolutely. That will be most satisfactory." He turned to Porter, who was off in a world of his own, practicing action poses. "It is settled; our little company is complete."

"Cool." Porter went back to posing.

"I suggest we meet in front of the tavern at dawn," said Revka. "We would like to get back on the road bright and early. Is that all right?"

"Of course."

"Then if you'll excuse us, we have to, uhm, do some stuff before we turn in. See you fellows in the morning."

**

A full moon bathed the warm summer night, as the two women made their way back to the inn.

"Well, this should be interesting," Revka observed. "Dragging those two turkeys along is going to be full of surprises. I can just feel it."

Iyarra clutched her hands in front of her. "I hope you're not mad."

"Nah, I'm not mad." Revka shook her head, waving a hand dismissively. "Just...you know what I mean. These guys are not good news. I don't know where you dig up a lunkhead like Hero Boy, but really! How can someone be that gormless and live?"

Iyarra smiled and patted Revka on the shoulder. "Oh, I'm sure he'll be fine. They made it this far, didn't they?"

"All right. But if he wanders off or plays tag with a weed snake or something, we're not sticking around, right? He's the old man's problem. He can look after the little pud."

"You know," Iyarra said, "Another thing I hadn't thought about is that we're going to have to be on guard with them around all the time."

"Well, that's what I'm say—"

"No. I mean *us*, as in you and me."

"Ohhh. Right." Revka kicked a stone down the rough path to the lake, where it landed with a muffled splash. "More good news. This is such a headache. And the old man looks just the type to rat us out."

"Mm." Iyarra looked down at her Revka and smiled a little bit. "The thing is, this may well be our last night alone for several days, you know? Perhaps we should take advantage of it, have a little walk in the woods?"

Revka wrinkled her nose. The ferry docks landed at an artificial clearing, with the woods cut back about fifty meters from the nearest buildings. Between the lake and the road, the forest loomed like a wall of darkness on either side. "Why would we do that? I mean, woods are woods. Not even very scenic in daylight if you—"

"No, no, no..." Iyarra bent her lips down to Revka's ear, walking her fingers along her shoulder. "Why don't you and I have a little walk...in the woods?"

Light dawned. "Ohhh."

"Mm-hm."

Revka allowed herself a grin. "Well...maybe a quick one. I don't want to be out there too late. And wear your bit. I don't want someone to hear you scream and come running."

"Deal."

***

The next day dawned clear and warm. The party assembled and was on the road in good time. Traffic was light, so the four were generally on their own. The alleged wizard rode a white donkey with the same air of complacent contentment found on the sort of people who go to great lengths to show how little they care of what others think. The boy was lunking along on foot but didn't seem to mind. The exercise certainly didn't tire his mouth. The chatter had started almost immediately and had been going on for a solid two hours by the sun. He carried on about the dangers of dire beasts and how he would deal with them, speculatory battle cries, and long, winding exploits of heroes gone before, augmented by extensive explanations of what he, personally, would have done differently.

"So like, he waited until the middle head was getting ready to strike, see, then he dove forward. So it couldn't, you know, turn its neck all the way around. Then the left head came in, and he did the same thing to it. The right head kinda tried to go over the other two, but they were trying to get around each other. So basically, he wound up braiding their necks together." He demonstrated, twisting his arms around in an unsuccessful attempt to simulate three entangled hydra necks.

"Uh-huh." Revka let her gaze wander to the scenery, listening with about half an ear. She had met heroes before. One thing she had noticed is that, by and large, they weren't big talkers. She began to wonder if hitching up with these two was such a great idea. After all, muscles are one thing, but who said he'd ever been in a fight? Maybe he just talked people to death.

"Anyway, that's not really something we have to worry about because, like, hydras really prefer mountainous and rocky areas, and this is all forest. They can't run through forests. So if you were worried about hydras, you don't need to be. If that's what you were thinking."

"Oh. Good."

"Yeah. This is totally wolf country."

"Actually," Alaman cut in, "wolves are very rarely a direct danger to humans. They may attack domesticated animals and so on, but only in the direst circumstances do they attack humans unprovoked. I've only heard of it happening during particularly harsh winters. Even then, it is an act of purest desperation. We really have nothing to fear from them at all."

Suddenly, silence sucked every sound from the forest. Iyarra stood in the middle of the road, ears pricked. The world went hushed, expectant. You could have heard a leaf fall.

The moment passed. Somewhere, a bird chirped. The others turned to Iyarra politely. She blushed, then just sagged. "Sorry," she muttered. "Thought we were about to..." The rest faded to mumbles.

Revka tilted her head. "What?"

Iyarra fidgeted. "Thought we were going to be attacked by wolves."

"What, just now?"

A hoof scraped at the dirt. "Yes."

"Why?"

"I dunno." Iyarra shrugged and muttered, "Just seemed like we were about to be attacked by wolves, that's all."

Revka sighed. She opened her mouth to say something but couldn't. That was when the morgas attacked.

For those who have been fortunate enough to avoid them, morgas are large apelike beings roughly the size of a man. They are generally covered with coarse, brown fur, with long arms that end in nasty, black claws. They like dense forests, where they can drop out of trees onto passersby and eviscerate them. It's believed they hunt in packs to overwhelm their prey through force of numbers, but it's possible they just enjoy eating out with friends as much as anybody. Iyarra reared up, nearly throwing Revka. Porter charged straight toward the largest morgas in the bunch, and Alaman...well, presumably he was around somewhere.

"Dammit!" Revka hung on and flipped a leg over and across Iyarra's back. She whipped around so she was facing Iyarra's tail and pulled out her sword. "Okay, ready!"

Iyarra reared again, and the two began to fight in earnest. The windmill was their go-to trick when they had to fight groups. Iyarra bucked and turned, relying mainly on her powerful forelegs plus a pair of handheld daggers. Behind her, Revka whirled her sword at anything that dared come close. Neither was a particularly experienced fighter, but with three blades and two hooves going at once, and no way of sneaking up on them, technique was secondary to the sheer potential for mayhem. Between the two of them, they could generally hold quite large groups of beasts (or guardsmen) at bay, or at least cause them to direct their attention to lower-hanging fruit. They capered and cantered wildly in the middle of a handful of morgas, managing to beat them back. Occasionally, one lunged forward and received a slash or a hoof-shaped dent for their trouble.

"Could be worse!" Revka shouted over her shoulder. A large morga tried to swipe her off Iyarra's back. She sliced deep along its forearm. The creature howled with pain and staggered back.

"Really?" Iyarra crouched and brought both hooves against a morga that had been getting too close. The sickening crunch confirmed the beast was dead before it hit the ground.

"Yeah." Revka leaned forward and slashed at a morga with its forelegs up, just about to strike. She got it neatly across the snout, causing it to fall backward and howl with agony. "Coulda been wolves."

Iyarra rolled her eyes. "Very funny." She ducked and just missed being raked by a set of claws.

"A true hero can laugh in the face of danger. Kick!" Iyarra's left leg shot back, just in time to send another morga falling directly onto Revka's sword.

"It's not my face I'm worried about." Iyarra yelped as the morga in front of her leaped. Too late to kick, she thrust her daggers forward and closed her eyes, bracing for the impact. There was a thump and a burst of hot breath inches from her face. Suddenly, her arms were full of dead morga. "Ugh."

Only one morga remained, keeping its distance to Iyarra's side. She tried to maneuver around so that Revka was facing the morga, but it moved with her. Damn. "I'm trying to get into position," she hissed. "Can you keep it off my back?"

"'Course." Revka kept her sword pointed at the last morga. This one was obviously smarter than the others. It had hung back and watched while the others attacked. Even as Iyarra tried to maneuver into kicking range, the beast shuffled, always keeping itself aligned with the middle and just out of the reach of Revka's sword. She watched it, saw the tensing of muscles.

"Iyarra," she whispered, never taking her eyes off the beast, "When I say jump, you jump forward as hard as you can, all right? In fact, when you jump, keep running so we get clear." She licked her lips and braced the sword's pommel against her leg.

"Got it."

Beneath her, Revka could feel Iyarra's muscles tensing, ready to spring.

The morga hunched down. There was a moment of perfect stillness. Revka and the morga locked eyes, then Porter brought the creature down with a flying tackle and proceeded to pummel the living daylights out of it.

Horse and rider stood dumbfounded, as the boy wrestled the beast to the ground, expertly ducking past its furious claw swipes, avoiding its attempts to bite him, and generally rendering it a massive, furry ball of impotent rage. Porter wrapped one beefy arm around the animal's neck, using the other to clench it down until the morga swayed and collapsed, unconscious.

For a moment, there was only the sound of Porter's heavy panting, accompanied by the retreating sounds of the wounded morgas. Revka finally freed her gaping jaw and turned to Iyarra. "Well," she said. "That's something you don't see every day."

Iyarra pointed wordlessly to a spot a few meters ahead. Sprawled in a rough circle, lay four other morgas, all unconscious. The two women turned back to Porter, who had stumbled to his feet. He was swaying slightly, but if there was a mark on him, they couldn't see it.

Revka leaned toward Iyarra, nodding at the boy. "Okay," she said. "Kid knows how to fight."

"An exemplary performance." And suddenly Alaman was leaning against a nearby tree. He lit his pipe with a leisurely air, looking almost inhumanly smug. "I can see my training has been most effective."

"Pardon me," said Iyarra, rather politely, Revka thought. "But where exactly were you in all of this?"

There came that smile again. "Oh, I was around, have no fear. Let us say I was lending...magical assistance."

"Yeah," muttered Revka, not quite under her breath. "Made yourself disappear."

Alaman blew a puff of bluish smoke. "I would not expect ignorant men or women to understand the vagaries of the sorceric arts. Nevertheless, I was able to do my humble part. And now, if you would be so good as to retrieve my donkey, we shall be on our way."

On cue, everybody looked around. Sure enough, the eminently sensible donkey had taken the first opportunity to remove itself. Revka groaned. "Well, this is just great. We do *not* have time to go rooting around the forest to find your damn donkey. You'll just have to walk to the nearest village and get a new one."

"*Walk?* My good woman, do you have any idea who you are speaking to? An enchanter of my prestige does not walk like a common burgher. We will retrieve the donkey at once, or I shall not proceed a single step!"

"Suits me fine, gramps. Come on, Iyarra."

Iyarra shushed Revka with a wave of her hand. She stood stock still, head tilted and an air of alertness about her face. She sniffed the air, moving her head slowly back and forth. "All right," she said. "This way." She trotted off into the underbrush. Revka scrambled to get herself turned the right way around on Iyarra's back.

Chapter Five

IYARRA'S NOSE TOOK THEM through the underbrush, away from the trail. The donkey had fled in a more or less straight line, which was fortunate. In fact, it seemed to Revka that there was the faintest hint of what might have once been a trail. The only trees in the path were young ones, and the vegetation on the ground seemed just a bit thinner. Nothing you could be definite about, but Revka had spent a long time tromping around in the woods. She'd picked up a few things.

They found the donkey after about ten minutes, munching unconcernedly at a patch of clover beside what appeared to be a large mound. Grown over with moss and patches of grass, there was something unwholesome about the way the mound sat, hunched up in the middle of the woods like an unpleasant memory shuffled off to the back of the mind to die forgotten.

Revka pursed her lips, giving the scene an expert once-over. "Huh," she said. "Weird."

"And decidedly not natural." Alaman strode up behind them, Porter in tow. The sorcerer moved past them and peered closely at a tangle of branches. He poked at them with his pipe for a moment, then gestured to Porter. "Cut here," he said.

Two slashes of Porter's sword were enough to send the branches and quite a bit of other debris cascading to the ground. Beyond, a suspiciously regular opening could be seen.

"It is as I thought," he declared. "An ancient temple, long forgotten by the passage of time, cursed and abandoned to the ages. Strange and terrible are the deeds that took place here, and long has it lain, far from the minds of men."

Revka peered closely. "You know, I think you're right. Iyarra, come look at this." The stony outcrops could very easily have been spires, and the grotesque shapes they'd assumed were the natural twisting of time and nature proved to be carvings. Iyarra examined one more closely, then quickly stepped away. Porter gawped at the mound, his mouth hanging wide open. "Whoa," he said.

Alaman patted Porter on the shoulder. "I know of this place. Deep in its heart lies a relic. Lain there lo these many forgotten years, in the great chamber below the surface of the earth. The cover of a wooden box joined with bronze bears the dread rune of its god, whose name even I dare not speak. You must go forth and fetch the box and bring it here. Touch nothing else. Do not attempt to open the box. Do not disturb those who sleep eternally within. Remember your training. Do you understand?"

Porter gripped his sword and put on his serious face. Behind him, Revka started counting quietly to herself.

"All right," he said. He nodded to the two women. "I won't be long," he said.

"Oh, but they will go with you." Alaman gestured to them with his pipe. "After all, a good hero never embarks upon a quest without his trusty assistants."

"Bingo," muttered Revka. "Wait. Assistants? Excuse me, we're just traveling with you two, all right? You want assistants, put us on the payroll. Otherwise, you can explore your own ancient temples."

"My apologies." Alaman bowed his head. "I merely wished my protégé to finish his errand before you two went in ransacking the place and plundering anything of value. I believe we would be best suited to resume our journey while you do so. You can catch us up at the next inn."

"Oh, right." Revka jammed an accusing finger in the old man's beard, where it stuck slightly. "Gonna take the good stuff for yourselves and leave us behind, right? I don't think so! We're going in with junior here whether you...like it...or..."

Revka sighed. She clapped one hand over her eyes, muttering and wiping her finger on her leather skirt. "All right, all right. Let's go."

"Don't forget the box," Alaman said.

***

Iyarra pushed aside a tangle of old vines, and the three stepped into the stygian temple. There was a moment of fumbling, and a torch was lit to reveal a largish antechamber. Two archways, one to the left and one right, allowed entry into the larger room beyond. Between the two archways, tattered scraps of what might once have been red velvet covered an old table. The floors, walls, and ceiling were uniformly carved of gray-green stone.

Here, sheltered from the majority of the elements, the carvings still held most of their hellish details of hideous lizard-like creatures dressed in human garb. The images portrayed feasts with dancing around fires, great horrible sacrifices, and everywhere the strange symbol of a deity so horrible that no stone could take its true appearance. Iyarra shivered.

They made their way slowly through one of the archways into the main sanctuary, a large room strewn with unrecognizable debris. At the far end, a dais held several thrones and a large altar, covered on all sides with scenes of violence and unholy wrath. They worked their way forward, pushing through the mess until they got to the back.

"You see this?" Revka poked at the altar. "This is your proper working model, right here. Not like the decorative kind you got in chapels nowadays. See, look. There are rivulets to catch the blood and funnel it down to the receptacle. Iyarra, bring the torch over here a second."

Iyarra shook her head. "I'd prefer not to," she said. "The smell of blood is...well, it's still pretty bad."

Porter nodded gravely. "Verily, grave were their deeds, and gravely have they paid for them. But come, we must do what we came here for." He moved toward a small door behind the dais and prodded it open with his sword. Iyarra leaned down to Revka.

"Verily?" she whispered.

"Hero talk."

"Oh." She shrugged and followed the others through the door.

They found themselves in a long corridor with darkened rooms on either side. Iyarra poked her torch into a few, but they all seemed to be more or less denuded of interest except for some old furniture and the occasional scroll. Only one room held any interest. About halfway down the corridor, a bit of green caught her eye. She ducked through the doorway and held her torch high.

These table and chairs were smaller than the others. The green she had seen was a board covered in tattered cloth, hanging on the wall. Grotesque figures cut from papyrus were attached to the board. Most were the same lizard people from the carvings; some were even more revolting. Their original garish hues had been preserved in the rarified air of the temple. Most had been colored in very poorly.

Revka appeared behind her, harrumphing at the cutout figures. Delicately, she tugged at one. It came away with only a little resistance. "Oh, look," she said. "They've got a bit of cloth on the back, see? Must be what makes it stick." She placed it back on the board, upside down. It stuck.

"Alaman did say we were to touch nothing." Porter hovered in the doorway. He kept shooting nervous glances over his shoulder.

"No, he said *you* were to touch nothing." Revka nodded to Iyarra, and they shuffled out of the little room. "Anyway, it wasn't anything important. So, where is this great chamber with the box?"

The stairs were at the far end of the hallway, turning in a small arc as they disappeared into darkness. Iyarra gulped, pawing at the floor. She was not, by nature, an indoors kind of girl, and definitely not the underground type. Staircases weren't too bad once you got used to them, but the smell...

Revka patted her withers. "What's wrong?"

Iyarra shook her head. "The smell," she whispered. "So much death..." She braced an arm against the wall and took a deep breath of the musty air from the hallway.

Porter quirked an eyebrow at Revka. "Is she all right?"

Revka tapped her nose. "Centaur," she whispered. "Very sensitive." Out loud, she said, "Iyarra, do you want to guard the hall here for us while we go downstairs?"

Iyarra pulled herself together and managed to nod.

"All right. We won't be gone long. Just keep your eyes open. If anything happens, shout. OK?"

"Oh, you can depend on that."

***

Porter and Revka made their way down the stairs, following the winding curve all the way around until it opened into a great hall lined with black marble pillars. The room stretched off into the darkness, easily as far as the entire area they had traversed upstairs. The floor was covered here and there with an unwholesome conglomeration of carpet, mildew, exposed stone, and mold. But mostly it was covered with bodies. Lots of bodies. The place reeked of old tombs, the smells of mold, decay, and death. Revka shuddered and almost wished she were back upstairs with Iyarra.

The two picked their way around the corpses, working their way forward. The bodies were all in various states of decomposition, but they had clearly once been the grotesque lizard creatures they had seen in the carvings upstairs. In person, so to speak, they were even worse than their carvings. Having sat rotting for hundreds of years had done little to improve their appearance.

Tables which had been laid end to end formed a corridor of sorts in front of the pillars. Unlike the great stone things before, these were simple, made of wood and cheap joinery. Each was covered with noxious, rotting heaps of indeterminate matter. Several had collapsed.

At the far end of the hall, a smaller dais held a few chairs similar to the ones they had seen upstairs. There seemed to have been a concentration of activity here, with several bodies clustered around. In the center, seated in a chair covered with strange and terrible carvings, were the remains of what could only have been the high priest. His robes, though torn and rotten with years, were still noticeably finer than those of the others around him. His ornate headdress had slipped off on one side, taking some flesh with it. In his lap sat a simple wooden box with brass fastenings. His hands, bones tattered with scraps of flesh, wrapped themselves in an iron grip around the precious box.

Revka wrinkled her nose. "Man," she said, "He really wasn't going to give that thing up easily, was he?"

Porter shook his head. "Oh, no. Probably died defending it from unbelievers or something." He prodded one of the many fallen bodies with his boot, and they watched it collapse in on itself.

Revka gave Porter a little nudge forward. "Well, off you go."

Porter licked his lips. He crept forward, easing his way through the bodies to the throne. Slowly, carefully, he worked at the fingers, trying to lever them away from the box. When that failed, he tried wiggling the box back and forth out of the priest's grip. The long-dead skeletal hands hung on, refusing to relinquish their prize. He pulled a dagger from its sheath on his belt, and tried to prize the fingers away, but to no avail.

He stood back, frowning. "It's pretty tight," he said. "I don't know if—"

"Oh, for crying out loud." Revka reached past him and yanked hard. The box came loose in her hand, dragging along the mortal remains of two hands and a forearm. These she pulled off without ceremony and tossed back into the priest's lap. "Dead guy," she explained. "Now, can we go?"

"I don't think you ought to have done that," Porter said, as they threaded their way back toward the stairs. "It was kinda disrespectful."

Revka shrugged. "Well yes, but who's gonna complain? Him? Besides, we came here to take his box. If he's not mad about that, I don't think wrenching his arm off is going to do it. Anyway, when you've been adventuring as long as I have—"

An almost insignificant shattering interrupted her boast. Behind them, the priest's head, jostled loose from the tug of war with the box, finally gave way and crashed down onto his lap. The skull bounced off the recently discarded arm bone and crashed into the legs of one of the few figures that, until then, had remained upright. The result was a sort of domino effect of crashing and clattering bones that grew louder and louder as the momentum built. Revka and Porter looked at each other and screamed, then ran for the stairs.

"Did you get it? Did you—oof!" Iyarra yelped, as Revka charged up the steps, swung a leg around, and leaped into the saddle. "Run!" Revka cried.

Iyarra galloped down the hall, ducking as they came to the anteroom again. The cacophony below crescendoed. In Revka's mind's eye, old bones snapped together, and shambling forms lurched toward the stairs, thirsting for the blood of the unbelievers.

They galloped down the aisle of the chapel, ducked their way into the foyer, and raced out into the sunlight in record time. Behind them, Porter lumbered along. He held the box tucked under one arm, sword in the other hand, trying to run backwards while stabbing and cutting at possible pursuers.

For a moment, all three stood staring at the entrance, waiting for hordes of undead to come streaming out. There was only silence, punctuated by the occasional loose bit of something falling over and echoing through the empty rooms.

"Ah, back are we? Excellent." Alaman was sitting on a nearby rock, puffing away at his pipe. He strolled over to Porter and took the box from his hand. "Yes, the very thing. Well done, boy. And you as well, ladies." He held the chest up to the light, examining it closely. A soft clattering of rocks, or something, dislodged and fell within the temple behind them.

"Yeah, we got your thing. Creepy as hell in there. Now, if you'll excuse me, I think I may have seen some silver back behind the altar." Stones shifted, and the entrance caved in, cutting off the temple. "Oh."

Iyarra patted Revka on the shoulder. "Probably just as well," she said. "We should really be moving on."

"Indeed. Let us find our way back to the road, and I shall tell you the history of this place." Alaman swung himself back onto his donkey and cantered off.

***

"An interesting and tragic case," Alaman declared as they followed the road. They had lost about an hour, all told, but with a good trot they would reach the next town by nightfall. "I suppose you saw that those creatures were of a race unknown to our age."

"Yeah." Revka fished around in a saddlebag for an oatcake, which she handed to Iyarra. "What were those things, anyway?"

"We know little of them, not even what they called themselves or what their spoken language may have been. Though I fear it must have been discordant indeed. We know only that they lived in these lands many centuries gone and erected sacred temples such as the one you saw. It seems there must have been other structures, but they were less sound, and have fallen to time.

"The temple you were in was their primary shrine. In it, they paid homage to one of the grotesque First Gods, beings as twisted and horrible as they who worshiped them. Terrible rites were enacted, savage rituals beyond the imaginings of you or me."

"We cannot know how long they lived and worshiped here, but it all came to an end on one cursed night, right there in that very temple. Their age ended, and the world has never seen their like since. Nor, with any luck, shall we ever again."

The travelers were silent for a spell, before Revka asked, "What happened in there, exactly? It was pretty nasty, by the looks of it."

"No one really knows. There are some who say there was a great schism, that some of the followers rebelled and turned on their leaders. There are others who declare that godless things invaded, seeking treasure and slaughtering the faithful to plunder the fine and fancy jewels with which they adorned their grotesque forms. There are even those who say they were having a bake sale and the high priest's wife was caught passing off store bought goods as her own, but this last I find doubtful."

"Interesting," said Revka. "So, what do you think happened?"

Alaman puffed on his pipe. "I? I suspect that, in their madness and arrogance, they attempted to call down their bastard beast-god from whatever noisome world in which it dwelt. They tried to summon a being that could not exist in a universe such as ours. They called it nonetheless, and it came."

Iyarra gulped. "What...what happened?"

Alaman stopped his donkey. He turned back to the others. "You saw what happened," he said quietly.

47

They rode on in silence. Alaman turned his attention to the box. He studied the lock, muttered a few charms over it, and wheedled at it with an old magic wand. After a few minutes of this, he cast his eyes to the ground and found a likely looking stone. He had Porter fetch it to him and brought it down on the lock with a resounding crack.

The lock fell off, and the box opened to reveal a heap of old coins. Though tarnished and discolored with age, silver is still silver, and gold is still gold, and there was a fair amount of each within. The old man lifted a coin for inspection and nodded.

Revka glared. "Money? That's what we were after? I thought it was supposed to be some holy thing."

"Oh, but it is." He tipped the box carefully, emptying its contents into a bag. "It was the temple building fund. Very important, you know." He threw the box into the bushes and put the bag away. "Now, on we go to the inn, I think. First round is on me."

***

In the dark depths of the once again abandoned temple, one of the collapsed skeletons slumped against that of the fallen priest. The old bones creaked and rustled, as they settled into a new position. A small slip of paper fell from between its fingers and fluttered to the floor like an autumn leaf. If there had been anyone available to translate the glyphs, they would have read, *"LEMON BARS. 3.49 THANK YOU FOR SHOPPI"*

Chapter Six

THE WESTERN GATE OF Kenning, a mining town, was still open upon their arrival in the late afternoon. They had argued over how to split the take from the temple. Revka pointed out that she and Iyarra had helped retrieve the box. Indeed, Revka had been the one to pry it from the old priest's grip. Alaman said that without him they wouldn't have known what was there at all, so clearly his management had brought the project to a successful execution and he should be suitably compensated. Iyarra quietly, but firmly, pointed out that without her nose they might not have found the temple, and Alaman would, most likely, still be searching for his donkey. Porter interjected that the donkey wouldn't have run away if they hadn't been attacked by morgas, so maybe *they* should get a share of the money.

Alaman told him to shut up.

In the end, they decided the best thing was to split it four ways, minus what Alaman called his "finder's fee." It was still a sizable sum. They ate and rested that night at the Filthy Ore, and Revka even treated herself to a bath with real hot water hauled up to her room in buckets. She spent the evening soaking in the tin bath, then doing some much needed armor maintenance.

Downstairs in the stables, Iyarra chatted with some new friends. A team of centaur couriers had come down from Port South en route to Rockwall, where they were to open a branch office. The sleek runners were bred for speed rather than strength, but they were friendly and full of gossip. A generous caldron of boiled oats had been laid on, so they all gathered around and ate and talked well into the night.

Alaman spent a very pleasant evening in the tavern, charming patrons with his charisma and performing ancient magical wonders in exchange for drinks. He knew a lot of magical wonders like Coin Through the Glass and Antigravity Ale. The end result was that he was more than a little bit tipsy as he strolled out into the night air to refresh himself. He lit his pipe in the shadow of the tavern wall and took a satisfied draw. It was a nice town, one worth investigating again when he had the time.

He sat and smoked for a good while, watching the few stragglers still on the city streets after dark. Between the free drinks he had won and the very excellent herbal preparation he always carried with him, he was in quite a pleasant little haze when he finally retired to his room. He never even noticed the figure watching him from an alley across the street.

***

Morning found them on the road again, trotting along and making good time. The landscape was rough. The troop was grateful for the wide road carved through the hills and boulders to accommodate the wagons that transported ore from the mines to the river. From there, the ore was loaded aboard the mighty ships that plowed their way up and down the Ataqua.

"I figure we'll get there tomorrow morning at this pace," Revka was saying, as they crossed a small bridge over a stream. "Assuming there aren't any surprises."

"I am inclined to agree." Alaman was only a little unsteady in the saddle, not so much as you'd notice. It really *had* been a good night. "I fear, then, that we will have to part ways. If Porter is to truly manifest as the Chosen One, we must head south toward his destiny. There are magic rings to retrieve, daemonic armies to sweep back into darkness, mighty deeds to be done. A great and terrible destiny awaits the Chosen One."

Porter grinned like an idiot. "Yeah," he said. "It's gonna be great."

"Huh." Revka looked askance at the boy wonder for a moment. She wondered if she should take him aside and give him a word or two of advice, one hero to another as it were, on the finer points of staying alive. She wondered if any of it would sink in. "Listen—"

"Maybe, when you're done with your quest, you can come and join us. Alaman says it's always good to have a barbarian warrior woman, because they fight almost as good as men. And when they get caught by a monster or whatever, you can rescue them."

"Well, I wasn't really planning on—"

"Then of course you'll totally fall in love with me and heroically sacrifice yourself to save my life. Although I'd prefer you didn't do that right away, as it seems kinda silly. I mean, sacrificing yourself right away and all. But Alaman says that's the way it is with heroes. You meet a warrior woman, you rescue her, and next thing you know she's throwing herself in front of a gruntbeast for you."

"Did he?" Revka looked daggers at Alaman, who was riding behind them. If he was listening, he gave no sign.

Iyarra turned back to Revka and grinned. "Why, Revka! You didn't tell me you were planning on falling in love with him. Shame on you!"

Revka snorted and nudged Iyarra in the back. "Watch the road, you."

Porter went on talking about...something or other. Revka wasn't listening. She was too busy seething. The *nerve* of that man! Actually, both of them. Men. They always seemed to assume everything was all about them. The old coot had filled the boy's head with all that sword and sandal garbage, and the boy was swallowing it hook, line, and sinker. If she had five minutes alone with him, she would give him such a piece of—.

Iyarra coughed. "Actually," she said, "We were hoping that perhaps Alaman might favor us with a bit of his wisdom." She looked back at Revka. "Weren't we?"

"Huh? Oh, right." She turned back to Alaman. "Listen, we're going to take a quick break. Can we talk to you?"

Alaman puffed on his pipe. "Well, we can certainly talk and keep traveling I should think. I dare say that should not be too difficult a task."

Porter raised his hand. "Uhm actually, I need to, uh..."

Alaman sighed. "Now, I *did* tell you to take care of that before we left this morning, did I not?"

"Well yeah, but...you know..."

The old man harrumphed. "When Zogar the Unquenchable battled the Firegast of Trull from sunrise to sunset, he didn't stop for breaks." He frowned at the landscape for a moment. "Very well. Be off with you, but don't be long."

After Porter scampered around a nearby hill, Iyarra moved over to Alaman and tugged up the sleeve of her tunic. "You're a wizard," she said. "Do you know anything about this?"

He leaned close, squinting his eyes for a moment. He tapped her arm with the bowl of his pipe. "Absolutely," he said. "It's a curse-mark."

"Yes." Revka radiated extreme patience. "We know that. We both have one. If we don't finish our job on time, it's supposed to take our skin off. So, is it possible to get rid of it?"

"Well, perhaps. Let me see." He guided them around until the morning light fell on the mare's arm. "Now then..." He fished in a saddlebag and brought out an old box, which he placed on the donkey's back. From it, he pulled a handful of crystals, two stones with holes in them, a rosewood wand (with a sequined star glued inexpertly to the tip), a lodestone on a string, two yellow frogs, a shrunken head, a deck of cards marked *Souvenir of Zan Vargas*, and a pair of gaily colored spectacles that proclaimed themselves *Another Fine Product of the Sacred Circle of the Seven Wise Mages*. Alaman applied each treasure against Iyarra's curse-mark in turn, muttering to himself all the while about semisacred geometries and quantum entanglements. Neither woman could understand anything he said. After about five minutes of this ritual, he sat up and shook his head.

"It is as I feared," he said. "The cryptoplast has bonded against the rhinosomes, rendering the geo-flangellates irreducible. I could disroute the parity runes, given several weeks, but I fear that doing so would almost certainly trigger the fault hex. Then, of course, you'd be even worse off. Er, how long did you say you had?"

"A couple of months. Maybe less."

Alaman winced and sucked in through his teeth. "Oh dear. Yes, that is a problem. I couldn't possibly interrogate the pelogronnis in time. Not without a circumflex oscillator."

"A circumflex, ah...?"

"Precisely. I'm afraid, out here, the best I could do is to conflate the rabinsplats until they temporarily deriddle the nitplomb. You wouldn't want that."

***

Alaman's words left a stunned silence in its wake. Iyarra's eyes had glazed over. "I...wouldn't?"

"Certainly not. No, I'm afraid there's just no way forward here. Sorry I cannot help you, but you know how these things are." There was a blur of hands, as the magical gewgaws were tucked back into their box, and the box stowed away again. "Now, where has that boy got to?"

"I'm here! I'm here!" Porter came trotting back around the side of the hill. "Sorry, kinda got turned around."

"Yes well, let us be on our way." Alaman picked up his reins and spurred the donkey into a walk.

Iyarra let them get a little ahead, then turned back to Revka. "All right," she said. "Did you understand any of that?"

"Not a word." Revka shook her head. "Something about a counter rune being faulted? And there was a carfulating...thing, wasn't there? Yeah, I have no idea."

Iyarra peered up ahead at the wizard. She half suspected the old man didn't know what he was saying either, but she didn't say so. It didn't seem like a helpful comment. She sighed. "Well, it was worth trying, I suppose."

"That's true." Revka peered down at her own arm for a moment. "You know what really worries me, though?"

"What's that?"

"I'm prepared to swear this thing is bigger than it was."

It was true. Iyarra had noticed the change on her own arm the other night, and here it was happening on Revka's as well. Twisted lightning tendrils were snaking out from the marks like roots in all directions. She wondered how much of their bodies would be covered before time ran out. She shuddered as they walked a little more.

"Revka?"

"Mm?"

"Do you think they would mind another stop? Only, we were so busy at the last one, and now I have to...uhm...."

"Oh, good grief."

***

The midday sun had burned away the chill of morning, and the day had turned out to be a nice one. Only a few clouds floated in the sky, on just enough breeze to keep things comfortable. There weren't many birds, but a few were around and singing a rather catching little warble Revka had not heard before. The disappointment over the curse-marks had faded a bit in the face of what was, admittedly, a beautiful day. As she rode along, Revka found herself slipping into a cheerful mood, right up until the screaming started.

The shrieking pierced its way through her reverie and sent the few birds flapping for air. The party stopped, looking around themselves in alarm. Porter was electric. "Come on!" He pulled his sword out of its sheath and ran off the road through the detritus of the stony country. Iyarra and Revka looked at each other, shrugged, and hurried off after him, with Alaman serenely bringing up the rear.

The source of the scream proved to be just beyond three smallish hills, in a sort of hollow. At the bottom was the mouth of a smallish cave, the opening of which was littered with bones and surrounded by scorched earth. Just outside the cave was a stake currently occupied by a princess. You could tell she was a princess because of the ruffled (if a bit grimy) pink dress. And the puffed sleeves. And the conical hat with the little strip of gauze hanging from it that Revka could never remember the name of. The princess struggled against the very stout ropes that bound her to the stake.

"Oh, fie! Oh, help! Oh, won't somebody *save* me?"

From the top of the hill, Porter waved his sword. "Fear not, fair maiden, I shall rescue you!" He made to scramble down the hill when Revka clapped a hand on his shoulder. "Hold up, there," she hissed. "A good hero always checks the situation before they act. Just diving in headfirst can get you in all kinds of trouble."

Porter blinked up at them. "Really?"

Iyarra nodded. "Trust us on this one."

Revka cupped her hands around her mouth. "Hey, down there," she shouted. "What's your story? What's going on here?"

"Oh, fie! Oh, tragedy! Oh—"

"Yeah, we've had that bit. Care to move this along, please?"

"Oh, I beg you, come and set me free! A group of ruffians have captured me and tied me to this stake to appease the dragon that lives in this cave. He terrorizes the people who live to the south of here, so they caught me traveling upon the road and have left me here in hopes that I will sate the dragon's hunger. Oh, you must rescue me before he comes!"

Iyarra looked back at Revka. "Aren't we a bit far south for dragons?"

"It is not unknown." Alaman crested the hill and dismounted. "They are attracted to the caves in this area, as I understand it. Very useful for hoards, caves." He pulled out a rope and carefully tethered the donkey to a nearby rock.

"Hoards?" Revka looked down at the cave and at the bones. Something had been there for a long time. Probably a lot of traffic coming off the road...*hmmm*...

Revka hopped off Iyarra's back and pulled out her knife. "Tell her we'll be right down."

Alaman's walking stick suddenly blocked her path. "Stay here. This task is a hero's task, one he shall accomplish alone."

Revka snorted. "Oh, come on. What, are you joking? You didn't have a problem sending us into that temple. But now we have to hang back?"

"Women do not rescue other women from dread peril. It simply isn't done. Besides," he added primly, "This situation clearly has destiny written all over it. No doubt it is his destiny to rescue the princess, which will undoubtedly lead him a step closer to his glorious fate. In any case, it only takes one person to free her. You may remain here."

"And you?"

"I will accompany him, that I may properly investigate the cave."

Revka wheeled around. "Ah-*ha!* Looking for the treasure, you mean! Going to cut us out now that there's the possibility of some real money! Well, you can—"

"*I HAVE SPOKEN!*" The old wizard raised his arms in the air. Instantly there was a peal of thunder, and the taste of imminent lightning in the air. Iyarra whinnied, and Revka stumbled back, falling onto her rump with a thud. "Now. Go back to the road and await our return."

Revka scrambled to her feet. "Now look, you old—"

Iyarra put an arm in front of Revka, blocking her way. "It's all right," she said quietly. "Let's just go back and wait for them by the road."

"Yeah, but—"

"Revka." And now there was something in Iyarra's voice, a note that hadn't been there before. "Let's go."

This was unusual behavior for the horsewoman. Revka blinked in mild surprise. She shrugged inwardly and made a show of dismissing the whole situation. "C'mon, Iyarra," she muttered. "We clearly aren't needed here."

"We shall join you shortly. Don't run off," Alaman warned.

"Yeah, yeah." Iyarra and Revka threaded their way back down the hill.

Behind them, the old wizard watched until they were out of sight, then rummaged on his donkey for a suitably large bag.

"I tell you one thing," said Revka, as they wandered back toward the road. "We're not carrying the loot."

"I wouldn't mind carrying some," said Iyarra, "as long as we were getting a share."

"No chance of that." Revka kicked a rock and watched it dance down the path. "Not after having to split with us last time. He's cut us out good."

"Look at it this way. Tomorrow, we'll be at the river and we'll part ways. We won't have to deal with them anymore. Won't that be nice?" Iyarra patted her on the shoulder.

"Yeah. Suppose."

"All right then. We can put up with them for another day, right?"

"Yeah, yeah." She caught up with the stone and gave it another kick. "Say, why did you stop me back there? I don't think he could have hurt us that badly, if that's what you were worried about."

Iyarra shook her head. "I just thought it would be a bad idea to stick around. No dragon would miss food that close to its lair."

Revka looked up at Iyarra. "Oh yeah? How do you figure that?"

"Let's just say herbivores get really good at learning the habits of carnivores. Especially big ones." Iyarra smiled back.

"I bet." Revka laughed and kicked the stone again. "You know what? It would serve them right if that dragon did come back."

There was a burst of noise. Revka jumped at the sudden sound, like thunder going off right behind you just when you thought the storm had properly passed. The deafening sound went on and on, echoing around the landscape for the longest five seconds in either woman's life. They stood still, neither daring to turn around. In Revka's mind, she could almost feel the blast of flame engulf her.

She opened her eyes. She was still there. Still in one piece, no burns or anything. Iyarra was still next to her, alive and intact. They each caught each other's eye, then turned back to see a plume of smoke rising beyond the hill from which they'd just come. Iyarra cleared her throat.

"Uhm," she said, "Do you think we ought to go and help?"

A tattered scrap flitted through the air, landing before them with a soft *wumph*. The debris was gray, for the most part, and slightly conical. Though charred and deformed, with a little imagination, one could easily see it as, say, the tip of a wizard's hat. They stared at it for a moment.

"Iyarra?"

"Yes?"

"Race you to the road."

Iyarra got there first, but not by much.

The princess leaned back against the pole, then delicately stepped out from the ropes that puddled at her feet. She eyed the remains critically.

"Your aim was a bit low," she said. "Always aim for the head, remember? They could be wearing money belts or valuable clothing." She poked at the charred bodies. "Sword's cheap, maybe get something for scrap." She wandered up the hill and fell to inspecting the donkey's baggage. Behind her, the dragon crawled the rest of the way out of the cave and started in on the day's catch.

"Let's see...provisions, couple of old books, deck of cards...ohhh, someone's been treasure hunting." She rooted through the purse, letting a handful of ancient coins cascade through her fingers. "Very nice."

She dumped the purse and the other valuables into a sack and turned back to the dragon. "Do you want the donkey? I know they disagree with you, but it's up to you."

The dragon looked up and eyed the donkey for a moment, then snorted and went back to its lunch.

"All right." She unhitched the struggling donkey, which immediately bolted from the scene and headed for parts unknown.

The princess slung the bag over her shoulder and sauntered back to the cave. On the way, she patted the dragon's flank. "Hurry along in when you're done, there's a good boy." She winked back at him, tugging her dress down off one shoulder. "I'll be waiting," she cooed.

The dragon grunted. He wasn't getting any younger, and competition with the younger bucks up north was getting worse and worse. At least here he had a decent hoard, no competition to speak of, and his meals practically delivered. All in all, it was a good deal, even if he had to put up with Miss Prissy Princess and her weird dragon fixation.

He finished up the last of the remains before they cooled and looked up at the sky. Still early yet. Probably could manage another bunch this afternoon, once she was done with him.

Best get on with it then.

He turned around and lumbered slowly back into the cave. Humans. Try and figure 'em.

Chapter Seven

PORT SOUTH WAS A good-sized town of several hundred people. That wasn't even counting the steady stream of traders, boat crews, and so on picking up and dropping off cargo on the progression of riverboats which plied their way up and down the Ataqua. Port South was one of the busiest ports on the river, and barges of ore were a regular sight. The city was always bustling, always on the move.

Through all of this, Iyarra and Revka bobbed and weaved their way toward the great harbor. Revka was frowning at her map. "So, we're headed upstream, according to this. That means we need to get across the river. Over there." She pointed to a spot where a giant drawbridge had been cranked up to let a riverboat pass. They got in line with the small crowd in front of the bridge's gate and watched as the boat passed and the bridge was lowered. Gates on both sides were opened, and traffic began to stream across the bridge in both directions.

"Neat, eh?" Revka took in the mechanics of the bridge with some satisfaction. "I was here a few years ago. They got oxen in the support towers that do the work. Look, you can barely see where the two bridges join."

Iyarra felt queasy. She wasn't particularly looking forward to spending the next few days on a boat. As for the bridge, engineering marvel it might be, but she could see the water through the gaps in the planks. And that gap between the two bridge halves was very visible, thank you very much. She didn't like it. If she looked too closely, she could almost feel herself plunging down between the planks and into the water, washing away forever...

A rear hoof caught on a knothole, and she stumbled forward with a yelp. Revka fell face first into Iyarra's hair. "Dangit, girl," she muttered. "You're holding up traffic, come on. People are staring." Iyarra mumbled an apology as she stumbled to her hooves and hurried the rest of the way across.

There were two boats scheduled to head upriver that morning. The *Miss Agnes* was basically a barge with a paddle wheel in back and a cramped cabin for the pilots. The *Autumn Blaze* was a true passenger boat, three stories high if you didn't count the wheelhouse. The floating hotel was draped in finery and painted up like the more enthusiastic class of wedding cake. In back, a giant wheel stirred the river into its wake. Iyarra and Revka stared in awe.

"Now *that*," Revka declared, "is what I call a boat."

"You know, we could just follow the river road." Iyarra's suggestion came too late. She sighed and trotted up the gangplank after Revka.

As in Peccaray, the travel warrants weren't good for transportation, but they did manage to swing a free upgrade to a private room, hastily refurbished to accommodate a centaur and human. Revka stood in the middle of the cabin, nodding her approval.

"How about that, eh? Finally, we get to travel first class for a while." She leaned against Iyarra, who was inspecting the large mattress on the floor that passed for a centaur's bed. "What do you say we get out of our traveling clothes and freshen up a little bit? There's a saloon at the front of the boat."

"I suppose so," Iyarra said. "But it is a bit snug in here. I mean, I can barely turn around."

"That's ships for you, I'm afraid. Anyway, we're lucky. The normal rooms here are just about the same size as the bed, and centaurs usually have to share stables down below." She unfastened Iyarra's saddlebags. "Now, let's wash up and see what we can scrape together that isn't leather or chain mail, shall we? I feel like kicking back for a while."

"All right." Iyarra started digging through the bags. "Though I don't know what we have that would be appropriate. Not a lot of evening wear in here, if you see what I mean."

"Well, we'll work something out." Revka elbowed her way past to the water closet. "Actually, it is a bit snug in here, isn't it? I think your stables aren't usually too much bigger than this. Though I'd hate being in close quarters like that. I like my privacy."

"Well, it's hard to explain. But it's nice, a bunch of us being together." Iyarra pulled some clothes out of one bag and began to fuss through them. "It's...reassuring. You know? Easier to sleep knowing they're there. It's a herd thing, I guess."

"I'll take your word for it."

Iyarra smiled sheepishly. "I feel the same way when it comes to you, you know."

"Do you really?"

"Mm-hm."

Revka smiled. She returned to Iyarra and stood on tiptoe to kiss her. "C'mon, gorgeous," she said. "We're gonna knock 'em dead tonight."

***

The lounge was the type you often got in the gaudier class of hotel, where no expense was spared in the cause of overdoing it as much as possible. Riding on a riverboat was something of an occasion, and the passenger boats that plied their trade up and down the Ataqua were masterpieces of sheer ostentatiousness. It was amazing what the right carpeting and a fresh coat of paint could do.

Iyarra and Revka moved through the early evening crowd, threading their way to a table near the front where floor-to-ceiling windows offered a sweeping view of the river. Iyarra had worked over the show costumes, removing frills here, adding a bit more modesty there. What remained were two perfectly elegant ensembles, entirely reasonable for evening wear. Revka had even put her hair up, something she almost never did. Iyarra gazed at her over the table and considered, not for the first time, that when she cleaned up, she cleaned up *nice*.

The evening went well, with plenty of talking and drinking and even a small combo in the corner playing music suitable for dancing. Revka had a glass or two of something, and before long her mouth had geared up to full speed. They had attracted a small group of listeners, as she expounded on their recent adventures.

"So, I was like, 'Look, pal. We went into your ancient, abandoned temple for you, weeded through I don't know how many dead bodies, found your treasure and got out of there in one piece. Now, you're trying to keep the whole thing for yourself? Sorry, honcho, that ain't gonna fly.' And then I—"

"Honcho?" whispered Iyarra.

"Not now," Revka hissed. "I'm rolling." She turned back to the audience. "Anyway, he kept threatening to curse us and turn us into all kinds of things, but I wasn't having any of it, not me. You just gotta show 'em a firm hand, wizards." She took a swallow from the tankard of ale someone had thoughtfully provided, while the audience digested this tidbit of wisdom.

"Very impressive." The speaker was seated by himself, two tables away. He was tall, thin, and exceedingly well dressed. He raised his wineglass in the ladies' direction and nodded. "Sounds like you are both particularly skillful and clever. Not just the usual hired swords, eh?"

Iyarra shuffled a hoof. "Oh, I wouldn't go so far as to say—"

Revka nudged her. "Oh, sure. You can't just go in swingin' these days. You've got to have smarts. Me and Iyarra? We've got brains we ain't even used yet."

The stranger's smile broadened. "You don't say! We may have to talk later. I may have a little business proposition for you."

Iyarra laid her hand on Revka's shoulder. "Well, that's awfully nice of you, but I'm afraid our time constrai—"

"Oh, this won't take any time at all. I assure you. Just a few hours of your time when we get to Port Mill."

"Well, that's very kind, but—"

Revka looped an arm through Iyarra's. "Excuse me a moment, mister," she said. "Gotta talk to my colleague."

In a quiet corner of the bar, Revka drew Iyarra to her side. "What are you doing?" she whispered.

Iyarra shrugged. "You know we don't have time for this. We've got a deadline. In fact, we've got a *very* dead line if we don't get back on time."

"Honey, listen. The man said it would only take a few hours. Why are you worried? We're making great time, for crying out loud."

"Well, for one, this guy. Who goes around hiring people on ships? And for that matter, who is he? Could be anybody."

"Well, he's probably some sort of merchant trader or something. Probably needs a guard. You know we can't turn down business."

"Our shares of the temple treasure should be plenty enough to see us there and back and you know it. I just don't like this guy. He smells wrong."

"Smells wrong?"

Iyarra just shrugged.

"Look, let me just talk to him, huh? You know I'm the one with the business head. I'll see what he has to say. If it's legit, great. If it's not, I'll take a pass. Fair enough?"

"I suppose." Iyarra sighed.

"All right." Revka gave the centauress a smile and patted her flank. "C'mon, you trust me, right?"

"Well, yeah..."

"All right then. Don't worry about it. I got this."

***

Later, back in the room, Revka draped herself against the horsewoman's body, eyes half closed, as they stretched out on the bedding. Iyarra was toying with Revka's hair. They rested as the boat calmly rocked with the waves. The sensation was almost hypnotic. Revka could feel herself getting pleasantly drowsy.

"Had fun tonight?" Iyarra nuzzled in.

"Hm?"

"Telling your stories." The centauress grinned. "I've noticed you never can resist an audience."

Revka chuckled. "Oh yeah. That's true." She managed a shrug.

"You know, when I saw you acting out our fight with the morgas, it reminded me of something."

"W'sat?"

"Well, remember when we first met? I was supposed to meet you in town one evening. I got there a little early, and I saw you with some children. A little girl was upset, because the other children wouldn't let her play. You made a little toy sword for her out of some scrap wood, remember? Then you taught her how to hold it right and the proper stance. I remember she was so happy when she ran off to join the others. I think that was when I really fell for you, I mean like felt serious."

Revka tilted her head upward. "You saw that, huh?"

"Mm-hm." She leaned down to kiss Revka. "It was very sweet."

Revka just shrugged. "Well I dunno about that," she said. "Just something to kill time. Besides, I kind of felt sorry for the kid, you know?"

"Did you?"

"Yeah, well, she…" Revka trailed off into a mutter. "She kinda reminded me of me at that age. Sort of."

"Oh?" Iyarra gently worked the tangles out of Revka's hair. "Is that so?"

"Well, when you're the only girl, it's… Well, it's tough sometimes. I felt sorry for her."

Iyarra leaned in and nuzzled against Revka. "You don't talk much about your childhood, I've noticed."

"Mm. Don't like to think about it, really."

"Had an unhappy one?"

"Not...not exactly. Just more like...well, it's in the past, basically. That's all."

"Okay." Iyarra gave her another squeeze. "Understood."

Revka didn't answer. She was lost in memories long tucked away. Funny, the things you remember sometimes.

Below decks, giant oxen trundled along, powering the gears that kept the giant paddle wheel turning. The boat cut its way slowly upriver, foam churning the moonlight reflected on the waves, and the night chugged its way toward the dawn.

***

The next morning brought a uniform gray sky from horizon to horizon. Iyarra reclined at what she assumed was the forecastle, drumming a hoof on the deck and trying to remember if it was 'night of red, dawn of gray, sends the traveler on his way' or the other way around. The air didn't smell like rain, just dullness. She leaned against the rail, watching the scenery drift by at a little over a walking pace. She spotted a patch of clover, ripe and ready to eat, and a glade of flowers, just within sight. The road along the river was wide and well-traveled. It was nice to have a bed and regular meals on the boat, but she had never been one for sitting in the same place, even if that place itself was moving. Her eyes glazed over, as she sat and ticked away the seemingly interminable hours.

When Revka joined her for lunch, she seemed very pleased. "All right. So, it's just like I said. He works for a trading firm, and he needs some hired muscle. There's a two hour layover in Carlin tomorrow, where he needs to pick up some goods. We escort him back to the boat, then when we get to Port Mill, we help him get it to his seller there. Bammo, no problem. We get paid for our time, and he says if we do a good job, then after we're done with this whole mishmash we can come back and work for him on the regular. You like that?"

Iyarra furrowed a brow. "What, riding up and down the river all the time? I'm not sure I'm ready to spend that much time on boats." Revka's pat on her flank wasn't exactly reassuring.

"Hey, I know you prefer running around, but it's not always gonna be up and down the river, right? Besides, a regular salary? Our traveling expenses taken care of? Not a bad deal at all. Don't I always take care of you?"

"Well, yes, but—"

"Well, all right then. Don't worry, we got this."

***

Carlin was smaller than most river towns but had a few trading routes coming up from just south of the mountains. Mostly, it was given over to warehouses and wholesalers moving goods back and forth. There was not much in the way of noncommercial traffic coming through, so the town tended toward the bland and prosaic. Mister David, as he had introduced himself, led them through a maze of dull, stone buildings. To all intents and purposes, the structure they stopped at seemed just the same as all the others. They were ushered into a small office, where he spoke briefly with a clerk. There were papers to sign, then a dull twenty minutes waiting for a little man to push a cart in from the warehouse proper. A fairly large, wooden trunk was duly signed over, loaded onto Iyarra's back, and hauled back to the ship, where it was locked away in the secure cargo hold.

"See?" said Revka, once the boat was paddling its way upriver again. "Piece of cake."

The box itself had not been particularly heavy, but boxes didn't lend themselves to horseback, no matter how many blankets you threw on. Iyarra was almost certain she had a splinter or two, right in the middle of her back where she couldn't get to them.

"Come on. We'll be in Port Mill tomorrow. We'll drop the thing off, with money in our pockets and a potential long-term engagement. What's not to like?"

"You're right." Iyarra took a deep breath, then let it out slowly. "I'm just...I worry, that's all. You know how I am, but I trust you."

"Do ya?" Revka raised an eyebrow.

Iyarra wrapped her arms around the other woman. "Of course. Always."

Revka grinned. "Well," she said. "That's better."

One deck below, Mister David leaned against the railing, his eyes on the road that followed along the river. Presently, he saw a courier on a fast horse galloping north, and he nodded to himself. The boat wouldn't make Port Mill til the next day. They would have plenty of time to prepare.

He turned and went into the lounge to see about lunch.

***

The sky was a perfect blue, as the three stepped off the boat and onto the streets of Port Mill. The previous evening's rain had washed the cobbled streets and left a post-rain smell that quickened the step and gladdened the heart. Even Iyarra was feeling rather cheerful as she followed Mister David off the main street and along a side alley to a small, unmarked building. Mister David had a brief word with the man behind the counter, and they were led through a door into the back room. A dignified, elderly gentleman waited for them.

"Well, Mister White, here I am, right on schedule!" Mister David beamed and patted the box on Iyarra's back. "Got it here safe and sound, all present and correct."

Mister White grunted. He nodded to two heavyset men, who lowered the box off of Iyarra's back. Mister White looked expectantly at Mister David. "Well?"

Mister David shrugged. "Well, what? You know I don't have a key for it. Go ahead."

The older man regarded him with a frown. "I am waiting for you to pay these two ladies off and send them on their way so that we can get down to work. I want them out of here before we open this thing up."

Revka stepped forward. "Not a problem, gentleman," she said. "Be out of your way in no time. Now, I believe the fee was five gold each. We can take silver of course, but not copper. Too much to haul around."

Mister David laid a hand on her arm. "Just a minute." He turned back to Mister White. "Actually, I wanted to talk to you about these two. You remember saying we need to bring a few more people in if we can? Well, I've had my eye on these two, and I think they can be trusted."

Mister White looked them up and down. "Really? They seem a bit scruffy to me. Besides, you know that what we really need are—"

"I know, I know. But they're adventurers. They've got brains and brawn, and they're successful, too. Just raided a temple and got away with half the treasure. They could help us with, ah, the other thing."

Mister White arched an eyebrow at his younger colleague, then walked toward the two women. He studied them for a long moment and paced slowly around them both. Without taking his eyes off the women, he asked Mister David, "Can they be trusted?"

"Oh, yes." Mister David nodded. "Miss Revka here and I talked on the way down. They are both quite scrupulously honest about work, dividing treasure up and so on. And of course, they are very discreet."

Mister White hmphed. "You said they took half the treasure. What happened to the other half?"

"Our traveling companions got that."

"And what happened to them?"

"Wrong side of a dragon. We found a hoard and, well, they shut us out of it. They thought the dragon was away. Turns out he wasn't."

"I see." He leaned back against his desk, appraising them. "And what brings you to this neck of the woods?"

Iyarra stepped forward, but Revka nudged her back. "We're just running a little errand for the Duke of Gainsburgh."

"Are you, now? You don't look the official type."

With a smirk, Revka flourished the travel warrants. Mister White took them and read them over for what seemed an inordinately long time. Finally, he handed them back. "I see. Well, very impressive. He's not one to just hire random persons off the street. I do know that much." He looked thoughtful. "And yet...it wouldn't do to unnecessarily delay you, would it? Perhaps we'd best just send you on your way, not involve you in this business. I wouldn't want to inconvenience you at all."

"Oh now, come on!" Mister David waved an arm at them. "You can see they're just what we're looking for, right? Brains and daring, honesty and resourcefulness. I've been looking up and down the river for weeks, and I haven't found more suitable candidates. We're just going to let them walk out the door? Besides, I'm sure they're curious. Right, you two?" He gave them a pleading look.

Revka held her hands up. "Look, whatever it is, we don't want to cause friction here. I will admit we are on a bit of a schedule, but we can spare you a day or so. If you need time, we can always come back when our business with the duke is finished."

Mister David waved his hands frantically. "No, no, no, no! No, please. Just hold on a minute." He turned to Mister White. "Come on, sir, you know what we've been looking for. These two fit the bill exactly! We can have the business done by this evening, tomorrow at the latest! What do you say?"

Mister White looked them over again, then back to Mister David, then back to them. Finally, he nodded his head. "All right," he said. "I'm going to trust you two. But I need an assurance of your complete discretion in this matter. Agreed?"

"Oh absolutely, yes."

"Yeah. Of course."

"Very well." He turned to the hired muscle, who were still lurking off to one side. "Targhan? Choss? I'll call you when I need you." The two gave surly nods and filed out the door, which shut behind them.

"Now then." Mister White produced an iron key and moved over to the box. Mister David rubbed his hands together in anticipation. The two women leaned forward.

There was a moment of metallic rattling and the creak of the lid being opened, then silence.

"Vegetables?"

"Not just vegetables." Mister White was seated in his office, a small corner walled off from the rest of the building. Every flat surface was covered in cryptic but important-seeming papers, leaving just enough room for a few chairs and Iyarra, who'd had to back in and wedge herself in the corner before Mister David had been able to close the door. "What we have here is better than silver, better even than gold."

Revka picked up a root and examined it critically. It looked like a potato and some ginger had gotten together on intimate terms and produced offspring. This had to be the runt of the litter, if she was any judge. "Okay. I give up. How?"

Mister White smiled. "Have either of you two ladies ever heard of the calamantrum? It's a small, greenish-brown plant, growing wild in rocky territory. Generally considered a weed as no one has ever found any use for it, and the plant produces no flowers. Animals generally avoid both plant and tuber, and it's about as aesthetically pleasing as a clod of dirt. In short, all it is good for is taking up space that could be used by other, more useful plants."

"They do taste terrible; I know that," Iyarra volunteered.

Mister White laughed. "I will happily take your word on that. Now, what you see before you is the calamantrum root. An unpleasant item, utterly hopeless for cooking or medicinal purposes. That is, until now."

He reached behind him and picked up a stoppered glass bottle. "This special preparation employs, among other things, an extract of the calamantrum root. I believe the alchemist, Quenda, was trying to create something else entirely. Interestingly enough, however, his potion turns out to be an excellent cure for...well, gentlemen's complaints."

"Uhm..." Iyarra sheepishly held her hand up.

"Oh, for Pete's sake." Revka rolled her eyes and stood on tiptoe to whisper into her ear. The centauress cocked her head at the whisper, then blushed furiously.

"Oh. Uhm. I see." She colored, flattening her ears against the sides of her head.

"Quite. Now, as you may imagine, there is something of a market for potions of this sort, especially for one that actually works. Quenda's has been extensively tested, and I hope you will forgive me if I say the results are remarkable. The fact is, this stands to make an absolute packet for whoever knows the secret to making it."

"Frankly, this alchemist is a dotty old bird, with no family or anything like that. He considers this an amusing side project but no more than a distraction to his real work. Consequently, he has agreed to sell the secret of his process for what, in all honesty, is a steal. I have been sent by my employer to purchase the formula on their behalf. Follow me?"

"So far." Revka nodded.

"Very good. Now, here's the thing. I am going to buy it all right, but not for them. No, indeed. I'm going to buy it for myself, or rather for the four of us gathered in this room."

Iyarra uhmmmed, "But isn't that a little...unethical?"

"Unethical?" The old man looked up at the horsewoman for a moment. "Let me tell you something about unethical. Old man Tomrolo took me on when I was a child. I have worked for him my entire life. I have traveled every inch of this kingdom, dragged caravans across deserts and snow plains, been attacked by skulldugs, cryptids, dragons, and every wild animal nature saw fit to throw at the commercial traveler. I have given my *life* to that man and his family.

"And we were family, in a way. The old man knew how to treat his people. He looked after us, you see. Many's the time he told me, 'There will always be a place for you under my roof.' A good man, you see. A saint, or as much as a merchant can be."

"What happened?"

Mister White toyed with a quill on his desk. "A fishbone," he said quietly. "I was away, running some spices down the river for him. One minute he was at dinner with his family, the next, dead on the floor. It was that swift."

"Of course, his son took over the family business. He'd been groomed, you see, from the very beginning. All slide rules and abacuses, going on about efficiency and trimming the fat. He called me in when I got back and thanked me for my service. He said that after this job I would no longer be needed. Can you believe that? He's bringing in a group of younger people, greenhorns. Who have no idea how to haggle. They won't know who to talk to, or the places to go and which to avoid. I have experience, but apparently that counts for nothing."

Suddenly, he looked very old. "Do you know what he said? He wished me luck in my future endeavors. What future endeavors? I'm old and tired. I was looking forward to coming off the road and resting, maybe working in the head office and supervising the young lads as they went out. But to be cast aside like an old rag?"

He shook his head. "No. I made up my mind, then and there. I was going to take care of myself. So here I am." He waved an arm around the office. "My retirement. A couple of rented rooms in a back street today, but tomorrow?" He held up the root. "With the secret recipe and an unlimited supply of these, we'll be set for life!"

He smirked. "And that smug little twerp won't be able to do anything but sit and watch."

Revka leaned back in her chair and put on what she considered a businesslike face. "Interesting," she said. "but I take it you're not actually planning on buying this formula or whatever with your boss's money. Are you? Besides, I still don't see what part we have to play in all of this."

"What? Oh, no, no, no." The old man laughed. "This will be a completely aboveboard transaction. I have some money squirreled away for a rainy day. Alas, not enough to meet the old coot's asking price. I brought in young Mister David here, an enterprising fellow with a lot on the ball. I've been training him up for a while. Between the two of us, we're close but not quite there. Which brings us to you two."

"We need to bring in a third, I guess third and fourth, party to get us over the line. To be blunt, if you can raise the funds, I am offering you a partnership in our enterprise. The percentage of the take to be determined by your contribution to the initial purchase. I, er, take it you have some funds?"

Mister David leaned in. "They've got their take from that temple I told you about. I'm sure that was a sizable sum, eh ladies?"

Revka leaned back, waved a hand dismissively. "Well, it wasn't that big a deal. Just a quick in and out to cover travel expenses. Par for the course, really."

"Still, if you have enough for us to proceed with the purchase, that would be splendid. May we see?"

Iyarra looked down to Revka, who nodded. Reaching back into her saddlebags, she fumbled for a moment, then pulled out the hemp bag into which they had stored their take. She undid the knot and tipped the contents onto the desk. Gold and silver spilled out in a pile, catching the glint from the afternoon sun.

Mister White lay a hand over the pile and spread it out across the surface. His eyes darted back and forth, doing swift mental calculations. He looked up at the ceiling, his lips moving as he ciphered. After a long moment, he looked back down at them and broke into a grin.

"Ladies, David," he said. "We are going to be rich."

Chapter Eight

THE REST OF THE afternoon was spent in delicate negotiation of the finer details. Iyarra tended to tune out for these parts, letting Revka do the talking, but eventually an agreement was reached. Iyarra and Revka conceded to stay another night, while the funds were collected. First thing in the morning, they would all count the money and Messrs. White and David would head off directly to complete the deal. They offered to store the money in their safe overnight, but Iyarra explained that they had some trifling little expenses to take care of that evening. In the end, they all shook hands and went their separate ways.

The sun was just beginning to set as Iyarra and Revka strolled along the shale beach that lined the river. The thin, gray stones made a quite satisfactory crunch beneath Iyarra's hooves. "I can't believe this is happening. You see, though? Our ship is totally coming in." Her girlfriend was practically bouncing, as she strutted along beside Iyarra.

"I don't know." Iyarra rubbed the back of her neck, looking down at Revka. "I'm still not sure how I feel about this."

Revka patted Iyarra's shoulder. "Oh, come on. I know it's taking a bit of a chance, but these guys are onto something big. Besides, it's too good an opportunity to pass up."

"I know you're better at this sort of thing than I am," Iyarra sighed. "But it doesn't..." She waved a hand vaguely in the air. "I can't explain it. If I say it smells wrong, that gives you the wrong impression entirely. It's more like...ugh. I don't know."

Revka sighed. She grabbed Iyarra's hand and stopped her. "Hey now. Listen. You know I trust you in things you know about, right? Well, this is business. Business is what I know about. You know that, right? So, I'm just asking you to trust me on this. He even signed that paper saying he'd refund us out of his own pocket if things went wrong. He's got bonds and merchandise. You know if we didn't jump at this and it turned out to be real, we'd be kicking ourselves for the rest of our lives. It's a calculated risk, right? Come on, now."

Iyarra gave Revka's hand a squeeze. "If you say so," she murmured.

Revka grinned and took a quick look around. They were alone on the beach. She stood on tiptoe to give Iyarra a peck on the chin. "All right," she said. "Now, let's go get some dinner to celebrate."

***

Later that night in her stable, Iyarra paced. She had been trying to sleep for ages, but it just wasn't happening. She leaned against the windowsill, gazing out into the night. She knew she should leave well enough alone, knew she should trust Revka in these things, but her senses were rebelling against the whole idea. She rubbed her temples, grumbling under her breath. Twice, she made to open the paddock door but stopped herself. She tried munching some oats but couldn't get past the first mouthful. She tried to sleep again. Nothing.

She gave up. Digging in her saddlebags, she found four cloth sacks and a few bundles of clothes. A few minutes later, the paddock door clicked shut behind her.

***

The next morning was clear and sunny again. They met back at the office right after breakfast. Revka and Iyarra's money was carefully counted out and returned to its sack. Mister White declared there was enough not only to buy the formula but to up the bid a bit, in case they had any surprise competition. He even gave them a small sack of coins to cover their traveling expenses in the meantime. "It should take us two weeks to get there and back again. If you like, you can just come straight here."

"I think we'll just breeze by in a few weeks," said Revka airily. "Depending on where our business takes us, you know how it is."

Mister White nodded. "Of course, of course." He went over to a corner and spent a moment fiddling with a safe. The door opened to reveal two large sacks. "My investment and Mister David's," he explained. "I need to do some wrap-up work this morning before leaving. You can see me off after lunch. In the meantime, let's store your money in the safe with the rest, shall we?"

"Of course." Iyarra picked up the bag and tried to turn around. She remembered too late that she couldn't do that in a room so small and yelped as she rear-ended a filing cabinet and dropped the bag.

"Sorry! Sorry!" She dropped down and scrambled for the sack, kicked it under the desk, then fished it back out again. She tried to get past the desk to the safe, but shamefacedly handed the bag to Revka, who placed it next to the others with a satisfying *chlink*. Mister White smiled and shut the safe, spinning the combination wheel.

"Well, that's it," he said. "Mister David, perhaps you'll show them around town for the morning? In fact, take them to lunch. My treat. I'll see you when you get back, right?"

Mister David beamed. "You bet, sir." There were handshakes and mutual congratulations all around, then a moment of awkwardness as Iyarra backed her way out of the office.

Mister David took them in a circuit around the town, pointing out the various sights. The mill, the town's namesake, was a monster, sporting a wheel larger than that found on the average riverboat. "Grain comes down from the vast plains to the north. The milled flour goes everywhere, all up and down the river. This mill made the city's fortunes and has been rebuilt three times, each version bigger than the last." He beamed. "It's a hell of a thing, you know? There are other mills, but none turn out so much flour of such a high quality and so fast. The river current is swifter than usual just here, you see. Adds an extra kick to the grinder."

A few hours later, they sat down to an excellent lunch. Mister David could not stop talking about the money. "Between you and me, ol' Mister White has always had a real nose for business. What the family is going to do without him is anybody's guess. Still, they brought it on themselves."

"Well, that's true enough. I guess you've worked with him a while," Revka observed.

"Oh, a few years. traveling up and down the river. He always tells me, 'Opportunity is where you find it,' and he knows what he's talking about. Guy can make money anywhere. Just let him get his hands on that recipe and boy, they'll have to dig more gold out of the ground for us!"

He took a sip of ale, and his gaze softened. "I really wanna thank you guys," he said. "This hasn't been in the works very long at all. We barely had any time to get our plan together. If you two weren't taking a flyer on trusting us, we'd never be able to do it at all." He raised his mug in salute. "You're good people."

"And centaurs."

"And centaurs." He laughed and drained the last of the ale.

A little while later, the three strolled back through the narrow cobblestone streets to the little warehouse, where it immediately became clear that something was wrong.

The greeting room was empty as they came in, and the door to the back was hanging ajar. There were signs of a scuffle. The three exchanged glances and dashed toward the small office. They found the safe open and empty, and Mister White slumped against the wall, covered in blood.

"Oh, no!" Mister David pushed his way forward. "No, no, *no!*" He slapped the old man's cheeks and shook his shoulders muttering, "Come on, you bastard, wake up!" Finally, the old man came back to a groggy sort of consciousness. His eyes focused on Mister David, then suddenly widened in alarm. "They got it," he cried. "The bastards got it all!"

"What? Who? Which bastards?" Mister David shook the old man by his collar. "Tell me!"

"Tell us!"

"It was Targhan and Choss," White groaned, trying to sit up. "Damn them."

Revka quirked an eyebrow. "What, you mean the two heavies that were here before?"

Mister White nodded. "Turns out they were working for the boy. He thought I might try something like this. They took the money and headed off a little while ago."

Revka groaned. "Dammit! Which way did they go?"

"East, toward the mountains. I heard them say they were going to meet some people on the pilgrim road."

Mister David looked up at the two women. "The pilgrim road! That was where you were heading, wasn't it?"

Iyarra nodded. "That's right."

Mister David nodded. "Right." He turned to Mister White again. "You said it was just a little while ago?"

"Yes, yes... I'm actually surprised you didn't see them."

"We came by the river road." He turned to Iyarra and Revka. "If you hurry, you can still catch them up, especially if they're on foot." He turned back to Mister White, who merely shrugged.

"Say no more." Revka slapped Iyarra's flank. "Come on, you. No time to waste. Let's get those guys."

"But—"

"Don't worry," said Mister David. "I'll look after Mister White. You just get those crooks with our money! No time! *Go!*"

***

Iyarra charged down the main street of Port Mill and out the Pilgrim's Gate. She raced down the dirt road, throwing a trail of dust over the other travelers. Finally, she rounded a bend and slowed to a steady, sedate trot.

"What are you doing?" Revka thumped her on the withers. "Come on! We'll never catch them like this. Get going."

Iyarra shook her head. "I don't think so," she said. "It really doesn't matter how fast we go. We're not going to catch them. I doubt very much that they even left town at all."

Revka's eyes narrowed. "What the hell are you talking about?"

Iyarra looked sheepish. "Well, last night, after you went to bed, I kind of couldn't sleep. Kept worrying about it. You know me and my suspicions. Anyway...uhm...I snuck out."

"Snuck out? Forgive me for saying, hon, but you're not exactly the sneaky type."

Iyarra rubbed the back of her neck. "Well, you know that one time in Fort Longran, when we had to get past all of those guards, and the streets were all cobblestone? You made those little booties stuffed with old clothes."

"Oh yeah, yeah. I forgot about that. That worked pretty good."

"Yes, it did. So I tried it again, you see. I kinda stood outside the window of their building, and I heard them talking and laughing. There were more people this time, so I peeked in, and they had turned it into a gaming house! There were people playing cards and dice and wheel of fate. Mister David was all dressed up, and everyone called him Darcey. Mister White pulled him over, and I heard our names. He said something about a 'blow off' after lunch, and that he would make it look good. And then I left."

Revka clapped her hand over her eyes. "Good grief."

"Yeah." Iyarra sighed, moseying down the road. "And when we came back after lunch? All that on his face? That wasn't blood. I know what blood smells like, and that wasn't it. Anyway, I'm pretty sure they were lying about everything."

Revka sighed. She stayed quiet for a while. "Yarra?"

"Yes?"

"Why didn't you tell me?"

Iyarra sighed. She reached back and gave her girlfriend's hand a squeeze. "I'm sorry. I knew that if you knew, then you would try to fight them, or trick them back out of their money as well, and what with one thing and another it seemed to me that we were better off just getting out of there as quickly as possible, you see? The last thing we needed was more trouble."

Revka sighed. "All right. You're probably right about that. But what you seem to have forgotten is that we took off, leaving them with all of our money. We were counting on that to get us to Kalazad and back again."

Iyarra reached back into her saddlebags, and rummaged around for a moment, then fished out a familiar cloth sack. This she passed wordlessly back to Revka. Revka opened the bag and peered in at its contents. "The hell?"

Revka reached into the bag. She let the coins trickle through her fingers. "But...how?"

Iyarra kicked a stone. "Well. Er...you remember when I picked up the bag with our money? And then dropped it?"

"When you had to fish under the desk for it? Yeah, I...*ohhhhhhh*."

Iyarra grinned over her shoulder. "Yeah. Pretty much. I thought for sure you would see it, so I kinda 'accidentally' bumped you out of the way. Sorry about that."

"It's all right, it's all right." Revka gave her a pat, letting the coins run through her fingers again. "Iyarra?"

"Mm?"

"If we've got the money, what did *they* get?"

***

Back in Port Mill, Mister White wiped the last of the 'blood' away. He fastened his collar, checking himself in the mirror. "Well," he beamed, turning to the others. "That is how you do it. A textbook example, if I may make so bold. Good job, everyone."

Targhan helped Mister White with his coat. "Thanks, boss. What's next?"

"I believe we have Master Gelf coming in this afternoon, with a mark from up north. Now, I figure we can string him with the Fiddler's Riddle for a few days, maybe even put him on the send. He sounds like the type we can milk for a good long while. So while we've got a moment, Mister David if you would, please?"

Mister David grinned. He pulled three cloth bags from their hiding place and put them on the desk with a healthy clunk. He opened Revka and Iyarra's sack and, with great ceremony, tipped its contents onto the desk.

The four men stared.

Eventually, Mister David managed to find his voice. "The *hell*?"

Mister White sighed. He reached down and spread the pile out, as if checking to see if a coin or two were secreted in there somewhere. But no, there wouldn't be any. He drummed his fingers on the desktop and glared.

On the desk, a small heap of gray shale stones stared back at him.

***

"So, we got our money back, and they got beach rocks." Revka chortled. "I swear, girl, I am rubbing off on you more and more every day."

"Undoubtedly." Iyarra preened and allowed herself a little canter, as they passed a merchant wagon.

"Actually, don't forget they gave us a little traveling money to be getting on with, too. We actually came out ahead on the deal."

"That's true!" Iyarra giggled.

Revka leaned forward. "Boy, can you just imagine the looks on their faces when they work that one out?"

There was a thoughtful pause.

"Yarra?"

"Yes?"

"Do you think we might want to start running again?"

"I...er, yes. Actually, I think we might."

"Yeah. Let's."

Chapter Nine

"WHEN THAT APRILLE, WITH its showers soote,
The drought of March hath pierce'd to the root,
Go pilgrimage to Tam menne surely would,
Were not the roads there reduc'ed to mudde."
—Geoffery Yarlsburg, "The Kalazad Tales"

By the time Port Mill was a good few hours behind them, the road was already beginning to incline, and the territory grew rough. A belt of stone stretched northwest to southeast across the landscape ahead. The Icarine Mountains.

They had moved off the road for a while, following little paths alongside and keeping an eye and ear out for pursuers. The afternoon dragged on. The sun grew hot in the sky, and it became increasingly obvious that if anyone was after them, they wouldn't be showing up anytime soon. Besides, Iyarra said she could smell water.

The pond was only a few minutes' walk from the road, nestled in a tree-lined glade. The water was a bit muddy but seemed all right. Revka busied herself hiding the trail and putting up a few noise traps, a trick she'd learned since the last time they'd been unexpectedly walked in on while bathing. Iyarra had never learned to swim, but she could horse paddle along fairly well. Revka, on the other hand, wasted no time in diving straight down to the bottom. She swam along the lake bed, poking around for interesting stones, dropped coins, ancient merchant galleons laden with treasure—well, you never knew. She had just surfaced with what was probably a perfectly good silver coin once you scraped the tarnish off, when she realized that they were not alone.

There were two of them, scruffy types. One was gangly and thin, with a leer on his unshaven face that was clearly trying for intimidation but happily settled for just plain sleazy. The other was shorter and more muscular. His piggish face wasn't built for complex facial expressions, but he managed to exude a fair amount of menace just standing there. Judging by their dress, the two were clearly highwaymen, and not very good ones at that. Skinny was leaning nonchalantly against a tree, picking his teeth with a dagger in a great show of aloof menace. He leaned forward.

"Well now, Charlie, look what we've got here. Must be our lucky day." He stepped over to the neat little stacks of clothing they had left on the shore and began to rummage through them. "Travelers in our woods, eh? And not even paid the toll. Dear, oh dear."

Revka groaned. That was the problem with swimming down deep; you couldn't hear anyone coming. She began to work her way along toward the shore and the bush where she'd hidden her sword. "Your forest? Don't see your name on any signs around here, Mister..."

"Spike. Well, our bit of it. Our little patch, you might say." He watched her for a moment as she eased closer. The bush was closer now, too far to reach but close enough to see that it was definitely swordless. Oh, hell.

Spike smirked, pulling her sword from behind his back. He waved it a couple of times. "Like I said, this here is our bit of turf. Nobody passes through without payin' their respects." He hefted her sword, testing it for weight. "Cor, this is nice. Could come in really useful, this."

Revka growled. "Those are government property, mister. Check the sigils. You take that, you'll have the Duke of Gainsburgh after you."

Spike laughed. "Oh, that's a real threat, that is. I'm sure he's gonna come all the way here to recover two sets of armor and a sword. Probably do it personal." He swung Revka's sword back and forth, grinning. "Of course, if yer really concerned, we might be prepared to accept an alternative payment. Gets a bit dull, out in the woods all the time. An' yer already dressed fer it. We may even let you keep some of yer stuff if you're good enough. Int that right, Charlie?"

The one called Charlie grunted. His facial expression hadn't changed a bit, but his lower lip wobbled in a way that probably meant yes. He was an ugly customer, clearly the 'hit first and fail to come up with any questions later' type. He squatted before Iyarra's stuff and started rummaging through the pile.

"L-look," Iyarra quavered. "If we... you know... will you let us go away?" She began wading her way toward the shore.

"Hey, now. Wait a minute!" Revka began to swim after her. "We haven't discussed this yet. I'm sure we can come to some kind of—" a stray bit of water went up her nose, and she had to stop and sneeze it out.

"I'm sorry, Revka," Iyarra said, barely able to keep her voice steady, "I don't want to see you hurt." She gulped and made her way toward the shore.

From the shore, the men watched. Iyarra had been just far enough in the water to protect her modesty. As she stepped slowly toward the shore, more and more of her became exposed. She wrapped her arms across her chest but was still blushing deep red. A stray shaft of sunlight pushed through the forest canopy and caught her torso as she rose from the water.

The two bandits had clearly been a *long* time without female companionship. The one called Charlie began to pant like a dog, dropping the saddlebag he'd previously been rifling. Beside him, the brains of the outfit forgot all about Revka's sword. "Cor...that's a sight for sore eyes, innit? That's right, you just steer your way toward me, luv. I like 'em dusky. Don't be shy. Let me see that—*Flippin' 'ell!*"

Iyarra's back breached the surface. She stepped out of the water, tilting her head at him innocently. "I'm sorry. Is there something wrong?"

The bandit spat. "Centaurs, Charlie. They're bleeding centaurs. I don't believe this. First chance at some tail in months, and it's going around on four legs. Right." He backed up, his face twisting into a snarl. "Change of plan. We take their stuff and sod off." He reached down for the dropped sword, but found it pinned beneath a hoof the size of his head.

Charlie, who was clearly somewhat slow on the uptake, made a grab for Iyarra's saddlebags. Without breaking eye contact with the other bandit, Iyarra planted a hoof in his chest that sent him sprawling.

Spike darted over to his friend. "What the hell did you do to him?"

"Nothing, yet." Iyarra's voice was cool and even; only Revka could hear the slight tremble in the horsewoman's voice. "Just discouraging him from trying something unhealthy. Now..." She leaned forward, glaring at them. Under normal circumstances, this would have afforded a very nice view, indeed. However, the one called Charlie just whimpered and shrank back. "I'm perfectly willing to let bygones be bygones. You can turn around and run away now, and we won't chase after you. That's about the best offer you're going to get today. Questions?"

There was a moment, then Spike put his hand up. "Er...just, speaking hypothetical, like...what would happen if I were to stab you and take your stuff anyway?"

Iyarra smiled. "Well, for one thing, you'd better be very fast with that knife, because if I've got any strength in me, I *will* kick a hole in your chest. Secondly, if you're lucky enough to escape me, you'd better be ready to take on my big sister." She nodded over her shoulder at Revka. "She's the fastest one in our family. And if you've made her mad, well..."

Revka picked up the cue. "That's right." She began to work her way toward the shore. "And don't forget we can track your scent, y'know, so running's not going to help you. Believe me, we got a nose full of both of ya the instant you showed up." She grinned and snorted like a shire horse. *Thank goodness this water is so muddy,* she thought to herself. *Now please, please be good little hoodlums and buy this...*

The leader of the brain trust sighed. He gestured to his partner. "Come on, Charlie," he groused. "Let's cut our losses, eh? No. Put it *down*, mate. This is a stra...teee...gic wit...draw...al; you remember? That thing I told you about. Now, come on!" He grabbed Charlie by the collar and backed them both out of the clearing. A few seconds later, footsteps sprinted into the distance.

Revka quickly swam to the shore, where Iyarra had sunk to the ground. Revka wrapped her arms around the trembling centaur. "It's all right. It's all right. They're gone now. They're not coming back."

Iyarra whimpered. "I thought they were going to... I thought about you, and I..."

"It's all right." She leaned against Iyarra, squeezing her tight. "You did good. Scared 'em right off. Couldn't have done it better myself."

Iyarra looked up at Revka. "I just... I mean, when they started talking about how they wanted 'alternative payment' and I just... I just wanted to..." She sniffed and wiped her arm across her face.

"Hey now. Hey." Revka smiled. "It's over, right? My Yarra coming up with a great plan just like that? You really showed 'em, girl." She gave an extra squeeze. "I'm proud of you."

"R-really?"

"You bet." Revka stood up and stretched. "Okay, that was a great swim, but we should probably head back to the main road. Who knows what other characters we got running around here." She frowned at something in her fist. "Oh, what do you know? It *is* silver."

They dressed quickly and loaded up, then headed away from the clearing and back toward the main road. A shape that had spent the last several minutes behind a particularly old and gnarled tree let out a quiet sigh of relief and melted back into the forest.

***

Traffic was fairly sparse; the main pilgrimage season wasn't due for another month or so. Iyarra and Revka joined a small group, who were more than happy to have a couple of armed and armored traveling companions. Pilgrim's road was a smooth and wide trail cut straight through the forest. Leafy trees bent over from both sides, creating a verdant tunnel. Here and there, shafts of sunlight broke through the canopy, and several trees were even beginning to bear fruit. Frankly, it was almost ridiculous how nice it was. Revka nabbed a couple of low-hanging pears and passed one forward to Iyarra. "So," she said to the rider next to them. "Tell me about this cousin of yours."

The miller beamed. He was a fat, red-faced man of about middle age, whose beard didn't actually hide his lack of a visible chin, however much it tried. He took another sip from his canteen and wiped his mouth on a sleeve that had been through enough as it was. "Well now," he said, "He works, as I said, for the kingdom of Mercia. He's a loader, and he told me—"

"Sorry, a loader?"

"Aye." He gave a nudge, and his burro grunted and picked up the pace. "You've not heard of them?"

"What, you mean like, loading cargo onto ships and things?"

The miller laughed. "No, no, like... Well, you're adventurers, right?"

"Well, yeah."

"Been in a few dungeons, I fancy?"

"Well, sure, but what's that got to—"

"And what do you find in dungeons?"

"Well, treasure, of course. And monsters."

"Healing potions," added Iyarra. "Don't forget those."

"Right, yeah. And all weapons and arrows and stuff. Why?"

The miller tapped the side of his nose. "Ahhh, ever thought about that? All those dungeons, and the potions are still good. Always a few monsters running about, some decent hardware to find? Even the torches are lit, aren't they?"

"Well, not always. I mean, there was this temple we found a few days ago. Mind you, the entrance had been blocked for who knows how long."

"Well, all right. Not all of them. But a lot of them, right?" The miller waved away undiscovered temples and got back on track. "Well, that's my cousin. He's a loader. Every so often, they go down into the dungeons, make sure there's plenty of goodies to find, enough potions to keep a body alive, enough monsters to keep it interesting, that sort of thing. He's with the royal tourism bureau, you know. It's all done through taxes. Gotta keep the adventurer dollar coming in, you know."

"Isn't that kind of...expensive?"

"Not so much, not so much. The adventurers usually spend what they find in the nearest town anyway, and a bit more besides. The gear and potions are pretty cheap, and monsters more or less make more of themselves. It all works out. Keeps the gold flowing, you see.

"Right, as I was saying, he travels all over the kingdom, getting to all the dungeons on his route. Him and the rest of the team, they see a lot of strange things out on the back roads. For example, they ran across a peddler a few months back, who told them a rather interesting story.

"Seems he was working his way through this forest, see, following this long trail between villages. It was two days since the last village, so he's tired. His horse is tired. They're both smelling about the same at this point. He's miserable, right? And the sun's coming down, so it looks like he's going to have to spend another night camping out in the woods, which he is entirely not looking forward to. All of a sudden, he sees somethin'.

"It's a light, just up ahead. Only a faint one, but the sun's almost down, so he can see it pretty decent. He figures, aha! Someone else on the road. And he leads his horse toward the light.

"Now, it's pretty dark by the time he gets there, but he comes out into this sort of clearing, right. The track's going along one side, and there, about halfway across, I kid you not, is an inn. Just right there in the middle of nowhere, right? The lights are on, and now he's there he can hear what sounds like laughin' and singin' and stuff. Not distinct like, but good enough. He's like, all right, this is what I need! So, he leads his horse down the path to the inn.

"But then things get a bit funny. There's no stables. I mean, you'd expect a stable at an inn, right? Or a hitching post or something? There's nothing. He looks around to see where the other horses are at. There's none. He thinks, all right, maybe everybody walked. But then he looks closer at the inn. It's all lumpy and gnarled, like if a kid made it with clay, you know what I mean?

"So he says to himself, all right, this is odd. He peers closer at the windows. Funny thing is, he can't see in. Oh, there's light all right, and maybe the windows are that cheap glass you can't hardly see through, but you'd expect to see shapes moving around, wouldn't you? Even the doorway looks a bit odd. It's all dark and that. Could be a foyer, right, but now he's suspicious.

"So what he does, he searches around a bit. He finds a big old rock, about the size of his head. He gets about five paces from the doorway and rolls the rock toward the door. The instant that rock went across the threshold, the lights went out and the doorway snapped shut. Scrunched up tighter'n a gnat's arse. So he's standing there, like, what just happened?

"All of a sudden, the doorway opens a little and it spits—*spits*, mark you—spits that rock right back out. Sails right by the fella's ear. He could feel it go by and all. Off it shoots across the clearing and into the trees opposite. When it lands, there's this metallic clang. Not what you'd expect in the middle of the woods, right?

"So, the peddler scratches his head. This is getting stranger and stranger. He grabs a lantern off his cart and lights it and goes into the woods where he heard the clang come from. And what do you think he found?"

"I, uh, really have no idea."

"It was this pit, right, and it was all full of bones. Horse bones, people bones, all kinds of animals. There was scraps of clothing and armor and like that. The rock must have landed on a bit of armor, right? Good gods, he thinks, 'cause every single one of those bones had been picked clean. Not a single bite mark on any of 'em. He figured the lumpy inn thing had dissolved all the meat and spat out the rest, just like it spit out the rock." The miller took another sip from his flask. "True story."

There was a moment's silence as the tale was digested by the audience. Iyarra looked positively ill, and all Revka could manage was a heartfelt "Damn."

"Yeah. Something, eh?"

"Well, yeah. But what was it? I've never heard of anything like that."

The miller shrugged. "Dunno. But my cousin says there's all sorts of things down that way. There's these mixed up things, like part one thing and part another. Like, plants with faces. He swears he saw a deer that had a shell on it, like a beetle. People do say there was some mad bugger lived there back a long time ago, liked making unnatural creatures. Mix up a little of this, little of that, so you'd get creatures that were all mixed up something terrible. Supposed to have died a long time ago, of course, but it wouldn't surprise me if some of those things of his are still around. Not natural, in my opinion, messing things around like that. Bound to be consequences."

Iyarra nodded. "Definitely." She shuddered again.

Just then, the head of the convoy called back. "Coach inn up ahead. We'll be stoppin' fer the night!"

Revka gave Iyarra a nudge. "You go in first," she said.

"Oh, *shut up.*"

***

The inn was large, built to accommodate the height of the spring pilgrimage. There was no trouble finding rooms and stabling for everyone in the off season. Dinner was in the main hall, where long tables stretched the length of the room. Humans and centaurs passed big bowls of food back and forth, more or less nonstop. The ale was not the best, but there was plenty of it. Before long, conversation was in full swing.

"Now you take Schwarzwald," the tall, thin character opposite Revka droned. The gratt resembled a stretched out humanoid, with gray-green skin and a distinctly amphibian cast to the face. You saw a lot of them nowadays. They'd formerly just haunted caves and moldering dungeons before discovering the civil service. They'd taken to the dull, thankless, and repetitive work like a duck to water. This one had introduced himself as a tax collector, and the conversation had gone downhill from there.

Actual conversation wasn't necessary; he was quite content to keep the thing going all by himself. Revka now knew more about the revenue adjustments for cows than she had ever wanted to know. She took another sip of ale. "Schwarzwald? Never been. Heard it's pretty creepy there."

"Indeed. Horrible place. We lose many tax collectors through there. But as I was saying, you can't run a barony like that, monsters and mad alchemists running about the whole time. Absolutely devastating to any sort of planned, political economy, I can tell you. Why, I recall two years ago, when we were performing a surprise audit and—"

"Sorry, was this going somewhere?"

"Well yes, *actually*." The tax collector sniffed. "In point of fact, I was going to say that they're finally doing something about cleaning up the place."

"Sending a few wizards in to fireball it, I'm guessing?"

"Certainly not. That would hardly make fiscal sense. No, the baron has been studying the matter. He's finally worked out the root cause and what to do about it. Turns out it's all terribly simple."

"Yeah?"

"Quite. They're going to change everyone's names."

Revka poked at her stew "Well, that seems perfec...wait, what?"

"The names. I don't know if you've ever noticed, but everyone tends to have names like Malidicto and Tarantulanya and Doctor Fango and so on. Turns out, that's been the root cause of their problems for going on centuries now. Basically, if you give someone a name like Von Evil, there are only a set few ways they're going to turn out. I mean, if you're Mister and Missus Shrinker, and you have a child who's scientifically inclined, sooner or later, someone is going to wind up finger height and stuck in a spiderweb. Stands to reason."

"I...suppose?"

"No supposing about it. They actually tested the theory properly. About twenty years ago, a pair of twins were born there. By the baron's order, one was named Fangarella, the other one Margaret. They left the two alone for twenty years, let them be raised in the same household, same friends, same everything. When the researchers came back, Margaret was married to a blacksmith and taking in sewing on the side. Fangarella, on the other hand..."

"Let me guess. Black leather? Skulls?"

"Exactly. She even had her own dungeon. Well, a bit of a dungeon. More like an extension to the root cellar, but she was clearly working toward more. After that, the baron made a new rule. Any baby born in the barony would have to be named from a list of approved names chosen for their social acceptability and lack of malicious character. They just released the official list a few months ago and are already holding everyone to it."

"Huh. Well, that's certainly a...unique solution they got, there."

"Oh yes. I grant you, it sounds like a good idea. Of course, nobody bothered to think about the record keeping. What am I meant to do when a village has a dozen John Millers, hmm? Nobody thinks about that. I mean, the revenue collection is going to be an absolute nightmare, you mark my words."

"Oh, dear. That does sound like a shame."

"Well, quite."

The salad bowl went by again. The tax collector heaped a healthy ladleful onto his plate and tucked in. Grateful for the reprieve, Revka turned to Iyarra, who was apparently entertaining a couple of the other pilgrims with some of their adventures.

"And so, I said, 'What do you mean novelty wrestling act?' And she said to trust her, it was going to be the talk of the fair. Which it was, actually, but not exactly in the way we would have—"

"Ah-*hem!*" Revka's elbow nudged urgently against Iyarra's ribs.

"Sorry, excuse me a moment." Iyarra turned to Revka. "Yes?"

"I thought we agreed we weren't going to talk about that," Revka hissed through her teeth.

"Oh, but surely the statute of limitations has expired."

"I don't care about the statute of stupid limitations. I don't want that story getting around any further than it already has, all right?"

"All right, all right..." Iyarra turned to the bemused pilgrims and shrugged. "Long story. Anyway, there was this other time when we wound up as bodyguards for this bishop..."

Revka tuned out from the conversation and let her mind wander. Her eyes drifted around the room, taking in the various people and centaurs and gratt and so on. Give it a few weeks and the place would be packed. By the time they were on their way back from the monastery the inns would probably be pretty near capacity. Might be a bit of a hassle, but at least it would give them a nice crowd to disappear into.

Hopefully, they would be moving along quickly. How long had it been, anyway? She counted out the days: there was that one lost to bandits, the journey to Peccaray, the boat ride...coming up on two weeks, almost. Okay, so they were making good time. If they took the same route back, barring bandits and other surprises, they should be all right. That just left the monastery and the theft.

That was going to be the hard part.

Revka would be the first to admit that she was not exactly a paragon of good citizenship. Heavens knew she'd had her share of mild misbehaviors. She'd plucked an apple here, stretched a truth there, but she'd never really stolen anything serious, and she'd never menaced an innocent traveler. Technically, doing little crimes was the same as big ones, but you couldn't fault a body for just surviving, could you? She had spent many a long night telling herself that.

Stealing a valuable relic from an order of monks was the big time, and not the kind of big time she wanted. You couldn't shrug that off. You couldn't make excuses. Okay, so they were being compelled against their will, but whatever god was in charge of that monastery would probably come after them. She just had to hope they wouldn't notice their treasure was gone.

Unconsciously, her hand drifted to her arm where the curse-mark rested under her armor. She had checked it surreptitiously every day. It was definitely growing. She hoped it wouldn't get all the way around her arm. Or up to her neck. That would be the worst. Maybe it would be all right. Maybe the duke would go ahead and take their curse-marks away, pay Iyarra's bounty, and leave them be. Maybe he'd even hire them for other jobs. Optimism, that was the thing. Do the job and hope for the best. But just in case…

Probably time for a backup plan.

In a far corner of the inn, a lone diner sat in a quiet corner. They didn't bother with much conversation, concentrating on their dinner and a quiet smoke. They left just as the beer was really beginning to have its effect on the rest of the guests. Nobody noticed them leave. But then, no one had noticed them arrive either, so that was all right.

***

A clap of thunder announced a torrential downpour that hit the ground before the thunder's echo had died away. An auspicious start to the morning. The convoy slopped along the road all day. Huddled up in their oilcloths, the travelers hardly spoke at all. The rain poured down into early afternoon, turning the road into mud and aborting the few attempts at conversation. The party finally passed through the great stone walls of Tam, at the foot of the Icarine Mountains, whereupon the rain immediately stopped.

"Typical," muttered Revka.

Tam was a smallish settlement at the bottom of Kalazad Mountain, one of the seven principal peaks that made up the Icarines. Originally a mining town, it had been built against, and eventually into, the former silver mine. These days, the town primarily served as a pilgrimage site and supply depot for the dozen or so monasteries that dotted the Icarines. A few inns and stables served the open air market between the walls and the mountain. There, one could buy goods or hire a guide to lead one up any of the mountains that loomed nearby. Behind the market a cave mouth that two dragons could easily have walked through side by side led into the mountain and the town proper. The interior of the old mine had been turned into warehouses, shops, and homes. Pit ponies hauled carts in and out of the gaping mouth, and the sounds of continual chatter echoed from below.

"Isn't it kind of odd, living down in a cave like that?" Iyarra asked. The pilgrims had settled in at one of the main inns and were having dinner. Everyone had more or less dried off. Hot food and cold ale saw their spirits considerably brightened. The miller, who had been there before on business and was therefore the self-appointed expert on the place, waved a hand airily.

"Well, it's not really a cave, you know. I've been down there. It's basically a long, wide avenue that corkscrews its way downward, you see. And everyone's got these chambers going off into their homes and that. It's comfy all year round, and the runoff from the mountain makes sure there's plenty of water. They even use water wheels to pump in fresh air. And, of course, you're safe from the elements. There are probably people down there right now who don't even know that there was a storm today, and more fortunate for them." He took another pull of his ale. "I've seen worse places to live. Hell, I've lived in worse myself."

"If you say so." Iyarra split open her bread roll and spooned in some apple butter. "I think I would prefer somewhere I could run around a bit. And sunshine. Sunshine's important."

Revka chuckled. "I know what you mean. Mind you, when you've got rain like we had today, I have to admit that a roof over your head has a certain appeal."

"Anyway," said Iyarra, after the miller went off for a refill. "Did you find out about the monastery?"

"Kalazad-Faan? Yeah. There's a road that goes up the mountain, takes the better part of a day to get up there. Pilgrims walk, but suppliers run a cart up a couple times a week. There's a guy says he can get us hired on as servants. Seems the holy brothers aren't all that great at cooking or cleaning. Anyway, he said we should show up at the gate to the mountain road before sunrise tomorrow, and he'll set us up. Even has uniforms for us, which is good, as I figure the armor would be kind of a giveaway."

"Well, quite."

"So, I figure we get up there, get a couple jobs that let us search the place over, find out where this thing is and—" Just then, the miller returned with his drink. "And so I said to 'em, 'Look, Mister, if you wanna call yourself Grunthaar and run around the woods in a loincloth all day, that's all very well, but don't expect supper to be waiting when you get home.' Am I right?"

"What?" said Iyarra.

The miller raised his mug. "Damn right!"

Chapter Ten

THE GATE TO THE mountain road was pulled aside just as the sun was pushing its way over the horizon, and a cart laden with supplies began its ascent. In the back of the wagon, a few women sat in shapeless gray outfits guaranteed not to inflame the passions of even the most devout monastic. Up front, the horses that usually made the trip found themselves augmented by one centaur.

The day was cold and brisk, and the road quiet. Most of the pilgrims wouldn't get going until the sun was up and the chill of the dawn burned away. From time to time, especially after they hit the higher altitudes, the travelers came across stray hikers who had got caught on the mountain and spent the night camped out by the wayside. But for the most part, the cart and its riders had the road to themselves.

Revka dangled her legs over the back of the cart, listening with half an ear to the gossip of the other women. It seemed they would go up in shifts, working for a week and then heading back home. This was the only life most of them knew. Someone had brought a jug of something along, and the jokes and gossip began to flow as the drink was passed around.

"Mind you, it's the old ones you have to watch out for." A middle aged woman waggled her finger at Revka. "Most of the younger ones are pious enough. You don't have to worry about them, but the old fellers seem to know what they're missing!" The women laughed, and the jug made another round.

"And watch out for Brother Dale. He likes to leave things around on the floor and ask you to pick them up for him. If you bend over to pick it up, he leeeeans all the way over, trying to peek up your dress."

"Not that he can see anything with these things," said another, younger woman. She tugged at the ankle length hemline. "It's like going around in a bag."

"That I'll grant you." The first woman nodded. "But that never stops him from trying. Mind you, he doesn't do it so much now with me. I just squat down to pick anything up. Quite ruins the old man's fun!" More laughter.

"I'll have to remember that." Revka gave a game little smile and let her mind wander back to the delicate question of how to introduce the subject of the jar. *Hey, speaking of which, these guys got any old relics lying around? Stone canisters, things like that?* No, that tack was liable to arouse comment, and just waiting for the conversation to naturally come around to ancient relics was probably not a winning strategy. She took a sip of the hooch as it went by and made herself tune back in to the conversation.

"Of course, the old abbot, he was the worst of the lot. I could tell you stories about that one." The old woman was plump, with a shock of gray hair. Her three teeth featured in her perpetual leer. "Not like the current gentleman. Very respectable, he is." She jabbed a pudgy finger at Revka. "You have any trouble from them lot, you just go straight up to Father Eliot, you hear? He'll set things right. He's a good man, he is. Not like some I could mention. And that goes for you too, miss."

The last part was addressed to another woman, leaning against the side of the cart with a disinterested air. She was lean and toned, with close-cropped blonde hair. She hadn't said much on the journey up, but Revka gathered she was also a first timer. Revka stole another glance.

There was something not quite right about the woman. Maybe it was her bearing, or the look in her eyes. Somehow, you couldn't see her scrubbing floors. Revka made a mental note to keep an eye on her.

The strange woman nodded to the old lady. "Thank you. I will remember." She went back to gazing off into the middle distance.

Definitely an odd one.

The cart rounded a curve and came to a halt. A trail wound up and away from the main path to a plateau surrounded by a wall of iron-black stone. Beyond the gates, squat old buildings could just be seen. There was some bustling about, and two of the women dropped off the tail end of the cart. "Oh," said Revka, "We're here already? That was sooner than I expected."

One of the other women shook her head. "Nah, this is Kalazad-Oyen, it's a different order. Bunch of bookworms. The whole place is just littered with books. Bad for you, in my opinion. Straining your eyes like that." She pointed along the road. "No, we're going to Faan, further along up the mountain." She smiled. "Just stick with us. We'll get you there all right."

A few bags were hauled up to the main gate. The old, worn sacks exchanged were carefully stowed away in a corner of the cart. The driver climbed back into his seat, grabbed the reins, and clucked his tongue. The cart started off again, working its way up the long and winding path.

The sun was an hour closer to setting when the cart pulled up at the gates that guarded the squat, old stone buildings within sight of the mountain's peak. The elevation made Kalazad-Faan noticeably colder, and Revka was grateful for the heavy wool uniforms they'd been given. The remaining women bustled off the cart. Iyarra was unhitched from the front, and they all headed up through the gates and into the compound.

Another group of women hurried down to the cart and clambered onto the back. *Must be the previous shift.* The driver turned the cart around and started back down the path. It would be a bit of a trot to get back to town before sunset, but the trip was all downhill and at least they'd be home and in their own beds. Well never mind, she had a job to do. She dutifully followed the other women to a long hut, which turned out to be a sort of dormitory. The beds were low, and each had a chest for personal items. Beyond the washroom, the centaurs shared a stall off one side of the building. As accommodations went, she'd certainly seen worse.

"Right," said the old lady from the cart. "I'm the senior person here, so I'm more or less in charge. Basically, that means I go report to the abbot, and he tells me what he wants done. Other than that, we just clean and try to stay out of their way as much as we can, right? You'll soon get the feel of things. The pay isn't marvelous, but the food's not bad and there's a decent enough amount of it. I'm Mother Grammidge, by the way. You can call me Gertie when the gentlemen aren't around. I don't suppose you can cook?"

"Well, a bit, yes."

"Oh good. I'll have you working in the kitchens, then. We're a bit short."

Iyarra wandered over. "How about me?"

"I think we'll have you outdoors, dearie. We're too high up for gardening, but there's always rocks and such that need clearing away. Loads being hauled, that sort of thing."

"All right."

"Now, everyone just wait here. I'll go report to the abbot, then we can get started. All right? Won't be any time at all."

***

97

Later that night, Iyarra and Revka were outside the barracks, staring up at the night sky. The evening's work had been fairly light but left no real chance to look around. Fortunately, the brothers were of the early-to-bed school, so the women more or less had the night to themselves. Revka chewed on a straw, leaning against a wall as they watched a few lone clouds drift by.

"So, how's the kitchen?" Iyarra asked.

Revka shrugged. "It's all right. Pretty big, actually. But not a lot of stuff to work with. Apparently, the brothers feel their asceticism should apply to the people doing the cooking as well. Actually, Gertie says they usually just bring stuff up from the town. Easier that way. Still, there's a good supply of food. We won't starve to death, that's for sure. What have they got you doing?"

"Moving rocks. They clear away rubble that's come down the mountain and chip it into stone blocks for building."

"Oh. Fun." Revka stared up into the night for a moment. There seemed to be something on her mind. "Iyarra?"

"Yes?"

"Did you see that other new girl that came up with us? The blonde?"

"Oh yes. I noticed her."

"Yeah. Anything odd strike you about her?"

"Well, it is interesting that she should be a new arrival at the same time as us. When we were settling in at the barracks, I could swear she smelled familiar, somehow. Can't really place it, though."

"No kidding?" Revka frowned at a passing cloud. "I think it might be worth keeping an eye on her. I mean, we'll all see a lot of each other, but maybe we should keep an extra eye on her. You know?"

Iyarra nodded. "Sounds like a good idea to me."

"Yeah." Revka got up and stretched. "In the meantime," she said, "we'd probably best call it a night. I suspect it's going to be a long day ahead, and it probably isn't a good idea to stay away from the other girls too much. They might start wondering what's up."

Iyarra nodded and hauled herself up. "Okay. If I hear anything about the relics or anything, I'll make sure and let you know."

"Same. And if either of us sees blondie doing anything odd or suspicious, we're to let the other know right away, right?"

"Got it."

"All right." Revka did a quick check of the immediate area and leaned up to peck Iyarra on the cheek. "We can get through this, right? Right?"

"Right."

"Darned right. Now, let's get back inside."

***

The next couple of days flew by quickly. Revka spent most of her time in the kitchens, helping cook simple but actually rather good food for the friars. She had picked up some herbs on her travels and introduced them into the recipes. This went over well, and she was rather proud, but she wasn't really getting out and around the place at all. Iyarra wasn't doing much better. Her knowledge of the outside and storage areas was becoming pretty comprehensive, but the brothers hadn't stored any valuable relics there. And she'd looked really, really hard.

"What with me stuck in the kitchen, and you outside," Revka said, "we're never going to find where this stupid thing is. In a few days, our week's gonna be up and everyone will be heading back down again. I don't much fancy us cooling our heels for a whole week before coming back up again, you know?"

Night had come, and the other women were gossiping in the dormitory. There was never anyone in the storeroom after vespers, so it made a good place for their quiet confab.

"Well," said Iyarra, "What do you suggest?"

"I've been thinking. I'll tell Gertie I'm getting a little sick of the view and ask if I can swap out with one of the girls who cleans the chapel. That's probably where the thing is. I don't know if you can do anything right now, not without arousing suspicion, anyway. Just bide your time tomorrow, and hopefully I'll have some good news. Sound good?"

"All right."

"Great. Shall we head in?"

"Uhm..." Iyarra shuffled a hoof.

Revka looked up at her. "What?"

"Have you...noticed anything odd about the other new girl?"

"What, blondie? Well, they've got her on the cleanup crew. Keeps to herself. Not a big conversationalist, but I haven't seen anything suspicious. Why, have you?"

"Well, the other day I was out moving rocks, and I saw her off by herself. She seemed to be snooping around the chapel area."

"Really?" Revka tilted her head. "What did she do?"

"Nothing much, really. She just sort of poked around for a minute, then left. I'm not sure why. It seemed a bit odd."

"Yeah." Revka jammed her hands into the pockets of her uniform. "That's...interesting to know."

"You think she might try something?"

"Could be, could be." She tilted her head back, lost in thought. "Okay. I have the bed by the door. I'm going to keep an eye open tonight, just in case. Most likely, if she's up to something, she won't do it during daylight, right?"

"Makes sense to me."

"All right. Shall we go inside?"

The two headed back to the dorm. Outside, a shadow that had been skulking next to a window tugged its coat closer around itself, swore quietly under its breath, and slipped away.

***

"Up and at 'em, girls! Come on, now, let's be having you!" Gertie's cheery greeting started their day. Revka washed, brushed her hair, and donned her uniform. She hurried across the courtyard to the kitchens and started fixing up breakfast. For people who didn't do much but shuffle from one room to another and stare at old books, the friars sure could put a lot of food away. Eggs, mostly, and porridge for when they got tired of that. The servants, not being under any particular holy injunctions, were allowed a little more extravagance. They enjoyed buttered toast and even the occasional bit of bacon brought along from town. There was the clearing away and washing up to follow, and that kept them going for a good while. All things considered, it was midmorning before she was able to step away into the pantry and take a quick break.

She leaned back against the cool stone wall and sighed. She'd told Gertie earlier that she wanted to ask her something, and the old woman had agreed to come by on her break. Revka closed her eyes, marshaling her arguments. *Don't make a big deal out of it. Act casual. Change of scene...tired of the kitchen every day...heard good things about the chapel. Play it by ear. If she seems dubious, drop it. Can build up some trust, come back to it later. Okay. Good plan.* She jammed her hands into her pockets and blinked her eyes open in mild surprise.

She pulled her hand out of her left pocket and...sure enough, a note. Addressed to her, even. She looked around, before unfolding the paper and hurriedly reading.

Revka boggled. She read it again. *Good grief.* She stared for a moment in mute disbelief. *How?*

There was the sound of the kitchen door opening, and Gertie's voice rang out. "Hello, dearie, sorry I'm late. His Graciousness was having me polish the silver in the nave. He always has me do it special, you know. Very particular about the silver." Gertie smiled from the doorway. "Now, Revka dear. You were wanting to see me about something?"

Revka started, then jammed the note back in her pocket. Her mind raced. "Huh? Oh yeah. Uhm...yesterday? When I used the biteweed with the chicken, did that go over all right? Only it can take some people badly if they're not used to spicy food."

"Oh, is that all?" Gertie furrowed her brow. "Well, I think Brother Maydril was complaining a bit after lunch. But really, he complains of just about anything, poor soul. I usually give him as bland a portion as I can manage. The other gentlemen seemed quite happy with it. Makes a nice change, I think. I do believe you've got a bit of an herbalist in you, young lady. Keep it up, you could be in charge of the whole kitchen one day."

"I'll bear that in mind, thanks."

"Was there anything else?"

Revka hesitated, then reached a decision. "No, that was all. Just wanted to check with you on the food."

"All right, dear. Well, it doesn't hurt to ask, I always say."

"Right, right. Anyway, I'd better get a start on lunch. Rarebit again, I'm afraid."

Gertie smiled. "All right, dear. Let me know if I can help you with anything."

Revka gave the old woman a smile as she bustled off, then fished the note out again. Yes, it still said what she thought it said.

Well, well.

She folded the paper very carefully and went back out into the kitchen.

***

After lunch had been taken care of, Revka wandered out to the back courtyard, where Iyarra was hauling some stray stones into position to be quarried. The actual hammer work was done by novices, by reason of physical discipline translating into mental and spiritual discipline, all of which were vital for a growing mind. And it meant that they didn't have to hire anyone from the village to do it.

Just at the moment, Iyarra was helping the novices move a stone into place for cutting. There was a lot of grunting and muttering under breath, as the heavy limestone was labored into position. The novices sat panting on the stone. Revka wandered over and nodded to Iyarra. "Got a minute?"

Iyarra mopped her brow. "We just have one more for today, I think. Maybe you can help me haul it over. Larence? Do you mind if she goes with me to get the last one?"

One of the novices got up, leaning back with a groan. He looked down at the stone, then over at the hammers and chisels that made up the extent of their equipment. "Take your time," he sighed. "No hurry here."

There had been a landslide at some point, or so it seemed. A large pile of rocks and rubble congregated at one corner, where the slope of the mountain continued upward. Several stones had been cleared away, but there were more than enough to keep novices nicely busy for quite some time. Revka helped roll a cartwheel-sized stone into position, then buckled the harness around and made sure everything was tight.

"So," said Iyarra, "Is she going to let you switch jobs?"

"I didn't ask." Revka handed the note over.

Iyarra licked her lips, as she peered at the paper. "Uhm…"

"Oh sorry, yeah. Here." Revka took the note back and read it out loud.

"The treasure you seek is in a room at the back of the main chapel, to the left of the pulpit. The door to the room will be unlocked tonight, so be ready. Be sure and burn this note before you go." She pointed to the end of the message. "It's signed 'A friend.'"

Iyarra hmphed. "That's awfully convenient."

"Tell me about it. Popped up in my pocket this morning."

"So…what do you think?"

"I'm not sure what to think. Could be the duke's got someone on the inside. Who here could know what we're up to?"

The idea hit them both at the same time. "Blondie?"

"Hard to see who else it could be. Everyone else has been here a while, as I understand it."

"May I?" Iyarra plucked the letter out of Revka's hand and dangled it in front of her own face, eyeing it critically. She took a deep whiff and closed her eyes. After a moment, she shook her head. "No."

"Not her?"

"Positive. She's got a completely different scent. This was written by a man. I'm sure of it."

"A man? Like, one of the monks?"

"Well, I suppose it's possible. Maybe the duke has been in contact with one, or sent a plant a long time ago."

"I suppose. But…I don't know. That doesn't feel right. Anything else you can tell?"

"Not really. I mean, it's kind of a familiar smell. I know I've smelled it somewhere before, and recently. I just can't think of where."

"All right. Do you want to hold onto the note in case you remember?"

"Yes, please."

Revka watched Iyarra stow the note away in a pouch, then gave her a quick pat. "I think we should pick this back up after the day is done. I should get back to the kitchens before they miss me."

"All right. I have to finish hauling this stone." Iyarra checked her harness. "I think I'd like to check something."

"Okay then. I'll get back with you tonight."

"Thank you."

Later that afternoon, after the day's work was done, Iyarra went on a little walk. She circled around the dormitory and stables. She wandered to the storehouse, then out the door and down the trail leading back down the mountain. She was gone for a little while. When she came back, she was moving fast.

***

Father Eliot had been with the monastery for nearly fifty years, ever since he realized that the alternative was to take over his father's shoemaking business. Over the years, he had worked his way steadily up through the ranks with a combination of scholarship, political adeptness, and plain old sense. He had spent considerable time making sure things at Kalazad-Faan were nice and quiet, as befit a place for learning, meditation, and divinity. Oh, occasionally there was a novice who wasn't quite cut out for the cloth. Or sometimes—very rarely these days—trouble with one of the servant girls. Generally speaking, life at the top of the mountain was calm and serene.

He picked up the note on the desk in front of him and read it again. He sighed. At the sound of a deferential knock on the door, he hurried the note into a drawer. "Come in."

"You wanted to see me, Your Grace?" Mother Grammidge put her head round the door and bobbed her usual half curtsey.

"Yes, yes. Come in. Close the door, if you would." He waited until she took a seat across from him. "Drink?"

"No thank you, sir. Not while I'm still working, you know."

"Oh, very well." He studied her for a moment. He may run the monastery, but she had the run of the place and knew every nook and cranny of it. She and her girls also got about and heard things, things that were generally too far out of range for someone sitting at the top to hear. He'd made it a point to cultivate her trust and, if not friendship, then at least a sort of understood partnership of mutual respect. Besides, it was always good to be nice to the person who was in charge of your meals.

"Tell me," he said, "has there been any unusual activity or gossip going around? Anything you can think of?"

Gertie furrowed her brow. "Well, I can't think of anything *particularly* unusual, Your Grace. Our Neviss had to sit out this week on account of her knee giving her trouble again, and I think the milk we brought up may be close to turning. I'll have a word with the dairy myself when I go back down, so it won't happen again. You may be sure of that."

"Very good. And I'm sorry for her knee. But other than that...?" He waved a hand vaguely.

"Nothing much to report, really. Everyone's doing their job. The new girls are settling in, I don't–"

"New girls? We have some new servants here?"

"Oh, yes. Two humans and a centaur. Came into town a few days ago, looking for work, so I was told. Seem all right, mind you. Hard workers and all that. The one gal is rather good in the kitchen. Why?"

"Oh, just...curious. That's all. Nothing else?"

"No, nothing comes to mind, Your Grace. I can keep my ear to the ground if you like. Shall I?"

"Please do, yes."

She gave him a nod. "You can count on old Gertie, sir. I shall let you know directly if I hear anything."

"I know you shall." He glanced at the window. "Day's nearly over," he said. "I won't detain you. I'm sure you're in the middle of getting dinner ready."

"Yes, Your Grace. It's sausages again tonight, I'm afraid. But I'm doing a bread pudding special for after."

"Sausages will be just fine, I'm sure. Good afternoon."

After she left, he took the note out of the drawer.

Abbot,

Tonight, there will be an attempt on Kalazad-Faan's reliquary. The thieves are desperate and dangerous. You will need as many people as you can spare to stop them. They will most likely strike after dark, so you have some time to prepare. Good luck.
A friend

Father Eliot tapped the note a few times. Desperate and dangerous, eh? Well, Brother Tice was a sturdy enough fellow. A couple of the novices were quite tough, but the only guard was old Orney who watched the gate, and he wasn't going to slow anybody down. Of course, they weren't the only ones on the mountain, were they...?

A few minutes later, a friar entered. "You rang, sir?"

"Yes." Father Eliot handed him a sealed envelope. "Run down to Oyen and give this to Father Goulding, will you? Tell him anyone he can spare will be fine."

"Yes, sir."

After the friar left, Father Eliot sat back in his chair, kneading his temples. He didn't need this sort of thing, not at his age. He just hoped that it could be handled quickly, and above all, quietly. Pilgrims were just beginning to filter up the mountain. It would be bad for everyone if word got around about desperate criminals running around what was meant to be a sanctuary from the problems of the outside world. That sort of thing bit into the all-important pilgrim income.

He sighed, then turned his attention to the minutes of the previous day's meeting. There might be no rest for the wicked, but they likely had less paperwork than the virtuous.

Chapter Eleven

THE MOON AND STARS were smothered in a thick, heavy cloud cover that draped the mountain in near-absolute darkness. Along one of the ebony stone buildings of Kalazad-Oyen, the lower of the two monasteries, a patch of darkness moved, blending perfectly with the surrounding night. Earlier that evening, they had watched a small phalanx of guards and some of the younger, fitter friars exit the gate and head up the path to Kalazad-Faan at speed. The figure had waited until after dark and the last lights went out in the library. The younger friars of Oyen tended to burn the midnight oil, but as most of them were up the mountain, that left only the older brothers, who liked their early nights.

Getting in had been no problem, nor had finding the item. Bless them, they'd stuck it right on the shelf, right in the first place one would look. And even a sign on the door. You had to laugh. The shape vaulted to the top of the wall that surrounded the monastery, found the black cord that hung over the edge, and began the climb downward. Probably not worth making the descent down the mountain in the dark; best to wait until dawn. Everything was going according to plan.

Feet touched down on firmness. Odd, surely the ground had been a bit farther down? And movement, like being on the back of a horse...

There was an edge of cold metal against his back.

"Don't you move," said Revka.

The thief twisted, lost his grip, and fell to the ground with a thud. Iyarra calmly pinned him to the ground with a single hoof. Not enough to crush him, just enough to make it clear that this was, indeed, an option.

Revka hopped off Iyarra's back and knelt by the thief. She brandished the note in his face. "All right, you want to tell us what this thing is all about?"

"What thing is all about?"

"Eh? Oh. Right. The dark. Sorry. Yeah, it's this note." She rallied. "The one you crammed in my pocket last night. You wanna explain?"

"I don't know what you're talking about. And get your damn horse off of me."

"Centaur, actually. And we know it was you. Isn't that right, Iyarra?"

"Yeah. Your scent was all over it. *And* at the inn on the way here. And at the bandit camp. You were all over that place. You've been following us."

The thief swore under his breath. "I was just trying to...to help you." Iyarra's hoof was beginning to get heavy.

"*Ohhh*, help us! You hear that, Iyarra? He was trying to help us. Well, that is nice. Only thing, if you were feeling so helpful, and you knew where the jar was, why didn't you just pinch it yourself and tell us to meet you somewhere? Why did you immediately head back down the hill to Oyen instead?"

"How...how did you know that?"

"Scent trail. Anyway, why did we see a bunch of Oyen's people come trotting through the Faan gate just before we were about to follow your trail? I call that suspicious, myself."

"Forget it. I'm...telling you nothing."

"All right, fine." Revka grinned in the darkness. "Be that way. I'm sure Iyarra's leg is getting awfully tired. Isn't that right?"

Iyarra yawned like a bad actor. "Oh, yeah. After a day of hauling stones back and forth? I don't know how much longer I can keep this one up, you know? In fact, I—"

"All right, all *right!*" There was a sigh. "The truth is...I was sent here by the Duke of Gainsburgh to steal a priceless item."

"Excuse me?" Revka tilted her head. "I'm pretty sure you mean *we* were sent by the Duke of Gainsburgh to steal a priceless item."

"No." And suddenly the voice was sneering. "*You*...were sent here to go up and get caught. You were just decoys, meant to lure attention away from here...so I could do the *real* job."

Revka hissed. "You're lying."

"Am I?" Even in the dark, there was the faintest glint of a smile. "Come on, now. A couple of random, traveling nobodies dragged off the road to steal a valuable holy relic? You believed that?" He barked a shallow, coughing sort of laugh, squirming below Iyarra's hoof. "Right now, everyone's up at Kalazad-Faan, waiting...for you."

"Well then, we'd better head up there, hadn't we?" Revka growled. "Only you're coming with us. And you're going to tell them *everything*. About shadowing us and killing those bandits and the duke setting us up and all of that."

"Right." Iyarra nodded, then a puzzled look came over her face. "Actually, that is a question. How is it you were able to take out that entire bandit camp single-handed, anyway?"

"Oh, that's easy." The voice was as swift and sudden as the knife at Revka's throat. "He had help."

Revka cursed. She made a show of putting her hands up slowly. "It's you, blondie, isn't it?"

"Nice guess. Now, tell your friend to take her foot off my colleague, if she doesn't want a demonstration of how we took care of those bandits. Silent kills are something of a specialty of mine."

"You heard her, Iyarra." Revka sighed. "Let the bastard go."

Reluctantly, Iyarra moved her hoof away. The thief scrambled to his feet. Blondie kept her knife against Revka's throat. "You all right, Dail?"

The thief dusted himself off. "I'm fine, just a little winded." He turned to the two women. "Now, I suggest you head up the hill and give us our distraction. Personally, I'd like to settle both of you once and for all, but we're going to need you to buy us some time. Get back up there and get them to chase you around a bit. I'm sure you can outrun a bunch of old monks."

"Oh yeah?" Iyarra folded her arms. "And why would we do that?"

Blondie tapped Revka's arm. "Because if you don't, you'll never get these off."

"That's right." The one called Dail chuckled. "If you keep them off our tail, we might tell the duke what a good job you did. Who knows? He might actually keep his promise. Or he might not. But you know what the beauty part is? You really don't have a choice."

Iyarra turned to Revka. "Is he serious?"

"He's right, you know." Revka glanced down at her arm. "They have us over a barrel."

Blondie removed her knife from Revka's throat. "Good thinking. Now, get up there and buy us some time. I'm sure I don't need to tell you what will happen if you get caught. Just run them around a bit. You can do that, can't you? We've seen you run." She pushed past Revka to the road, and quickly disappeared into the darkness.

Dail nodded to them and gave a sardonic bow. "Ladies." And he was gone.

Revka sighed. She hauled herself up onto Iyarra's back. "Come on."

Iyarra groaned. "You mean we have to head up there *again*?"

"Afraid so."

"Yeah, but…" Iyarra began to pick her way up the trail. "We're not really going to go through with it, are we?"

In the darkness, Revka's face was unreadable. "Trust me," she said.

***

It had been several hours since Brother Bartolo and the others took up their positions. He was beginning to wonder if anything was going to happen.

They stared at the chapel doors, straining their ears for any suggestion of sound. Aside from the occasional muffled cough, there had been absolutely nothing.

Brother Bartolo was not a small man. He had been a woodcutter before he heard the call, and as such was not at home crouching behind a very small table for several hours. He kept having to shift position as his legs cramped up. By rights, he should have been in bed and asleep hours ago. Not that you could call the straw pallets they gave the novices around here *proper* beds. Mind, the way he was feeling, a four poster with goose down pillows couldn't have been more welcome. Also, he was pretty certain he was going to have to pee pretty soon.

There was a noise.

Just the faintest hint of a sound from outside, but it was a noise. Around him, he sensed the others stirring. All eyes turned toward the door. Bartolo held his breath, tightening his grip on the iron candlestick in his hand.

Any moment now…

The door swung open with a sound like a thunderclap. Two silhouettes stood in the torch light.

"Surprise!"

***

The sun climbed its way up the mountain, finally lighting upon the buildings of Oyen. It had been a busy night. The initial surprise was quickly followed by a somewhat hasty explanation, which led to a rather longer explanation and a quick pilgrimage down the mountain to Oyen. There, the whole rendition was made to Father Goulding, who now sat in his private rooms, listening to Father Eliot and the two women.

"Well," he croaked, "I must say this is the most extraordinary thing I've heard in quite some time." He was very old, bald, and thin. Hunched in his robes, he tended to put people in mind of a bespectacled turtle. His skin was pale and delicate, as if spending a lifetime around books had given him the consistency of old paper himself. He gazed down at the two notes in his lap. "And you're quite sure you believe them, Robert?"

Father Eliot nodded. "Take a look at the notes," he said. "They're quite clearly in the same handwriting. What they've told us seems to add up. Besides which, I can't think of another explanation that fits the facts so well. Certainly, I can't imagine why anyone would travel this far just to steal that old jar."

"Actually," Revka cut in, "What is the deal with the jar, anyway?"

"It holds part of the wheel upon which Saint Ulgat was martyred," said Father Eliot. "Though, I have to say, probably fake. We acquired it during a time when there was no real governance on the authenticity of relics. I believe we still have two of his skulls – one from when he was martyred, and one from when he was a boy."

"Wait, what now?"

"Exactly as I said. But they were someone's skulls, so we keep them and look after them in memory of their previous owners, whomsoever they might have been. That does rather bring us back to the question of the hour. Can you honestly not think of why someone would go to so much effort to steal from here?"

Father Goulding shook his head. "I really fear I cannot. I mean, we have no treasures, no relics of any note. Just...well, just books."

Father Eliot smiled. "Now, I seem to remember a certain someone telling me that there was no such thing as 'just books.' Many times, in fact. I'm sure there must be some valuable works in your collections, or possibly even some dangerous ones?"

"Well yes, of course. We keep them separate, where our visitors cannot get to them."

Father Eliot brightened. "Ah, good. Locked away somewhere, I presume?"

"Naturally. We keep them in a room upstairs, where visitors aren't allowed. Anyone who wants to read from any of those books has to apply for permission. Even then, only supervised reading is allowed. The door is always locked when one of our staff is not inside."

"I see. Well, I think it might be a good idea if you sent someone up to pop in and see if anything is missing."

It only took about two minutes after the order was given for a breathless monk to come pounding down the long hall to Father

Goulding's chambers. The door to the restricted collection was not only unlocked, but was in fact, hanging wide open. An immediate inventory of the collection was underway.

Father Eliot turned back to Revka and Iyarra. "While we are waiting," he said, "did these people make any mention of what they were after?"

Revka shrugged. "He just said that they had been sent to get a priceless artifact. He didn't say anything about books."

Iyarra raised her hand. "Maybe it *is* an old book. He did say artifact."

Father Goulding shrugged. "I'm afraid most of the restricted books are rather old. Quite extremely so, in many cases. Can you think of nothing else?"

"Sorry, mister."

"Father."

"Father, yeah. Just what we said already."

"I see. Thank you." Father Goulding sat back and kneaded his temples.

"One thing puzzles me," said Father Eliot. "You mentioned those curse-marks. As I understand it, they wouldn't remove them if you got caught or betrayed them, and yet you came straight to me. Why is that?"

Revka frowned. "I...well, you know, they just had me so mad. Frankly, I kinda figure they're not going to take the stupid things off no matter what. So, why not tell you?"

Father Eliot chuckled. "An interesting argument. And probably true, I regret to say. I'm afraid we don't have any magic people here—quite against the rules of the order, you know. But I might be able to make inquiries...?"

"Would ya? Because these things are a real pain in the...uhm, you know."

There was the flap of leather sandals on stone as another friar came bolting down the hall. He swung into the room on the door jamb and nearly slipped as he tried to stop. He stumbled to an awkward halt, panting and leaning on his knees. Father Goulding patted the young man. "It's all right, Brother Kurz. Take a moment. Collect your breath."

Brother Kurz shook his head. "It's the...the book, sir..." He shook his head and wheezed.

"Yes, yes. It's all right. Which book?"

"The... The Words of...of Ashkahn..."

A collective gasp stole all sound from the room. The already tense atmosphere shifted quietly but unmistakably into serious, cut-with-a-knife territory.

"Er...? That's...bad, I take it?" said Revka.

Father Eliot's face was grave. "Ashkahn was...well, he was generally regarded as the single greatest homunculist of his day. Possibly of all time."

"Hom...?"

"Homunculist. That means he was able to create living creatures using alchemical processes. He could create beasts of land and sea, large ones, small ones. There are even those who say he created the first dragons, though why he would do such a thing I cannot begin to imagine."

Iyarra perked her ears. "What, like any kind of creatures?"

Father Eliot nodded. "Oh, yes. I know for a fact he commanded quite high sums to animate pets for the gentry, modeled on creatures from their favorite stories and so on. There's a rather good painting of Queen Arra the First, as a child, accompanied by a miniature horse that he had created for her. It was pink, you know. Apparently the little creature could sing simple songs and play games with her."

"Well," said Revka, "That doesn't sound too bad."

"Yes. Well. His real money was in creating less...innocent creatures. Guardians. Slaves. And soldiers."

"Soldiers?"

Father Goulding nodded. "The book is essentially a diabolic recipe book for creating creatures of any description. It took the combined efforts of three nations to subdue the army Krun the Conqueror commissioned from him. It is said that Ashkahn's creatures were more machines than animals. They could move as freely as any beast but were utterly without souls. When Krun sent his troops into battle, they marched like toy soldiers, slashing and blocking even when their limbs were cut away. They had no notion of pain or fear, we are told. Cogwork soldiers, made of flesh and bone."

"O...kay," said Revka. "That's pretty horrible. And you think that the duke is going to try to whip up his own army?"

"Well, I hardly think he has gone to all this trouble to make singing ponies."

"In the end, they wound up putting Ashkahn to death," Father Goulding explained. "A small team from the three allied kingdoms hunted him down. They destroyed his workshop and all its secrets. His servant escaped with the book. The dangerous tome passed through various hands, until we were able to acquire it and lock it away. It has been here ever since. Well, until now."

"Uhm... Pardon me for asking." Iyarra stepped forward shyly. "If the book was so dangerous, why didn't you just, you know, get rid of it?"

"Get...rid of it?"

"Yeah," said Revka. "Like burn it. Light a match, end of problem."

Father Goulding was trembling. He had somehow managed to turn even whiter as he stammered "Buh–buh–b–"

Father Eliot hurried over and patted the elder abbot on the shoulder. "It's all right, it's all right. She didn't mean it. Take a deep breath. There's a fellow." He turned to the women. "You must understand that to destroy a book is... It's unthinkable. No matter what the contents."

Iyarra furrowed her brow at this but shrugged it off and said nothing.

"So what," asked Revka, "are we going to do?"

"I think, first of all, that you need to get back there as quickly as you can."

"What?" Revka screwed up her face. "Why?"

"Primarily to stop them using the book. If you can intercept those two on your way back, then so much the better." He nodded in Iyarra's direction. "I understand you, young lady, have quite the sense of smell. If you hurry, you might be able to pick up the trail and catch up with them. Even if they do make it back to the duke before you can stop them, you can at least delay their use of the book, stall them somehow. I will send messengers to certain lords I know. We will have troops there as quickly as possible to nip this whole thing in the bud before it has a chance to become Krun all over again. Also, I will see if we can locate someone who can do something about those curse-marks of yours. How long did you say you had?"

"Well, they said two months, and it's been a few weeks, so..."

"You should be able to get there with plenty of time to spare. If we find someone, we will send them with the troops; I give you my word. Time is of the essence. We will see to it that you have adequate supplies for the return trip. Have you any weapons?"

"We have weapons and armor down in Tam."

"Very well. Do all you can to stop or slow these people down. If possible, retrieve the book. We will send troops to aid you as soon as we can. And may the gods help us all."

K.L. Mitchell

Chapter Twelve

"I DON'T BELIEVE THIS," Revka muttered for the seventeenth time, as they threaded their way down the mountain trail. The morning had brought with it a slow but steady trickle of pilgrims working their way up the mountain. Iyarra had to dodge and weave her way around several groups that insisted on taking up the entire width of the trail.

A rather large, old woman was apparently too intent on grumbling over her prayer beads to watch where she was going. Iyarra swerved to avoid a collision. "Oh?" she said, "Which particular part don't you believe?"

"Oh, all of it." Revka sat on Iyarra's back with her arms folded, and sulked. Just for a while, she had thought they really might have a chance at the big time. She had pictured them getting steady work, high risk but high reward special missions. She imagined them becoming the specialists in delicate jobs that needed doing quickly and quietly. Now, it turned out that they were not only conscripts but sacrificial lambs, sent out to be caught, expected to fail.

Expected to fail.

Somehow, that was even worse than the curse-marks.

It wasn't as if they were particularly good at what they did. Even in her more boastful moments, Revka would freely admit that they were just a couple of jobbing adventurers trying to make a living. They were Jills-of-all-trades, so to speak. But they'd managed to get by, hadn't they? There had been lean times, but there was always food about if you knew where to look. Neither of them was afraid of hard work. The times had been good, really.

And then along came this stupid duke and his stupid horse thief business and these stupid, stupid curse-marks. She wished she'd never heard of him.

Actually, now that she thought of it, she rather wished *he'd* never heard of *them*.

Anyway, too late now.

It was midafternoon by the time they got down to Tam. It didn't take long for them to change back into their armor and begin a slow circuit of the town. Iyarra sniffed the air, trying to track down their adversaries. The town was bustling, and multiple scents jostled for her attention. She had paced back and forth across the front gate before declaring that they could not have left town, at least not by that route. A slow examination of the walls stretching around the town and all the way to the mountain revealed no trace of them. They had just begun to check the various inns when Iyarra froze, ears pricked.

"What is it?" Revka hissed.

Iyarra tilted her head just a bit. She bit her lip, then turned with glacial slowness to the mouth of the tunnel leading into the mountain. She took a few steps forward, closed her eyes, and took a deep breath. If Revka had been in the habit of traveling in more sophisticated circles, Iyarra's attitude would have put her in mind of an expert sommelier tasting some familiar vintage. As it was, she just kept still. A moment later, Iyarra snorted and started trotting toward the mouth of the tunnel.

Revka leaned forward. "In there? Really?"

Nod.

"But why would they do that? You'd think they'd hot foot it out of town."

Shrug.

Revka sighed and sat back again.

The main tunnel was spacious and wide, with torches all along the walls. If Revka had stood on her saddle, she might just have been able to touch the roof. People strolled up and down the path, chatting amiably or quietly going about their business. Somewhere down below, someone laughed. The echoes bounced up and down the tunnel above the general susurration. Periodic light wells punctuated the darkness, where copper mirrors caught the sunshine and sent it flowing into the darkness.

They followed the tunnel, down in its slow corkscrew, into the depths of the earth. Down here, the air was a tad stale. That meant the scent hadn't drifted, so Iyarra began to move with more speed. She followed the trail through a side tunnel, then a smaller corridor. A long ramp opened into a large chamber, which seemed to be a sort of indoor market. Stalls and tents lined the walls of the room, and a large bonfire in the middle provided additional light. There was a furtiveness to this place. Normal market noises were replaced with whispered conversations, and there were too many hooded cloaks for Revka's liking. The whole place felt shady, the kind of place where vaguely defined "businessmen" went about their business in a nice, informal way, well away from the vagaries of law. She was pretty sure this market wasn't on the tourist maps. She slipped a hand down to her sword hilt, just in case.

A few of the denizens glanced up as the two went by, then quickly turned back to their own affairs. Iyarra picked her way across the room. Revka knew the horsewoman wasn't comfortable underground, and as they picked their way forward she could feel Iyarra's muscles tremble beneath her. She gave the centaur a reassuring pat and kept her eyes open.

A ragged curtain near the far side of the room opened up into a smaller area set up as a sort of pub. Shadowy figures hunkered around small tables in hissed conversation. Dim candles were the only source of light. Iyarra slowed to a walk, letting her nose do the work. Revka peered into the gloom, trying to pick out the shapes, many of whom slunk back away from the light.

The team worked their way between the tables, trying to look inconspicuous. Occasionally there was a muttered comment, but most of the patrons studiously avoided paying them the least bit of attention. There weren't many centaurs down in this part of the cave. There were a couple, so Iyarra didn't completely stand out. This was the kind of place where it paid not to notice things, or to be noticed. Revka expected they could have painted themselves purple and tap danced across the room without arousing too much comment.

In the end, it was Revka who first heard the familiar voice in urgently whispered conversation off to their left. She gave Iyarra a nudge, and they worked their way closer in a roundabout way. There were three of them. The lean shape was the male thief, with his back toward them, hunched in close to the two toughs, who sat opposite. Tall, broad, with arms and legs that bulged with muscle, they looked like serious trouble. Ram's horns sprouted from their bald heads and curled out and away to tips filed down and topped with metal spikes. They looked like the type that would kill someone for money, or simply because they couldn't think of a reason not to. They listened intently to the thief, who seemed to be giving them some urgent instructions.

"...and armor, but burn the papers, all right? Every bit of paper or anything with writing on it. Got it? Brilliant."

One of the thugs narrowed his eyes and peered up at Iyarra. He muttered something to the thief, who stiffened, put down his mug, and turned around. "Ah. Ladies."

Revka hopped down off of Iyarra's back. "Hey. Thought you'd be well out of town by now. Where's your friend?"

The thief shrugged. "She had some business to take care of. In fact, so did I." He inclined his head toward the two thugs. "I take it that all went well?"

"Well, we're not locked away in a dungeon somewhere, so I'd say that's a pretty good guess."

"Very glad to hear it."

"Anyhow, it's just as well we ran into you. We might as well head back together, now we're all friends and so on." Revka smirked. "You can tell the duke all about how helpful we were, and he can take these damned things off our arms. Then we can all go our separate ways. Won't that be nice?"

The thief smiled. "I'm afraid not. We'll be heading back without you. These two gentlemen here will be taking care of you." He dropped a little money pouch on the table and drained his mug. He stood and bowed, then turned to the men. "All yours, boys. Remember your instructions."

"Now, hold *on!*" Revka stepped forward to intercept him. "You're not welshin' out on us, are you? We've done everything your dumb duke wanted us to do! Are you seriously going to—"

"Not everything." His smile was positively diabolical. "But the boys will take care of that last detail." His hand moved, and there was a sudden, blinding flash of light. Revka staggered back, swinging wildly in the air, but the soft patter of stealthy feet told her that her quarry had gotten away.

She shook her head and tried to blink away the green and purple splotches that wouldn't fade from her vision. There was the telltale *skrrrunk* of chairs being slid back, and the sinister, ringing hiss of weapons being drawn. That would be the two uglies. She started backing away... To her left, she could hear Iyarra rearing up in surprise, followed by the crash as she destroyed the thief's chair on the way down. This caused Iyarra to stumble backward, bumping into another patron, who immediately gave her a kick. The one he got back sent him flying into the next table.

At this point, things got complicated.

Through the curious alchemy by which these things work, the brawl spread through the tavern like wildfire. The chain reaction of violence—fueled by darkness, carelessness, and plenty of alcohol—turned the room in a matter of seconds into a glass-smashing, wood-splintering, free for all. Some of the more secretive customers nipped to the edge of the room and slipped out the door, but the majority seemed more than happy to dive right in. Had the women been in a position to observe, they would have noticed several tables of men jump up and join the fracas just for the sheer hell of it. But at the moment, they had other things on their minds.

Revka felt one of the thugs coming toward her. She paused, then ducked just as a spiked club swiped the air where her head had been. She dropped to the floor, scurrying away on all fours. She could just begin to see shapes again. She dove under a table just ahead, then out the other side. Her pursuer ducked below the table and began to crawl after her, but he wasn't really built for dexterity. He managed to get himself tangled between chairs, while Revka doubled back to Iyarra.

The centauress was standing right where she had landed, squirming as the other goon closed in on her. Even worse at moving than he was, she'd grabbed a chair and was holding him at bay. That wouldn't last forever. Revka cursed. If only she had some kind of a—

Oh. Right.

She pulled her sword out of its sheath and crab walked around behind the assailant. His attention was taken up with trying to swing around Iyarra's chair. If she could just...

There was a shout, and a tankard clanged against Revka's shoulder. She looked as the other thug, having disentangled himself from the table, came charging toward her. She swung the blade, just managing to slash Iyarra's goon in the side before haphazardly parrying the other one's club. They started to fight in earnest. The tough guy was obviously stronger than her, but not what you would call nimble. She managed to keep ducking and parrying, making him do the work, as she lured him away from Iyarra. Just let them get to one of the more open spaces...

There was a splintering crash. It was hard to see much between the darkness and the speed at which the thug went by, but Revka guessed he'd just received one of Iyarra's special kicks. Revka and her assailant both gaped as the brute sailed by to a rough landing on a table. There was no doubt that he was dead; no one could look like that and live. The other thug stared at the body in disbelief. Revka managed to recover and stabbed him haphazardly, but effectively, in the chest.

She shouldered her way through the two to three person bouts back to Iyarra, who was in the middle of a small circle of wary fighters. They'd seen what she could do at close quarters. Most were choosing to carry on their business with other, less dangerous partners. A couple of other centaurs zeroed in on her but got waylaid by some other patrons and were happily occupied. Revka tapped Iyarra on the shoulder. "Let's go," she hissed.

They tried to worm their way toward the door, but the path was blocked. Revka could squeak through if she was careful, but Iyarra wasn't going to be able to work her way around the various punch-ups between them and the way out. In theory, they could fight their way through. In theory. Revka darted her eyes around, looking for inspiration.

Nearby, against the wall, a rough wooden bench with legs formed a large L, about as long as Iyarra was tall. Revka gazed at it a moment, then smiled.

"Okay," she said, "Here's my plan..."

***

Targon the Mighty brought a table leg down with a satisfying *crack* on the skull of his opponent. He'd had a few ales and had a good buzz going. Not enough to throw off his technique, mind you, just enough to get him in the mood. Good thing the brawl had started early this evening. Someone *bit* his lower leg. He cried out and turned to give them a kick.

Suddenly, there was a commotion—check that, an even bigger tumult. His friend, Hogarth, cannoned into him, sending them both spilling to the floor. Targon opened his mouth to curse the clumsy fool into oblivion, then caught a glimpse of what had knocked him down.

A tall wooden V, two long boards nailed together, was plowing its way through the crowd. Anyone caught in its path was shoved to one side, where they inevitably crashed into several others. From the ground, he couldn't quite see the ram's six-legged pilot, but he heard their battle cries.

"Higher! Higher!"

"It *is* higher!"

"I'm scraping the floor, here!"

"Sorry!"

"And watch out for my feet!"

And then they were gone. The cloth flap that served as a door flopped back into position, and the room went silent. A long empty gap led straight through the tavern to the door. Fallen drunks on either side eyed each other. One or two got up and took a few half-hearted swings at each other, but the fun had gone out of it. By ones and twos, the rest picked themselves up, along with what was left of their tables.

Targon eased himself up and cracked his neck. He grabbed Hogarth and helped him up, then they both staggered back to their table. He looked at the tankards knocked aside and the ale spilled all over the floor. He shook his head sadly. Some people just did not know how to behave.

***

Iyarra shoved the bench out of their way. Revka climbed on her back, and they darted through the open area back into the tunnels. Iyarra kept moving, putting as much space between them and the tavern as she could. After a few wrong turns, they found their way back up to the surface, where the sun was just beginning to set.

The two moved to a convenient alley back behind a warehouse and paused to catch their breath. "Well," said Revka. "That was unexpected."

Iyarra tilted her head. "Was it?"

Revka shrugged. "No," she said. "Not really." She stretched and began to rummage in Iyarra's saddlebags. "One thing's for sure," she said. "We don't want to be spending the night here. They've probably hired all sorts of goons to come after us." She sighed and gave Iyarra's back a pat. "I'm afraid it's back to sleeping rough for us, kiddo. At least for a while."

Iyarra shrugged. "I don't mind so much." She held still as Revka climbed back on. "But I agree, yeah. We should probably keep off the road, too." She set off at a trot, heading for the gate. There were the usual guards there, but Iyarra suddenly felt a wave of paranoia kick in. Were there that many guards when they first came? She couldn't remember. She stared straight ahead, trying to look nonchalant.

Revka, too, picked up the vibe. She leaned forward. "Hey," she whispered, "Think they ratted us out to the guards?"

"Don't know," Iyarra said. At the gate, two guards were in conversation. One of them seemed to look their way for a moment. Iyarra's heart skipped a beat.

"Well, he probably wants us taken care of quietly. If they got officials involved, there's always the possibility we'd rat out both them and the duke."

"So, what do you think?"

123

"I don't know. Trot casual, but be ready to gallop."

The two approached the gate. Another guard had appeared from somewhere. There seemed to be some sort of conversation going on. There were only a few people heading out of the gate at this hour, so there wasn't any sort of crowd to disappear into. Still, Iyarra shuffled in with a small cluster of folks and tried to look inconspicuous.

They moved toward the gate, almost level with it now. It definitely wasn't her imagination. There were more guards, clustered about and giving special attention to departing travelers. Behind her, Iyarra felt Revka shift her weight, ready for fight or flight. She took a deep breath and stared straight ahead as they crossed their way through.

"Oi, you!"

Iyarra nearly jumped out of her skin. She froze in place, watching in panic as several guards converged on them. She tried to get herself to run, but somehow her legs just weren't getting the message.

The guards clustered around the little group. Suddenly, swords and crossbows were everywhere, and it was too late to run. Iyarra felt her stomach drop. They were going to be caught, and it was all going to be her fault.

The man next to her spat and drew a stiletto from nowhere. "Just try it," he growled.

"Now, Schaunnacy," the speaker's insignia identified him as a sergeant. "I know, sure, you can count. There's five of us, and all your friends turned tail on you. You've no chance at all."

"You bet?" Suddenly his knife was pressed against Iyarra's withers, just beneath the breastplate. "I think I've got a very good chance. Looks like I've got a hostage and a way out of here in one." He turned to Revka. "You. Get off."

"But I—"

"Get off, or I'll gut 'er."

Revka opened her mouth to reply, then seemed to think better of it. "All right, all right," she said. She raised her arms with exaggerated care and slid off the other side of Iyarra's back. "I just feel I ought to warn you, that's all."

Schaunnacy, who already had one foot in a stirrup, paused in the act of hauling himself up. "Warn me?" His eyes narrowed. "What about?"

"Oh, Iyarra here. She comes from a long line of Mesopotamian fainting horses. Keel over at the first sign of danger. Isn't that right?"

"Eh?"

"Huh?"

"I *said*," Revka repeated, her enunciation slipping into overdrive, "That she faints *at any sign of danger whatsoever.* Isn't that so?"

"Oh! Oh, right." Iyarra slapped the back of her hand to her forehead and rolled her eyes. "In fact, I..."

"Wait a minute," Schaunnacy said through gritted teeth.

"Oh, yeah. Here it comes."

"Whooooaaaahhhh....!" Iyarra flopped onto her side. There was a muffled crunch, as a leg tried to take on half a ton of horse and lost, then a stream of curses. Schaunnacy flailed helplessly, unable even to notice as the city guards closed in.

After the guards carried the hobbling Schaunnacy away, Revka climbed back onto Iyarra's back. "You okay?" she whispered.

Iyarra nodded. "Yeah. Yeah, I'm okay. Let's just go."

Revka pursed her lips, peering at the guardhouse. "Say, you think there might be a reward?"

"Revka?"

"Mm?"

"Please. Let's just go."

"Ah. Right."

They rode in silence for a while, until the light of day began to fade away. They moved away from the road, setting up camp in an isolated glade near a small stream. Iyarra was quiet all through setting up the camp, and during dinner. It was only as they sat watching the fire that she sagged and let out a little sigh.

Revka scooted over to her. "Yarra? You all right?"

Iyarra shrugged. "I'm fine, yes. I mean, considering."

"Hey, it's all right. We got rid of that guy in no time flat, right? You did good."

"Oh, it's not just that." Iyarra plucked a blade of grass and toyed with it. "It's all these thugs and thieves and fighters and other people we seem to be running into lately. Ever since we got this job it's been nothing but trouble. I know you love adventuring and all, but I'm really wondering if I'm actually cut out for it."

"I'm sorry, hon. I guess I just assumed since your people are nomads..."

"Well yes, but your entire tribe goes with you everywhere, and you stick to the same general area. In any case, it's...different, you know? Like it's all your home, and you're just in different parts of it."

"All right." Revka moved around to face Iyarra. She took the horsewoman's hands in hers and looked up at her. "I tell you what. If we get through this and you still feel this way, then no more wandering, okay? We'll find a nice village to settle down in and get regular jobs. We'll have a nice little cottage, and a field to run around in. We'll come home every night, and there won't be any more adventures. You can even pick the place, all right? Does that sound nice?"

Iyarra nodded. "Yeah. Yeah, it does."

"All right." Revka leaned up and gave Iyarra a hug. "We'll get through this. You just wait and see."

Chapter Thirteen

MORNING TRAFFIC HEADING AWAY from Tam was relatively light as they set off down the pilgrims' road again. They were able to make good time despite the gentle, persistent rain that came down every step of the way.

"Are you sure you can't pick up either scent?" Revka scowled at the road ahead that was rapidly turning into mud again.

Iyarra shrugged. "Sorry. Just no way. The rain, you know?" She sludged along the path, pausing to tuck an ear back under her oilcloth hood.

"Hmm, assuming they're heading straight back, they're probably following the same path we did. We just have to retrace our steps, and we'll catch their trail sooner or later."

"I hope so." Iyarra stepped gingerly around a puddle. "The trail won't last for long, you know."

That evening, Revka lay awake in the roadside inn, listening to the rain drum on the roof and thinking of Father Eliot's final words to them. He'd walked with them down the trail a while before beckoning them to stop.

I didn't like to say anything in front of Father Goulding, but the book is dangerous enough that if you have to destroy it...well, go ahead and do so. We really cannot allow those secrets to fall into the hands of one ambitious for power. If it comes down to it, don't hesitate to destroy the damned thing. Don't worry about Father Goulding, all right? You let me worry about him.

It seemed to her a curious sort of request. Didn't those guys basically worship books? But she supposed it made sense when you thought about it. A book like that could cause serious trouble. Of course, if it had been up to her, she'd have torched that sucker first thing, no question. She was never terribly at home with books. Her mother had insisted she learn to read and write, but given the choice between reading about something and actually doing it, Revka always knew which she preferred.

In her stall below, Iyarra couldn't sleep. The rain usually made a soothing backdrop, but she couldn't stop worrying about the mysterious stranger and that stupid book he'd stolen. She'd always found it easy to just trust in Revka and assume that she would see a way through. Somehow though, Iyarra couldn't stop wondering if this adventure was too much, even for her intrepid friend. She shook her head, trying to banish the terrible thought from her mind. The worry persisted. She paced and fretted, and watched the rain come down.

***

Morning brought them and the rains back to Port Mill, but by midmorning the sun pushed its way through the clouds. The city gleamed. Iyarra spent a little time wandering around the main city gate, testing the air. In the end, she had to admit that any scent the thieves had left was long gone.

They wandered toward the docks. "The way I see it," said Revka, "they're going to want to get back as quickly as possible, right? Well, the paddle boats move upriver a little faster than trotting pace, but going downriver is a whole different story. You'd have to gallop to keep up with them, right?"

"Right."

"Okay." Revka looked around the open marketplace. "And as far as we know, they didn't have horses anyway. You hungry?"

"They could buy or steal some," said Iyarra. "And I could eat something."

"All right." They wandered toward a corner, where several food stalls were clustered. "I don't think they would, though. I think they're probably traveling light. Besides, it's probably more trouble than it's worth, getting a couple of horses like that. I expect they're mostly staying off the main roads, keeping to themselves."

"Makes sense."

"What I figure is, grab a riverboat going back down to Port South and basically retrace our steps back to Gainsburgh."

"Works for me."

"Cool. Looks like that stall over there has fritters. Let's check them out."

A little while later, Revka was strolling alongside Iyarra toward the docks, carrying a greasy paper bag and sharing a fried pastry with melted cheese. Iyarra stopped dead in her tracks.

Revka managed to stop in time and only just managed to avoid smooshing the pastry into Iyarra's shoulder. She stumbled and looked around. "What's up? Why've we stopped?"

"Look." Iyarra pointed. Not ten paces away, a genial older man was chatting with some well-dressed men who had just come off of one of the boats. Revka gawped.

"Well, I'll be," she growled. "It's Mister So-Called White." She handed the pastry over and fumbled for her sword. "I've got a score to settle with that no good—"

"Ah-ah-ah!" Iyarra laid a warning hand on the woman's shoulder. "We already got back at him, remember? The stones?"

"Oh. Right." She looked around. Now that she was paying attention, it didn't take long to locate Targhan and Choss lurking off to one side. They were keeping an eye on their boss. "Should we make ourselves scarce?"

"I think so."

"Yeah." The two women began to back away from the scene, maneuvering around a seafood barrow until they were out of sight. Revka let out a sigh of relief and relaxed...just in time for Iyarra to tread on a man's foot.

"*Grnnnnnrrh!*" he said, if only less coherently. Iyarra pulled her hoof away quickly.

"Watch where you're going, you rat-damn stupid *nag!*" he swore, hopping up and down.

"Look," said Revka, "We're sorry, we were just—"

"Sorry?" The man's face was red with rage. Two men who were standing with him drew out some nasty looking clubs. "We'll give ya sorry!"

Revka reached behind her, grabbed the first thing that came to hand, and brandished it at him. "Stay back!" she cried, waving a small octopus at the men. A tentacle waved back at her.

"Arse-pimples." The octopus splatted against the nearest man's face, and Revka swung herself onto Iyarra's back. "Change of plan," she said. "*Run!*"

The man flailed around, trying to bat the creature away. He tried to shout and received a mouthful of ink for his trouble. Iyarra bolted down the road, dodging and weaving around the carts and pedestrians that packed the docks. A long, flat barge was being unloaded, and several bundles of wool blocked the way. Revka could feel Iyarra's legs bunching up. "*No!*" she screamed, "Don't try to jump it!"

129

Iyarra's hooves skidded. She swerved at the last second, galloping up the ramp and onto the barge. Iyarra bolted along the length of the boat, past bundles of cloth, bales of cotton and wool, over a line of rain barrels, and down another ramp onto the docks, moderately inconveniencing several men who were hauling provisions onboard.

Revka ducked as an angry stevedore threw a boat hook at her. "Nice trick," she shouted. "How did you know that barge had a second ramp?"

"I didn't!"

"Oh. Right."

They hurried along the quayside, weaving their way through the crowd as quickly as they could. Behind them, Revka could hear more men shouting and running after them. The shouts sounded awful unhappy about something. She yelped as they vaulted over a crate and came down in a mud puddle, dousing two or three innocent bystanders who immediately joined the chase.

Ahead, several men were unloading cages from an old farm cart and passing them up to a riverboat in a kind of bucket brigade. "Move it!" Iyarra waved her hands frantically. "Gangway! Coming through!"

The men, to their credit, had the presence of mind to scatter out of the way. Unfortunately, not all of them had the presence of mind to take the cages with them. Too late to stop, Iyarra bounded through a gauntlet of panic-filled chicken crates. Revka shut her eyes. She heard the splintering of wood, a terrified squawk, then a panic of frantic wings. She risked opening one eye.

A chicken glared back at her.

She gingerly lifted the chicken away and blinked in mild surprise at the contents of the saddle blanket. "Say, Yarra?"

"What?"

"Do you like eggs?"

"Uhm, kind of busy right now."

"You sure? It's fresh."

"Yes, I'm sure!

"Okay then." She tucked the egg into a saddle bag. The chicken regarded her with the wild eyed, manic stare that is a chicken's natural state. She looked behind. Some of the cage men had joined the pursuit. She hefted the chicken and weighed it carefully in one hand, then took aim.

"What was that noise?" Iyarra called back, as she skidded around a corner.

"The noise? Oh. Uhm, nothing important. Keep running."

Revka snuck another peek behind her, watching the chaos unfold. "As the gods are my witness," she muttered to herself, "I thought chickens could fly."

"What?"

"I said, keep running!"

By this time there were some dozen or so men chasing them, all of them looking pretty angry. Iyarra turned right, heading inland from the docks and toward one of the smaller market areas. Booths lined both sides of a long street mobbed with people. Iyarra staggered to a walk, desperately trying to thread her way through the crowd.

Revka groaned. Any second now their pursuers would round the corner and they'd be trapped. There'd be no way to get away with all these people here. If only she—

"Left!"

"What?"

"Left! By that booth! Right now!"

The pursuers came charging into the market street and slowed to a halt. The troublemakers were nowhere to be seen. The original pursuers pushed their way to the front, two of them supporting the still-hobbling third between them. They glared at the crowd. "Come on," one shouted, "they can't have gotten far!"

The men began to weave their way down the street, peering into stalls, poking at large hanging tapestries, keeping their eyes peeled. It would have gone very badly indeed if one of them had looked behind them, as a centaur and rider, cloaked and smelling faintly of chicken, tiptoed out of an alley and headed back the way they had come.

***

Iyarra slowed to a trot, panting as she made her way out of the city gate. Revka guided her to a small clump of trees by the side of the road. They sat for a few tense moments, listening. It soon became clear that no one was coming after them. Revka dabbed her brow.

"Okay. That was a little too close for comfort. You okay?"

"I'm fine, I'm fine...can't believe we nearly ran into him like that."

"Yeah, I should have thought about that." Revka slid off Iyarra's back and stretched. "Still, it's not all bad. I suppose we can head down the road to Port South, and..."

"And...?"

Revka didn't answer. She was peering at the river in a quizzical manner. It seemed to be bothering her for some reason.

"Uhm, Revka?"

A long quiet moment passed before Revka turned. "Yarra?"

"Yes?"

"We just came out of town, didn't we?"

"Right, yes."

"And that's the river, right there, right?"

"Yes."

"So...why is it on the left?"

"I'm sorry?"

"The river. If we came out of town, it should be on the right, shouldn't it? I mean—" she stopped in midsentence, her eyes narrowing. A piece of driftwood floated toward them, bumped gently against the shore, then carried on its way past the gate and toward the mill. Revka sighed.

"Iyarra?"

"Yes?"

"What direction were we traveling in, when we escaped from those guys?"

"I didn't really notice. I was just going for the fastest possible route."

"Iyarra..."

"Yes?"

"We came out the wrong gate. We're at the north side of town. We need to be going south."

"Sorry."

"It's all right. Can't be helped. We'll just have to go back through town."

"With all of those men looking for us?"

"Oh yeah."

"And those people we upset at the docks?"

"Yeah, all right, I get the—"

"And possibly running into Mister White and his friends, who will *not* be happy to see us."

"I think you've made—"

"And probably someone's alerted the guards by now."

"All right, *all right*." Revka threw her hands in the air. "Forget the town. We'll just head up the river, all right? Bound to be another port before long. We'll get a boat there, or something."

"Okay."

They started up the road, watching the river drift by alongside them. They were quiet for a while.

"Revka?"

"Mm?"

"Do we have any more of those cheese fritters? I dropped mine in the excitement."

"Oh. Hang on." Revka peered into the bag. "Looks like pig meat, apple, and uhm…" She shook the bag. "Some sort of fruit. Could be cherries."

"Don't like cherries."

"There's the apple. You like apples."

"Okay. Thanks."

Revka patted Iyarra's side. "Any time, hon," she said. "Any time."

K.L. Mitchell

Chapter Fourteen

THE NEXT TOWN UPRIVER turned out to be Port Carlin, which was a good long trot along the river. In fact, it was already dark as they dragged themselves through the city gates and found their way to the nearest inn.

The next morning, after a quick breakfast, they headed down to the docks to find a ship heading south. Port Carlin had a lifting bridge just like at Port South, which didn't improve things. Eventually Revka had to lead Iyarra across while the centaur kept her eyes closed.

A quick survey of the docks showed there was only one passenger boat getting ready to go downstream. There was a problem, though.

"The *Autumn Blaze*," Revka read out loud.

Iyarra frowned. "Isn't that the boat where we—"

"Mm-hmm."

"You think Mister David is...?"

"Quite possibly."

"And he won't be happy to see us either, will he?"

"Can't see how he would be."

Revka sighed, her hands on her hips as she looked around. An important looking man with a clipboard was standing by the gangplank, muttering to himself. From time to time, he would jot down a note. She went over. "Excuse me?"

The man didn't look up. "Yes?"

"Yeah. Hi. Is this the only passenger boat heading downriver today?"

The man looked up. "That's right, yes. We should have the *Sweet Abissiniya* here tomorrow morning, though, if you like."

"I see. Thank you."

Revka went back to Iyarra and shrugged. "Well, we can either take the chance and get on the boat, or wait til tomorrow. Or we could start walkin'."

"Sorry."

"Of course, by the time we get all the way down to Port South, they'll be out of there and down the road a ways. There's no way we can catch up with them then." Revka scratched the back of her neck.

"I wish we could take a shortcut or something, but there's only the river road." Iyarra sagged.

"I suppose I could..."

Iyarra politely waited a few moments. When nothing else seemed to be forthcoming, she gave Revka a little look. "Uhm, could what?"

Revka didn't answer. She was too busy looking west, away from the river, where the rocky hills had been replaced by grassy plains. The hills undulated gently. Here and there, the occasional tree punctuated an otherwise unbroken expanse of grass.

She turned to Iyarra and smiled. "Fancy a run?"

***

A few hours later, they had left the river well behind. Rolling hills of grass stretched away as far as could be seen in any direction.

"Great idea, huh?" Revka was in full preen mode. "I figure we'll cross right over, pass Kenning altogether and hit the lake district in no time. Heck, we might even beat him there, especially if we keep up the pace."

Iyarra snorted. *We.* She trotted over the crest of a small hillock and allowed herself a gallop down the other side. It was, she had to admit, pleasant. Her clan was nomadic, and she had grown up on very similar lands to these. Even the grass tasted like home.

And yet...something about the arrangement kept nagging at her. She couldn't quite put a finger on it, but somehow, she just couldn't let go of the idea that something was wrong. Revka, on the other hand, was practically crowing.

"I mean, there's tons of grass for you, nowhere for bandits to hide, we've got enough provisions to last me a few days. This much grass means there's bound to be some water around here somewhere. Streams and whatever. And best of all, we got the whole place to ourselves."

Iyarra began to slow down. Ah. That was it.

"I mean," continued Revka, "You think of all those suckers going down the river, and basically taking the long way around the plains when they could just go across. It's ridiculous. Makes you wonder why nobody ever does this, you know?"

Iyarra crested a hill. Far to their right, she could see a handful of large gray shapes lurching toward them.

"I think," she said, "it's because of the drakuls."

***

Drakuls, for those who have not had the pleasure, are large carnivorous creatures that live in grasslands, where they prey on herbivores, carnivores, insectivores, and pretty much anything else that happens by. They travel in small family groups called damnations and are generally considered some of the nastiest creatures you could ever hope to avoid.

To get a good idea of what a drakul looks like, cross a praying mantis with a Komodo dragon and grow the thing to the approximate size of an upturned refrigerator. Cover the body with a variety of horns, fangs, tail spikes and whatever sharp or dangerous objects you can find. Paint the whole thing battleship gray. You now have something that resembles a drakul.

It is at this point that you should probably start to run.

***

Revka did a double take. "Holy hell," she muttered. "Run!"

Iyarra had already broken into a gallop. She bunched up her fists, pumping them back and forth in an attempt to build up speed.

Revka sneaked another look. "Can you outrun them?"

"Me? No. They'll go for ages."

"All right. Let me see what I can do."

Revka clambered around so she was facing their pursuers. This was no easy task even when they weren't moving. At full gallop, it was a pain. She lashed herself to Iyarra's harness, then fumbled for her crossbow. The military issue from the duke's armory was fairly old, but someone had at least thought to restring it and give it a bit of oil. Fine. That only left the bolts. She clenched her legs around Iyarra's barrel, then started to rummage through her saddlebags. *Bolts, bolts, come on...ah!* She pulled out a leather roll and triumphantly tugged the knot that held it closed. The cloth unrolled on Iyarra's back, revealing several wicked-looking crossbow bolts, most of which immediately fell out and tumbled to the ground.

"No!" Revka grasped frantically at them, holding the roll to her body and grabbing as many escapees as she could. She scooped them back into the roll and tucked it under one leg. There were still about a half dozen or so, and...let's see...five drakuls coming after them. Could you kill a drakul with one bolt?

Probably not.

She sighed and pulled the latch back hard. "Okay," she shouted back at Iyarra, "Here's my plan. It looks like we got a couple of adults and a few younger ones. I'll try to take out the adults once they're in range. Maybe we can outpace the juveniles, or they'll go away or something. Do drakuls eat each other?"

"Dunno," Iyarra called back. "They eat everything else."

"Okay. Maybe we'll get lucky." She patted the scabbard hanging from her belt. If worse came to worse...best to not think about it. Get ready to open fire.

They were noticeably closer now.

Revka slotted a bolt into the crossbow and tried to sight along the barrel. This was not easy; archery was not her strongest suit at the best of times. Riding on the back of a centaur, galloping at speed with most of her ammunition gone, was about as far from the best of times as you could get. Also, the sudden rush of activity and fear had joined forces for a full-on assault on her bladder. She groaned and tried to concentrate on her aim.

The first drakul was coming into range. She waited for it to get a little closer and tried to aim for the head. She said a quick prayer and pulled the trigger. The bolt flew from the crossbow, sailed through the air, and right through its ear. It bellowed, staggering just a moment, and then redoubled its pursuit. If anything, it seemed to be coming after them faster. Still, she had managed to make it angry. So there was that.

She quickly shuffled another bolt into the crossbow. This time she didn't take quite so much time on her aim, but sent it wildly flying toward the beast, just as Iyarra leaped over a small stream. The bolt flew low, hitting the ground with a thud. "Farg!" she muttered and fished out another. This one did better, hitting the lead drakul's left foreleg with a good meaty *thwack*. The beast howled and stumbled off to the side. It didn't stop, but suddenly it was a lot slower. The others darted past their injured mate, eyes fixed on their quarry.

Revka grunted and fumbled for another bolt. OK, they might be able to leave this one behind. Go for the legs, that was the thing. She sighted along the length of the bolt, taking aim at the other adult. It was getting pretty close now, shouldn't be too hard to hit something. There, something to be optimistic about. Did she feel better yet?

No.

She pulled the trigger, and the bolt shot out. The tip wound up grazing the side of the beast, just scratching its hide before tumbling uselessly to the ground. She swore and grabbed another one. Better. This one caught the beast in the chest, not enough to slow it down, but perhaps it would buy them a moment.

All right. One more bolt to go. She took a deep breath, aimed at the wounded drakul, and pulled the trigger. The bolt flew wild. Revka had mistimed her shot and let go just as Iyarra's hooves hit the ground hard. The bolt flew past the lead drakul and managed to hit one of the three smaller ones right in the face. The young one howled and reared up, managing to crash into one of the other juveniles right behind it. They tumbled for a moment, before the uninjured one regained its footing and resumed the pursuit.

Okay. No bolts left, three beasts still in pursuit. She groaned and tossed the empty crossbow at the drakul, where it hung off a horn like a particularly tacky earring. She tugged an old throwing dagger from its sheath in her boot and looked up to make sure the beast was close enough. By now she could see flecks of spit coming off its saber-like teeth. Revka dug in her heels, waited til Iyarra was in midstride, and took her shot. The knife whirled through the air and landed straight in the beast's cheek. The adult drakul shook its head wildly, trying to dislodge the blade, but this wasn't any cub. The huge creature didn't even slow down.

Only a half dozen or so meters separated them. She fished in the saddlebags, not taking her eyes off the pursuing creatures as she groped desperately for something, anything. Her hand closed around the handle of their iron frying pan. She whipped it out and flung it toward the leader. The pan bounced off the drakul's armored chest with a metallic bong. The beast barely stumbled.

Desperate now, she started grabbing fistfuls of items from the bag and hurling them at the pursuing beasts. Metal cups, cutlery, her lucky rock all flew toward the pursuers, but still closer they came. After a moment's hesitation, even her helmet went flying. Her precious protection merely bounced off the lead drakul's snout and pinwheeled away.

Too close now. She could see the mottled texture on the skin of the lead drakul, mark the battlefield of scars across its face. She pulled her sword from its scabbard and eyed the leader warily. Any second now it would leap. The others would too. She might be able to impale one, but wouldn't get all three.

Stupid bladder's not doing me any favors, either.

She could see the leader's rear thigh muscles bunching up under its skin. She narrowed her eyes, licked her dry lips, and edged forward—well, rearward—sword ready. *Well, here goes...*

The adult drakul leaped. Revka gripped her sword, aimed at the approaching creature, and braced for impact. Half a ton of snarling savagery sailed toward her. She squeezed her eyes shut. *Please let this be quick.*

There was the noise of the wind and a series of muffled thumps. Iyarra slowed and came to a halt. Revka tilted her head. In theory, the world should have been a red-hot hell of teeth and claws. Not that she was complaining. She risked opening one eye and peeked around.

The massive drakul lay on the ground, several arrows stuck in its flesh. Those weren't Revka's little crossbow bolts, either. She counted five serious hunting arrows, the kind designed to take down big game. A quick survey revealed that the two remaining juveniles had met the same fate. So, someone with enough firepower to take out a bunch of drakuls. Could be good, could be bad. She chanced a look over her shoulder.

***

They had come to a stop at the base of a hill. Centaurs lined the crest, stretching for a good way in both directions. Nut brown and bulging with muscles, their upper torsos practically gleamed with sweat. Each one carried a longbow. For a moment, they stood absolutely still, looking down at Iyarra and Revka. A huge, hairy fellow with a long, gray mane and beard stepped forward. He peered closely at the two for a long moment, then cupped his hands around his mouth. "Puya?" he called.

Iyarra squealed. "Papa!" She galloped up the hill to her father and hugged him tight. Revka, who had only just managed to keep from falling off at Iyarra's sudden uphill sprint, managed to fumble her way onto the ground and shake some circulation back into her legs. Beside her, Iyarra was practically dancing with joy. "Look, Revka, it's Papa! This must be our herd! I should have realized you might be out here somewhere!" She capered from side to side in her excitement.

The old man nodded. "Iyarra, girl, what are you doing out here? And who is this?"

"Oh! Papa, this is Revka. She's my friend."

"Hi." Revka waved.

"We've been all over the place! We've been up to the mountains and down the river, and there was a temple, and we got chased by those drakuls, and I thought we were gonna get it!"

Her father ruffled the girl's mane. "Yes. Well. You're very lucky we happened to be in this area, yes? You could have been very badly hurt." He peered closer at her. "Are you hurt?"

Iyarra shook her head. "I'm fine, Papa. Just a little winded, that's all." She turned back to Revka. "Are you okay, Revka? Revka?"

Revka stood slightly apart from the others, a preoccupied look on her face. Her thighs were locked together, and she was bouncing up and down on the balls of her feet, looking around with apprehension. There seemed to be something on her mind.

"Uhmmm," she said. "Is there, maybe, a bush or tree or something around here? Somewhere close, preferably. It's, uhm, it's a bit urgent."

K.L. Mitchell

Chapter Fifteen

THE CLAN HAD SET up camp a little way away, by a creek that wound its way around the hills. The water was not very wide but shallow enough to wade through. It was enough. "The plains are covered with little creeks and ponds like this," Iyarra explained. "Our people basically go from one to another, hunting and grazing."

Revka pulled a blanket around her shoulders. They sat before the central fire, surrounded by a few dozen round tents. Each belonged to an individual family. Above, the sky was fading blue-black into night. "Hunting?" she said, "I didn't think you guys hunted."

Iyarra shrugged. "Well, mostly we hunt things that would otherwise hunt us, if you see what I mean. Drakuls. Other predators. Just because we don't eat them doesn't mean we have to stand there and let them eat us."

Revka nudged a baked apple away from the coals. "I thought you just ran."

"Run?" A shape moved behind her. "Oh yes, but only when we run out of arrows." Iyarra's father sat down and gave Revka a smile. Iyarra had explained that Toth was the chief of the clan. In the firelight he seemed even larger, more solidly built. He was old and age toughened, like teak. The centaur looked like he would just keep on getting tougher, until at some point he'd be indestructible. Something about his eyes echoed that. Their steady gaze said, *Here is a man who will never back down from a fight and who will protect his family with every ounce of strength he has.* He turned to Iyarra. "You haven't told her much about us, I think? She thinks the Greatfoot are runners?"

Iyarra blushed a little. "Sorry, Papa. No, I haven't told her much about us." She turned to Revka. "The Swiftfoot and Fleetwind clans are more, uhm, built for speed, you might say. We're more, well..." She tapped one of her large dinner-plate hooves on the ground.

Revka smiled. "Heck," she said. "I know that. I've seen you fight." She grinned at Toth, nodding her head toward the centauress. "Why, you should see this one. Only a couple of weeks ago, we got ambushed by some morgas down south. She kicked one so hard his chest caved in."

Toth roared with laughter. "What, this dainty little thing?" He slapped an arm around Iyarra's back and squeezed her to his side. "Sounds like my girl is learning a thing or two out in the great wide world! And to think, she was always the shy one." Iyarra blushed, her ears flattening against the sides of her head.

Revka picked up the baked apple and brushed it clean. "Oh, she still is. But I gotta say, she will hold herself in a fight. Nice singing voice, too." She grinned wickedly at Iyarra and took a bite out of the apple.

Iyarra made a face. "Okay," she said. "Now you're just doing it on purpose."

"Guilty." Revka chuckled. She looked up at Toth. "Seriously, though. She's doing really great out there."

"Very glad to hear it." He patted Iyarra's mane affectionately. "I have to admit, I was worried when she wanted to go out and see the world a little bit, you know. But it sounds like I had nothing to worry about. Isn't that so, Mother?"

There was a soft rustling, and an older woman sat down next to Revka. Her lower half was slate gray, matching the mane that tumbled down her leathery brown face. She wore a deep green robe bedecked with beads and polished waterstones that flowed down to her back and over her lower half. Her mane and tail were strung with ribbons and braids, and bangles hung on her neck, wrists, and ankles. She settled by the fire in a quiet clattering of metal, then smiled to Toth. "Indeed, so it would seem."

Iyarra brightened. "Oh! Revka, this is my mother, Anyala-Hua-Si. She's originally Fleetwind," she explained.

The woman turned to Revka. "You may call me Anyala, most do." In the firelight, she seemed...well, it was difficult to say. She was a handsome woman, probably middle age or not far past. Though something about her seemed older. Perhaps it was the gray hair. Or the light catching the contours of her face. Being out in the sun all the time tended to bring out the wrinkles early, didn't it? Well...something, anyway.

Revka extended a hand. "I'm Revka. Good to meet ya."

The older woman nodded gravely. "Likewise. My daughter has told me much about you. She visited my tent earlier, while you were resting. I think we have many things to talk about."

"Oh?" Revka glanced over to Iyarra, who was suddenly very occupied with something or another. "Do we?"

"Indeed yes." The old woman gave Revka a pat on the arm. It was an innocent gesture, and possibly a coincidence that she patted the spot where, underneath the beaten leather armor, the curse-mark still lurked. Revka caught herself stealing a glance down at the spot, then turned herself away.

"I was thinking," said Toth, "I might take you two out hunting with us tomorrow. Still some more of those drakuls about. We shall need all the help we can find getting rid of them. Nuisances, they are. It's a constant fight against them."

Anyala shifted to one side, as a couple of other mares approached. They set up a tripod over the fire and hung a large cauldron. As the contents began to heat up, the scent of spices wafted through the air. "I think a hunt would be a fine idea," she said, "but I should like to spend some time with Revka. I wish to get to know her better, if she does not object?"

This time, Iyarra's eye caught Revka's immediately, and there was just the faintest nod. "Oh, sure," Revka said. "That would be great." She smiled. "I think I've had enough of drakuls for a couple of days, in any case, and I'm sure I'd only slow you all down."

Toth laughed. "Very well," he said. "Another time."

Anyala leaned forward and stirred the cauldron, dipping in a long wooden ladle and taking a taste. "Ah, yes. It's ready." She pulled out a small hemp bag and extracted a pinch of some dried plant matter. This she crumbled into the pot and stirred it round again.

The smells coming out of the cauldron weren't familiar, but they certainly were beguiling. Revka felt her mouth water. "What is that?" she asked.

"It is nothing special, just a simple stew." Anyala smiled. "We make it from the various plants we forage as we go from place to place." She gave the pot another stir. "Plus, certain herbs we have collected over time. We call it *chuv*, or cluster, because once you have the base, you can add whatever you have on hand."

"Mother always says you never eat the same *chuv* twice." Iyarra smiled.

"Well, I should hope not!"

Iyarra rolled her eyes. "I mean, you don't eat the same combination of ingredients twice. It's always a little different. I remember, when I was little I would always think, 'this is the first and last time I will ever eat this.' It was kind of a momentous occasion, to a five-year-old."

Toth laughed. "You should have seen her! She would wait until she got to the last mouthful, and wave bye-bye to it. You remember that, Puya?"

"*Daaad!*"

Revka snorted, biting down on a guffaw.

Just then, a young colt stepped to the cauldron for a taste of the chuv. He tilted his head to one side in a reflective attitude, then glanced at Anyala, who nodded. He ladled a scoopful of the stew into a bowl made from a large hollowed-out nutshell. There followed a sort of general movement of the herd to the fire, as everyone filled a bowl and broke off into little groups to eat.

Bowls were passed around the central fire, and everyone helped themselves. Revka blew carefully on her first spoonful, then tasted. The base stock was very flavorful, even if she couldn't quite identify it. There were mushrooms and boiled roots, some kind of chopped leaves, even some berries that gave it a just tart enough edge. It was really quite good, actually.

There was a period of silence while everyone ate. Revka had been around Iyarra long enough to know that centaurs could put the food away like champs, but she'd never seen a full clan having dinner before. One thing was for sure; they really liked their chow.

After a while, conversations started up again. A few came back for second helpings. Out in the darkness, an old man made a comment that was met with laughter. By one of the smaller family fires, someone started playing a harp. Revka found herself humming along, tapping her foot in time. The melody was simple, but no less graceful for that. Around the various campfires, there was a settling, a quieting of conversations as the tune drifted out into the night.

Iyarra moved around the fire to sit by Revka. "Like it?" she whispered.

Revka nodded. "I think I've heard you sing this one before, haven't I?"

Iyarra smiled. "Sometimes. It's an old song. It's about...oh, about running along the plains, feeling the wind, being free...that sort of thing. I could translate, but it isn't really the same."

"Nonetheless, I am sure your friend would love to hear it." Anyala smiled at her daughter. "Why don't you give her a little of it?"

Iyarra flicked an ear. "Oh, I don't know," she whispered. "You know I don't like singing for people."

146

"You used to love it when you were younger. Besides, you do have a lovely voice."

"She's right about that," Revka agreed. "I mean, I've heard you sing lots of times. And it's not like busking in front of strangers this time. It's us, right?"

Iyarra nodded. "Well, I suppose that's true." She looked around the camp, then shrugged. "Oh, all right." She took a breath and began to sing.

The warmth of sun, the coolness of the breeze,
The sky is free of cloud and water-blue,
The ground is firm, the grass is soft and sweet,
The land stretches before me and awaits.

The vile jackal cowers under skulking-tree,
And in their stony den the wolves do sleep,
The plain-hawk glides above, the chitter-bird it sings,
I raise my head, and in reply I sing.

It was about this time that others out beyond the light of the central fire began to sing along. Some harmonized with Iyarra, but there was also a current of voices singing words Revka could not recognize. She had heard Iyarra sing in Equine before and recognized the sound of it. The individual words were hard to discern, but the overall impression was melodious, and flowed in a way her own tongue did not. Fascinated, she tilted her head, the better to hear both versions at once.

Swift the hoof upon the turf, and smooth the way,
And through the wind I flow, it binds me not,
And by my side my herd, as thunder rolls
So does our coming sound upon the earth.

And long and far we run, the ground beneath us flies,
The earth we only touch with lightest tread,
There are no chains, no walls of stone, no winter's chill,
There is only Herd, and Freedom, and the Run.

In the darkness, the harp's music stopped. Now there was only Iyarra, her voice flowing out into the night.

There is only Herd, and Freedom, and the Run.

The last note died away and left behind a silence that spread across the camp, holding all who heard it for a single sublime moment. It seemed to Revka that the whole world was suspended, clinging to that one perfect silence, until it gently unraveled and time came flowing back.

She gave her head a shake, willing herself out of the spell. "Wow," she whispered. "That was...really something, there."

Iyarra gave her a faintly worried smile. "You really liked it?"

"Oh yeah." Revka nodded vigorously. "The words were...I mean, I've never heard lyrics like those. I don't mean they were bad or anything. Actually, they were really nice. It's just sort of, uhm..." She waved an arm vaguely, trying to conjure up the right words from the air.

"Our language is rather different than most," Anyala explained. "We never developed a written language of our own, you see. And our spoken tongue is more based on emotions and sensory impressions, that sort of thing. As you can imagine, it's difficult to translate to the common tongue. I'm afraid it loses rather a lot."

"Well, even so...!" Revka grinned and gave Iyarra an affectionate pat. "That was really good. You never cease to amaze me, you know that? Always something new with you."

Iyarra flattened her ears but smiled. "Thank you," she whispered.

Toth stood up and stretched himself. "Well," he said. "If you ladies will excuse me, I think I will make my rounds. Got some of the other families to talk to about tomorrow, and of course, I need to check in on the sentries." He leaned across the fire to Revka and confided in a stage whisper: "I often catch them dozing on their hooves, especially when there's been music in the air."

Revka laughed. "Well, that I can understand."

Anyala smiled to her husband. "I will see you when you return, dear."

After Toth left, she turned to the two younger women. "Now then, I think Miss Revka can join us in the family tent. I've got several blankets, and I'm sure we can make her quite comfortable. And of course, we still have your old bedding, Iyarra. I trust that will be suitable?"

"Yes, Mom. Thank you, Mom." Iyarra smiled and nodded in agreement.

"No problem here," Revka smiled. "I can bed down pretty much wherever."

"You're quite welcome." She got to her hooves, gathering up the dinner things and toting them off to a nearby tent. "Don't stay up too long, girls. The night gets cold quickly."

"Nice folks," said Revka once they were alone. "Real tight-knit group you've got here, it seems like."

"Yeah." Iyarra nodded. "Always have been, really."

Revka grinned. "It shows, you know." She leaned against Iyarra's flank. "You can really tell when someone's had a good home life."

"How about you?" Iyarra gave Revka a playful nudge. "I know you don't like to talk about yours, but..."

Revka's face was turned away, which was just as well. When she finally spoke, her answer was hesitant.

"My family? Well, they're kind of...I mean...well, they're not like this."

Iyarra sighed and patted Revka's shoulder. "Bad memories?" she whispered.

"What? Oh no. No." Revka shook her head. "Not for the most part, anyway. It's just..." Her hands started waving around again, as though the air could speak for her. "Well, have you ever been to the mountain country? Up north, I mean?"

"Me? No."

"Well, the people up there, they're different. You know? I mean your family. They sing and talk and you all *feel* stuff so deeply. Up there..." She sighed and shrugged. "When they call us 'people of ice,' they're not always talking about the glaciers."

Iyarra wrinkled her nose. "Ohhhh, I see."

"Yeah. I think that's a lot of why I came down here, actually." She stretched out her legs, leaning against Iyarra's side. "I take after my mom, you see. She met Dad when he came down south on business one time. He married her, brought her back home, and for the rest of her life she was 'that southern girl' who didn't fit in. She was very fiery, very passionate. That's what Dad loved about her. Everyone else...well, they didn't hold with being overly emotional, if you see what I mean. Dad did his best, but she was never happy there. Years and years of everyone acting like you just blew into town yesterday, it gets to you.

"But she had me. My brothers, they all took after Dad, but I always took after Mom, which got me into a *lot* of trouble as a kid. She did her best, tried to raise us up right, you know how it is. Sometimes, she'd tell us stories, or sing old songs while she worked around the house. I remember she didn't sing so much as she got older. Then one day..." Revka shrugged.

Iyarra rested a hand on her shoulder. "One day what?"

"Oh, Mom never was suited for the winters we had up there. Every year, when the snows came, she had this thing where she would sometimes go quiet and just stay that way for a while. Like she was lost in her thoughts. She'd be busy chopping vegetables for dinner and just sort of forget what she was doing and stand there for ages, staring into space. It just kept getting worse, you know?

"One day, she said she was going out to the market to get some food. She headed out the door with her basket, and...that was that. Never saw her again. There were footprints, but they weren't heading toward the market. Just off into the wilderness, onto the ice plains. Dad and the men from the village tried to search for her, but there was a blizzard that night. By morning, her footprints were gone."

"Oh, dear..." Iyarra slipped her hand down to Revka's and gave it a squeeze. "I'm so sorry."

Revka stared into the fire. "I think she just gave up, to tell you the truth. Couldn't live there anymore. Probably just started working her way down the mountain and walked until she couldn't anymore." She tucked her legs under her chin and hugged them. "After that, Dad kind of shut down himself. I mean, he'd do his work and did his best to raise us, but it was like he was just going through the motions. It wasn't a real surprise when he didn't last too long after. Most of the family stayed up there, but I had to get out, you know? Didn't want to end up like Mom."

"And that's why you came down from the mountains?"

"Aye. That's about it." She looked up at Iyarra. "I mean, don't get me wrong. We were a good family. We all loved each other in our own way. But...well, you've heard the joke about the ice warden who loved his wife so much he almost told her?"

Iyarra wrinkled her nose. "Ouch."

"Yeah. And then I see a family like yours, you running up to your dad and hugging him like that, and everyone so happy to see each other, and it's...well, I get to thinking, that's all. What it might have been like."

"Well, for what it's worth, I think they like you, too." Iyarra gave her hand a squeeze.

Revka squeezed back. "I'm glad," she whispered as she stared into the fire.

Chapter Sixteen

REVKA HEARD STIRRING BEFORE even the sun was up. By the time she trudged out of the tent, the camp was bustling. Iyarra and her family were already dressed and having breakfast.

Iyarra scooched over, offering her a spot in front of the fire. "We'll be heading out in a bit. They think there's another drakul pack a little ways north. We should be home well before sundown."

"You sure you're okay to hunt? I know you're not big on fighting."

"I'm sure." Iyarra handed her a bowl of hot oats. "It's different like this. The clan hunts together, you see? It's like we're stronger, somehow. We fight better in groups."

"All right," Revka smiled. "Just making sure." She sat down and made herself comfortable and tucked into her breakfast. After a while, Toth came up to them. He was carrying a couple of bows and several quivers of big, nasty looking arrows. "All ready, Puya?"

Iyarra hopped up. "Ready!" She took the smaller of the two bows and slung a couple of quivers over her shoulder. Her legs were wrapped in thick bands of leather. "Bites," she explained, when Revka raised a brow.

Revka helped cinch down the saddlebag filled with spare weapons and provisions for the day. She gave Iyarra a pat. "All right, you. Be careful out there, okay? I want you back in one piece."

"I promise." Iyarra and Toth trotted off to the north side of the camp, where a couple dozen others were waiting. There was some quick discussion, then a sharp whistle rang out and the party galloped off into the distance.

Revka watched until they disappeared over the crest of a distant hill.

Anyala approached without a word. For a moment, her expression was unreadable as she regarded the young human woman. She laid her hand on the girl's shoulder. "Come," she said, "There is much to discuss."

***

The interior of the tent was simple, just a few sleeping mats, some pelts, and tools. Revka had come to associate the musky, horsey smell inside with Iyarra, but here it had a slightly different feel. Anyala beckoned her to the sleeping mats. "Sit down, dear." A small fire pit had been dug into the earth, and a triangle of leather suspended over it held a dark, simmering liquid.

Anyala took a leather cup, scooped it through the liquid, and passed it over to Revka. "Drink," she said, "but slowly." Revka sniffed at the brew uncertainly. It smelled of herbs and fruit and things she could not identify. In the dim light of the tent. it had a sort of bluish-green color, which lingered even in the steam that curled up and away. She blew gingerly across the surface and took a sip. The taste was not at all bad, actually. A bit fruity, and earthy, but with a savory note to it as well. She regarded the cup curiously.

Anyala scooped a cupful for herself. "Do you like it?"

Revka nodded. "It's very...interesting. Nice flavor to it. Uhm, what is it, exactly?"

Anyala stirred the liquid some more, watching it carefully. "The tea is made with the infusion of meadow hay, but with juniper and other berries therein, plus some special ingredients I have been fortunate to gather over time." She took a delicate sip and nodded to herself. "I thought you and I might have a bit of a talk today. I wish to get to know the young lady who has captured my daughter's heart."

Revka froze. She looked down and away from the older mare, not daring to say anything. Anyala chuckled. "Oh come now, dear. Do you think that I have no eyes? Iyarra has always shown where her heart lies without reserve or hindrance, and it is easy to see your mutual devotion. Mind you, I am mildly surprised she has chosen a female, but such is not unknown among our people. Now, a human on the other hand... Well, it has happened from time to time, but I never understood the appeal. No offense meant, of course." She took another sip of her tea. "So, I think perhaps today we might get familiar with each other."

"Oh. Well, okay, I suppose we can, yes." Revka shuffled uncomfortably.

Anyala patted her arm. "It's all right, I assure you. I hope we shall get along very well. If Iyarra regards you as highly as she seems to, then I think it quite certain that we shall. Now, just relax and tell me...yes, tell me how you first met."

Revka nodded and took another sip. She could feel the tea warming her inside. She began to relax a little, feel more comfortable in the other woman's company. She felt that she could tell the older woman anything, and her tongue began to loosen.

It really was very good tea.

***

It was a few hours later, and anyone passing by the tent would have heard two voices raised in laughter. Inside, Revka was in full story mode, waving her hands expansively as she painted the scene out for the older mare. "So, this family, they were really rich, all right? I mean, just *disgustingly* rich. Like one time, we were at this inn, and they sent me down to see what the bill of fare was. So I go and I get a list of everything they got. Fifteen minutes later, they send me back down with a note saying, *We'll take it.* It was like ten minutes before I could get the innkeeper to understand they meant some of everything."

Anyala laughed, shaking her head. "Oh, you're kidding!"

"Not a word of a lie! Anyway, they went crazy cooking every different dish and sending it upstairs. The poor serving girls got their exercise that night, I can tell you. The family wound up taking only a few bites out of each dish, then sent me round the corner for some meat pies off a guy on the street!"

Anyala shook her head. "Oh, dear." She sipped some more tea from her cup. The leather skin was nearly empty now, and the fire had been fed twice to keep it going. "And how long were you with them?"

"Oh, just as far as Rivergate. They had their boat waiting for them, so that was the end of that job. Fortunately, they paid well, so we got to take it easy until the next one came along. Not that we mind living outside, but in the winter it's nice to have the option of an inn, if you know what I mean."

"I see, yes, and I do know what you mean. We always migrate south when the time comes. No use sitting around waiting for winter to catch up with you."

"Exactly, right." Revka smiled and sipped some more of her tea. "I don't mind it so much, but it's sure different from how I was raised. Back home, most folks hardly ever left their village, you know? I mean, once in a while someone would get restless and take off. And there were a few people who traveled down to the flatlands for business sometimes, but it was not a normal thing for most folks."

"I see." Anyala nodded. "It is...different for us. Home is where the ones we love are. All else is background." She reached for a small pouch of herbs. "I think it might be a good idea if we tried a little experiment," she said. "I think it could help you understand us better and vice versa. Would you be interested?"

"Well, sure. I mean, what exactly did you have in mind?" Revka put her cup down, tilting her head curiously at the older woman.

"I propose to look into your dreams." She reached into the pouch and took a small pinch of something greenish-brown and crumbled it into a wooden bowl. "This powder will make you sleep and cause you to dream in a...well, in a special way. There are things you need to know about us, I think, and words alone cannot answer to the task. We may both come away with a better understanding of each other. Does that sound all right?"

"I...think so, yes." Revka nodded slowly. "But it won't be anything bad, will it?"

Anyala shook her head. "No, nothing bad, I promise. But it does take a certain amount of trust. I hope that we may have that trust between us, if not now, then at least when we are done. If you wish to leave the dream at any time, only call out my name. All right?"

Revka bit her lip but nodded. "All right."

"Very well." Anyala dropped the powder into Revka's cup and stirred. "Now, drink it all down. That's good. Now, lie on the mat behind you and relax. Listen to the sound of my voice. Already you are getting sleepy..."

***

Revka blinked and looked around. She was in a large field that stretched out in all directions, reclining in the shade of the only tree in sight. She turned her head this way and that, trying to take in the scenery—what there was, anyway. She was alone, as far as she could tell. Something about the place seemed awfully familiar. If she could just work out what...

"Revka!" And suddenly Iyarra was there. She cantered in place, her body haloed in the bright sunshine. She smiled over her shoulder and called out, "Run with me!" She galloped away.

Revka scrambled to her feet and hurried after her girlfriend. She laughed, feeling the warmth of the sun on her skin as she ran. Pumping her arms, she closed on the cantering centauress. Iyarra always looked her best when she was running. Revka watched her muscles move under her skin, her mane and tail streaming behind her. And yet, there was still that discordant note. Still that something nagging quietly. Revka shook her head clear and concentrated on the chase.

They ran through fields and copses of wildflowers. As Revka got closer, Iyarra sped up a little bit, then a little more, until Revka was having difficulty keeping up. She waved a hand at the centauress, wheezing a little. "All right...slow down a bit...some of us don't have so many legs..." If Iyarra heard, she gave no sign.

Faster and faster Revka ran, and further and further away her Iyarra seemed. Revka began to gasp for air, her legs failing beneath her. She signaled frantically for Iyarra to slow, but the mare kept going, farther and farther away. And Revka remembered.

The field. The sun. The running and never being able to keep up. It was *that* dream, the one she'd had so many times since they'd gotten together. She didn't get it so often these days, but it was always ready to come roaring back, and here it was again. She knew how this would end. The harder she ran, the farther away Iyarra would be, until she would be just a spot on the horizon, then not even that. Revka hated this dream, *hated* it. Every time she found herself having it again, she tried to will herself out of the scene. She tried to change the dream, or wake up, or anything. This time, at least, it worked. She groaned, felt her real body shift, and blinked herself awake.

Anyala was seated beside her, watching impassively. "A very interesting dream. One you've had before, if I am any judge."

Revka took a moment to pull herself together, then managed to nod. "I...yeah. Sometimes."

Anyala smiled a little and patted her gently on the shoulder. "For what it is worth, I think I may safely say she will never leave you behind. Understand, that is not how we are. It is... Well, it is best that I show you." She passed a cup over to Revka. "Here, drink it down again, just like before. Now, listen to my voice..."

Revka blinked and looked around. She was in a large field that stretched out in all directions, reclining in the shade of the only tree in sight. She turned her head this way and that, trying to take in the scenery—what there was, anyway. She was alone, as far as she could tell. Something about the place seemed awfully familiar. If she could just work out what...

"Revka!" And suddenly Iyarra was there. She cantered in place, her body haloed in the bright sunshine. She smiled over her shoulder at Revka and called out, "Run with me!" She galloped away.

Revka scrambled to her feet but found this suddenly more difficult than usual. There seemed to be a whole lot more of her. She looked down at herself, down past her belly to the spot where her body blended into the white and brown pelt and the legs... The legs.

Revka felt herself about to faint. She braced herself against the tree, heart thumping while she waited for the scenery to stop spinning. She risked a look behind her. It was true. A chestnut brown body with white splotches stretched out behind her, what she'd heard the horsemen call Pinto. She eased herself gingerly to her feet—her hooves—and tried a step. She stumbled a bit, overcorrected, tried to consciously track all four legs at once, got thoroughly confused, and was about to fall flat, when a hand took hers.

Iyarra smiled down at her, giving her hand a squeeze. She helped Revka up and guided her forward. Revka kept her eyes on the cen—on the *other* centauress. If she didn't think consciously about it, then...yes, she was walking. They were side by side, moving with a slow and steady gait. Iyarra kissed her cheek and whispered, "Now, run!"

They cantered across the endless field, cutting and capering all the way, laughing and calling out to one another. They ran faster and faster, the field spreading out before them. Revka felt the landscape rolling underneath her, the incredible sense of speed. She'd gone this fast when riding on Iyarra's back, but this time it was *her* legs pounding, *her* muscles working. It was intoxicating. They fell in together, side by side, and for the longest time galloped together. No words spoken, no words needed.

Then somehow, they weren't alone. It was the herd—no, *her* herd, racing alongside them. Behind were the older ones, those who had come before and moved on to the Grazing Lands beyond. There were others behind them, stretching back generation after generation, all going forward, all moving as one. The Herd, strong and indivisible. Generations and ages, young and old, any corner of the world, and it was still The Herd, always and forever.

There was a light up ahead, a certain truncating of the scenery. The field and sky dissolved into a whiteness. Revka regarded the oncoming void with uneasiness, but once again Iyarra's hand found hers. The centauress gave her a smile. All around them, eyes on the horizon, the rest of the herd surged forward. Revka felt herself speed up to match their pace. The rumble of hooves upon the earth built to a steady climax. Revka and Iyarra, hands still clasped, galloped together into the light.

***

The light faded into darkness, the thunder of hooves into the sound of her own breathing. She lay still for a moment, feeling herself settle back into the waking world. She pushed herself upright, fumbled awkwardly for a moment, then tumbled onto her back. She blinked in mild confusion down at her legs. There didn't seem to be enough of them.

Anyala chuckled a little and helped her to sit up. "Slowly, now. I didn't realize it would take you in quite that way." She waited, sipping the last remnants of her tea, while Revka pulled herself together. Revka groaned, staring ahead of her at nothing in particular for a long, silent moment. She whispered, "Is that... I mean, is that really what it's like? Being a centaur?"

"For the greater part, yes." She patted Revka's hand. "Granted, some of that was allegory, but you have to expect that in visions." She looked up, gesturing around as though outside the tent. "Our world is always changing, moving from one location to another. It is our ties to each other that give our world stability, that keep us grounded. No matter what happens to the outside world, the world inside is strong and unchanging.

"To be allowed into that, to be a part of it, is a truly great honor. *But*," she added, "it is also a stern responsibility. With the herd, there is no easy come and go. The herd demands the most serious commitment. Our Iyarra has given you a place in her heart that very few outsiders receive from one of us. I need you to understand this, and to honor it as it deserves. Do you understand me?"

Revka managed to nod. "I... Yes, I think so. I mean, not all of it at once. But I think I've got the fundamentals, if you see what I mean." She sighed. "It's just so... Well, I mean, if you could only see how it is where I came from. But never mind. It's not important. I guess I've always been fascinated by how strongly she seems to feel things. This really puts it in perspective, actually."

Anyala nodded. "Oh yes. Yes, indeed. Even among our people, Iyarra is a passionate one. It is quite a heart that you have won. I hope you know that."

Revka allowed herself a chuckle. "Oh, don't you worry about that," she said. "I've known that for a long time." She idly tugged a blade of grass from the ground and twirled it between her fingers. "A long time."

"Good." Anyala's hand was on her shoulder, the older woman smiling. "I can see that you do. Now then. Let's have a look at this curse-mark of yours, shall we?"

Revka started. "The curse-mark? Oh, yeah. I guess you know all about that, don't you?"

"Well, not all. Iyarra did tell me a little bit, when you two first arrived. She said some baron or—"

"Duke."

"Duke. Thank you. He put one on each of you as a means of making sure you ran this little errand for him. Now, I'm not an expert by any means, but I do know a thing or two about medicine and dispellation. Let's have a look at it, shall we?"

Revka obliged, pulling off her tunic. She turned her arm to the firelight, and the older woman moved in close. "Right, now. Let us see." She began tracing her fingers over the symbols of the mark, murmuring quietly to herself. "A very complicated one, I have to say," she said after a time. "I had almost hoped that perhaps he was bluffing, but it is, indeed, the genuine article. Have you had anyone else look at this yet?"

"The monks up at the monastery, but they didn't know anything about it, couldn't make head nor tail of it. Oh, and there was this wizard we met. He had a look at it, too."

"Oh?" Anyala arched an eyebrow. "And what did he say?"

Revka made a face. "Oh, all sorts of stuff. Like how the cryptoplast had bonded against the rhino thing, and he couldn't do something without a circumflex thingamajig. Apparently, our pelogronnis need to be oscillated. Or something."

Anyala's face was a mask. "Your pelogronnis? Are you quite sure that's what he said?"

"Yeah. I definitely remember that. The word sounded familiar, but I couldn't think where from, so I didn't say anything."

Anyala rubbed her temples. "Revka, a pelogronni is a type of mushroom found near swamps and marshes, best known for its use as a laxative. I can't imagine what that would have to do with curse-marks in any form."

Revka thumped her fist on the ground. "I *knew* it! I knew that old man was just blowing smoke at us! I bet he didn't have any more idea about removing curse-marks than I do!" She folded her arms, snorting.

Anyala patted her arm. "Well now, consider that a life lesson learned. But let's have another look at this, shall we?" She rummaged in another cloth bag. From this one, she brought out a reddish-brown powder which she poured into a bowl. A little water from the waterskin turned it into a paste, which she applied carefully over Revka's curse-mark. It only took a minute to harden and crumble away, leaving a layer of traces going across the curse-mark in strangely regular patterns. Anyala studied them for a long moment, then sighed.

"Sealed, I'm afraid," she said. "I could perhaps get through it if it were not so, but without the key I'm afraid I'm quite stuck."

"That's right." Revka winced. "The guy said something about it being sealed with the duke's house, or something."

"Ah. A family rune, no doubt." Anyala sighed. She leaned over and gave the girl a gentle hug. "Well, there's nothing to be done about that but to go forward and hope you can get him to be merciful. I hope you can. If not, come back to us, and we will try what we can. If worse comes to worse, we can always... Well, there are ways of removing the cursed area relatively painlessly, but I rather doubt you want to go around with one arm."

Revka made a face. "Not if I can avoid it, no."

"All right. Well, I will meditate upon this and see what I may come up with. In the meantime," she pulled herself up to her hooves. "There are chores to be done, and I would welcome your company. Shall we?"

Revka nodded. "Of course."

"Good." The older mare smiled. "We have a couple of hours before they get back. Should be plenty of time. Off we go, now."

***

In fact, it was nearly sunset when the hunting party returned, tired but in high spirits. Toth was first into the camp, leading the others in song. He spotted Anyala, and galloped up to her, pulling her into a tight embrace. "Ho there, my lady, and what do you think? Three damnations of drakuls we found! Sixteen of 'em sent back to the dirt! And three leancats as well! And is your stallion a great hunter?"

Anyala laughed and hugged her husband. "And I trust none of our own hurt?"

"Only young Chas, a nip to the flank. Nothing that won't heal, and I daresay he won't be quite so reckless when next he hunts." He beckoned to Iyarra, who trotted up to his side. "And who laid the killing blow on the biggest one today, eh? Her father's daughter, that's who."

Iyarra blushed a little and shrugged. "Well, it's not like I was the only one fighting it."

"Yes, but you finished him off. Good and proper, too. Why, we—" There was a roar from the hunting party, as two mares came out of a tent. They carried between them a pole on which was suspended a water sack, sealed tight. The pole was lowered onto a pair of tripods, and a bucket placed beneath. Someone produced a mug, and passed it along to Toth, who used a spigot at the bottom of the bag to fill it. He took a long gulp, seemed to ruminate on the contents, then turned his eyes to the sky. He nodded to the others. The hunting party cheered, and soon a long line was snaking toward the water sack.

Revka fell into line with Iyarra. "You okay, sugar?"

"Oh, I'm fine, yes." Iyarra nodded. "A little tired, of course. It's ages since I hunted. But other than that, yes, I'm all right. How about you? Did you have a nice talk with Mother?"

"Oh yeah. It was definitely interesting."

"Good." Iyarra fished in her saddlebags and brought out a couple of mugs. "On the way back, I spoke to father about the duke and all. He says they'll be happy to escort us back west as far as the lake district. Mother should be able to look at the curse-marks, as well."

"She already did. Says she can't do anything about 'em 'cause they're sealed."

"Oh." Iyarra made a face. "Well, maybe there's something else we can try. She is rather good at potions and things."

"She does make some interesting drinks. I'll give her that much."

Iyarra giggled. "Oh, did you have some of her medicinal teas? Yes, she definitely does."

They moved further along the line. "So," Revka said, "You really found three groups of those things?"

Iyarra shrugged. "Well, more like we found two and the third bunch found us while we were heading back, but yeah, good day's hunting. Dad was pleased. The drakuls aren't good for much. I doubt even you would want to eat their meat, but their fins are handy for tool making. Nice and sharp, see. And their hide makes decent armor if you can stand the smell."

"Good, good. Uhm…" She peered ahead of them. "What are we in line for, exactly?"

"Celebratory drink. We always have some after a successful hunt." The centaur ahead of them filled his cup and moved aside. "Go on, try some."

Revka shrugged and filled her cup. The liquid was dark auburn and frothed like beer. She stepped aside and sniffed it curiously. The smell was not unpleasant, just...very different. Kind of an outdoorsy smell. Iyarra joined her and took a healthy swig. She held her eyes closed a moment, a beatific smile on her face.

When she didn't move for a moment, Revka gave her a gentle nudge. "You okay?"

Iyarra blinked, then smiled down at Revka. "Oh! Sorry. Yeah. I was just thinking how long it's been since I've had some of this." She gave Revka a little bump. "Go on. Try it."

Revka took a careful sip. It was some sort of alcohol. Not strong, but definitely flavorful. The familiar note in the scent rang again, as she felt the drink fill her senses before sliding down her throat.

"Wow. That's, uh..." She searched for a word. "Robust."

Iyarra giggled. "You like it?"

Revka waggled her head back and forth a moment, then nodded. "W-e-l-l, yeah. I mean, it's odd, but not in a bad way."

"We call it bread beer or sometimes liquid bread. It amounts to the same, basically. We take our old bread, see, and—"

"Wait. You have bread?"

"Well, sure. We spend half our lives running around in fields full of wheat and barley and rye. We've always got plenty of flour."

"Oh. Okay. Carry on."

"Well, we basically take our old bread and soak it in water. We let it ferment, usually with berries or whatever else we can find, wherever we happen to be at the time. Then you just put it in skins, find a nice cool stream to keep it in until you're ready to drink, and there you are." She smiled. "Dad always has some waiting when they get back from a good hunt. Puts everyone in a celebratory mood without being *too* celebratory, if you see what I mean."

Revka took another sip. "Yeah..." She nodded a bit to herself. "Not bad. Kind of grows on you."

All along the camp, fires were being lit. There was laughter and singing and the smell of dinner just beginning to spread itself over the camp. Iyarra tugged Revka toward the main fire. "Come on," she said, "Old Raff is going to sing about the hunt. He always does that."

"Oh?" Revka hurried alongside her. "Like, a play-by-play sort of thing?"

"Pretty much."

Revka grinned. "Will you be in it?"

Iyarra smiled back and shrugged. "Dunno," she said. "Let's find out."

Chapter Seventeen

THE NEXT MORNING, THE herd was up with the dawn. Breakfast was a quick bowl of porridge, then they set to breaking down the camp. Revka watched as tents were taken down and rolled up, poles disassembled, goods bundled away with speed. Within an hour, the entire camp had disappeared. A few centaurs had carts for some of the larger items, but nearly everything had been bundled up into backpacks and saddlebags.

"Pretty good, huh?" Iyarra smiled at Revka. "We've got a lot of practice at packing up and heading out, you know. Everything's made to be broken down into something that can be easily carried. We don't have much more than we need, and we can pull up stakes at a moment's notice. Just like us, you know?"

"True." Revka nodded. "But I wouldn't mind one of those tents."

Iyarra giggled. "I'll see what I can do. Now, come on. Up."

Fifteen minutes later, they were away. The hunters formed themselves into a perimeter around the rest, with Toth at the front. Anyala and Iyarra followed just behind him. The fields stretched out before them in a seemingly endless vista of majestic splendor. The sun was up. The sky was clear. Perfect traveling weather.

An hour later, the fields were still stretching out before them in an increasingly endless vista of majestic splendor. An hour after that, the majesty and splendor had worn off but were being made up for by extra helpings of endlessness.

Sometime later, there was a rock. Revka watched until it disappeared behind them.

There were plenty of conversations going on around her. They were a sociable folk, centaurs. It wasn't that she was bored. She and Iyarra had spent enough days on the road that she was more than used to long journeys, but generally there was at least *some* scenery to look at. These fields... It was like they hadn't gone anywhere at all. She could close her eyes for an hour, and when she opened them again the scenery would look the same. She tried closing her eyes.

A sharp whistle brought everybody to a halt.

Revka peered around Iyarra to see what was going on. The herd stood at the crest of a hill, overlooking a sort of shallow valley. A stream trickled along the bottom, and brightly colored flowers bordered both sides. Toth turned around to the rest of the group and cupped his hands. "We'll stop here and eat," he bellowed. "Be sure and replenish your waterskins."

The herd quickly made itself at home, setting up fires and congregating into groups. Most seemed busy with preparing bread or rye cakes, or oatmeal, or some other variation on the theme of lunch. Revka wandered down to the stream and peered into the waters. The fish swimming around would barely make a mouthful. She began to trace the creek back, looking for a deeper pool with bigger fish. She rounded the corner of a hill and followed along to a new area.

This place was a curious one. The right hand bank followed the curve of the hill, but the left hand bank was completely flat for quite a way. The grass was different, too. The deeper shade of green had just a tint of blue if you looked at it properly. She crept forward cautiously and yelped when her foot went right through the grass and into some cold, brackish water.

Iyarra came around the corner at speed. She groaned and helped Revka back onto the dry land. The flat area rippled in slow motion like a giant waterbed. Revka stared. "What in the world is *that*?"

"Hobb's grass." Iyarra helped her to her feet. "It's this weird kind of grass that only grows over water. Here, look." She knelt down, and gingerly tugged at the edge of the patch. The grass came up as if it was all one piece. Underneath, the individual blades came together in what appeared to be a series of interconnected strands from which dangled tiny, hairlike roots.

Revka poked at the underside of the turf. "Good grief," she muttered. "Where on earth does that come from?"

"It grows out here in the grassy areas, usually near creeks or in the lowlands. Basically, you get an area with a lot of standing water, like when this stream overflows. The water just sits here, and the grass grows its way over it. Papa says that the seeds come down from the mountains and flow through all the rivers and streams, but they can't grow unless the water is standing still."

Revka gave the grass another tap. It wobbled a bit, then subsided. "I don't suppose there'd be any fish down there, by any chance?"

"Possibly. I can't say I've ever looked. We don't really 'do' fish, you know?"

Revka tugged off her boots. "Only one way to find out." She went over to Iyarra's saddlebags and pulled out a tunic. She tied the top in a knot, closing off the sleeves and neck, then waded into the water, pushing a path through the layer of grass.

Iyarra cocked her head. "What are you doing?"

"Shhh." Revka began to methodically drag the garment through the water, open-end-first. She waded in deeper, pulling her improvised net back and forth. From time to time she'd haul it up to peer at the contents, make a face, and try again.

Iyarra settled by the bank. "Is this likely to work?"

"Way I figure it," Revka said, "If there are fish down there, they're probably not used to predators. They'd be pretty big and lazy. No survival instinct, see? No need for one. So, if I just...aha!" She hauled the shirt up and watched the water drain out. Something inside flopped frantically. Revka beamed and held on tight.

"Look at that!" The fish she pulled out was long and silver, a good ten pounder. She dropped it back into the shirt and began to wade ashore. "How's that for clever, hm? I — Ow!" She staggered, nearly falling face first into the water.

"Eeek! Revka, are you all right?"

"Yeah, hang on, hang on. Stepped on a rock." She fumbled around in the water with her free hand. "Funny thing, you wouldn't think you'd get many rocks out here. *Ohhhhh.*" She pulled her hand out of the water. This wasn't a rock. Rocks didn't have facets, or come in translucent blue. They also didn't catch the light in that particularly entrancing way, even covered with all the muck and grime. She held up the gleaming prize. "Will you look at that?"

"You found a crystal?" Iyarra's eyes widened.

"Yeah, believe it or not. Big one, too." She looked back down at the water. "Probably been down there for ages."

"Well, what's a crystal doing in there?"

"Search me. Probably somebody dropped it while traveling, then it rained and this thing filled up and the grass grew. Next thing you know that was it." She began to wade back to the shore. "Still, it's a nice one." She rinsed the gem off in the stream and gave it another look. It was about the same size and shape as her thumb and didn't have a scratch on it. "Hmm, funny thing." There seemed to be a light to the stone that had nothing to do with the sun.

She tucked it into her belt pouch. "Anyway, what was I doing? Oh, yeah." She turned her tunic upside down and dumped the fish out onto the ground. "That'll make a good lunch, right there. Some trick, huh?"

Iyarra smiled. "Yes. Very clever. We can cook it up at the fire for you. Just one thing..."

"Yeah?"

"You may want to wash first." Iyarra pointed to the green-brown slime that covered Revka's legs. There was an awful lot of it.

"Er, yeah." Revka looked down at herself. "I'll get right on that."

***

After a quick wash and a grilled fish lunch, Revka was in considerably better spirits. The herd moved on, and before too long, she and Anyala fell to chatting.

"...then she came around from behind the tree and pointed at the ground. She said, 'Look, Mommy, I made apples!'" Anyala covered her mouth, giggling softly.

Revka stared for a moment, then nearly fell off Iyarra's back. "Oh, no!" she cried. "Oh, that's just—oh now, that's the best." She fell backward, sprawling herself along the centaur's back, and cackled with glee.

"Mother," Iyarra groaned. "I can't believe you told her that story."

"I'm sorry, dear." Anyala reached over and patted her hand. "But it is a time honored, mother's prerogative to embarrass their children when they grow up."

"Yeah, she's got a point, you know. Anyway, come on." Revka managed to get back enough of her breath to sit up. "You have to admit it's a cute story."

Iyarra snorted. "It's not cute. It's embarrassing."

"Yeah, but you're cute when you're embarrassed."

"Oh, shut up."

"Was she always this easily embarrassed?" Revka asked Anyala.

"Oh, absolutely. Whenever we met anyone from outside the herd, she used to hide behind me and peek out in the most adorable way. Of course, that didn't stop her parading around naked whenever she could. You see, most of our young—"

"Mother..."

"Well, they don't bother with clothing until they're three or four years old. But she just wasn't having it at all."

"*Mother...*"

"Eventually we had to lay down the law, you know. You should have seen her, stamping around in her little tunic and making this big frowny face at us any time we looked in her direction."

Revka laughed. "I think she still makes that face, as a matter of fact. I bet she was adorable."

"Oh, she absolutely was!" Anyala brightened and began to rummage in one of her saddlebags. "I have…if you'll just give me a moment. Where are they? Ah!" She pulled out an old scroll of leather, rolled up and bound with cord. "I had paintings of her done when she was just a little foal. Would you like to see them?"

Revka grinned. "Would I?"

The leather scroll was unrolled, Revka and the older centauress holding it between them. "Now, here she is as a newborn. You see? Fast asleep. And here's her first bath."

"Aw, would you look at that."

"*Mom!*"

And the herd moved on.

***

Evening found them setting camp by a small grove of trees near a pond. The water attracted a few animals, mostly ungulates but a few predators here and there, all milling about. The mix seemed odd to Revka, but they all seemed to be leaving each other alone. She watched the sun work its way down toward the horizon.

"You would think 'twould be a bloodbath, wouldn't you?" Toth moved beside her. "But it never is. Have you noticed how they come and go yet?"

Revka furrowed her brow. "How they…? Well, no, not especially. Why?"

Toth grinned. "The plant eaters always come from the west, the meat eaters from the east. Everyone stays on their side and departs the way they came. Such has it been since we have roamed these plains."

"Wow." Revka watched a young drakul drink its fill and saunter off, ignoring the antelope not ten paces away. "Does anybody know why?"

"The animals themselves, I suppose." Toth gave a shrug. "But they're not telling." He scratched his arm absently. "I think perhaps it is just…what do you call it…neutral territory. There is an understanding that no hunting happens here. It goes out from here, too. I once stalked some animals as they approached this place. They actually go around for quite a distance until they come to the eastern or western side. Only then do they approach the water."

"That's..." Revka shook her head. "That's really weird."

"It is, yes. But I suppose it works. As I say, it has been this way for a long time."

"I'm amazed some hunters don't just camp out here and shoot what they want, whenever."

Toth snorted. "You're not the first to think of it. There was a man once, name of Great N'pa. A great hunter, so he was. He came once to us and asked the way here. This was in my grandfather's time, you understand. We were heading that way ourselves, so we pointed him in the right direction. We were in no great hurry, mind, so he planned to get here a day early. 'By the time you arrive', he boasted, 'I, Great N'pa, will have many pelts for you, and much meat for N'pa!' And off he went."

"What happened?"

"Couldn't say. The herd got here two days later. All of the animals were here, drinking the water as usual. There was no sign of Great N'pa. His camp was empty, only his gear remained. His boots sat right by the shore of the pond. They were just"—he gestured vaguely—"*standing* there, you know? The lacings were still done up and everything. No footprints, either, though that place was very muddy." He thought about it. "There was a bow too, Grandfather said. A very good one lay on the ground by the boots. Anyway. The herd waited three days for him, but Great N'pa never returned."

"You don't say."

"It's true. We still have his bows, you know. Except the one found by the pond. Grandfather told me he tried using it for a while and couldn't hit a dead tree at ten paces. So, he burned the bow and buried the ashes. Maybe it is back with its master now."

"Could be, I suppose."

There was the sound of voices from the camp. Toth pricked his ears. "Ah! It sounds like supper is ready. Come along."

They left the watering hole behind. From time to time, a new animal would arrive, or another would leave. Sometimes a mother would yip at her cubs, or one of an ungulate's many stomachs would churn noisily to work.

The rest was silence.

Chapter Eighteen

THE NEXT MORNING, THE herd departed the watering hole and continued their way east. Revka was starting to enjoy herself. She seemed to be getting along well with Iyarra's family, thank goodness. The herd's life was quite pleasant, if a tad on the monotonous side. Still, things could definitely be worse.

The wind picked up a little as they made their way along. The hills flattened into fields of taller grasses. Here and there were even the occasional trees or shrubs. "We'll be getting to the lake district in a couple of days," Toth said while they took a short break. "Making very good time, I think."

About an hour later, a shimmering white shape appeared on the horizon. As the herd approached, the shape resolved itself into a shining white city surrounding a castle, straight out of a fairytale. Gleaming spires of blue topped the towers, from which multicolored banners streamed against the cloudless sky. The walls around the city shone pure white, and the wind carried the scent of fragrant spices and sounds of harp and lute.

Revka leaned over Iyarra's shoulder and pointed. "What is *that* place?"

Toth smiled. "That is the lost city of the elves. A wondrous place. I think perhaps it would be good to stop there for the night. What do you think, dear?"

Anyala nodded. "I believe that would be an excellent idea. It has been so long. Hasn't it, Iyarra?"

"Oh, gosh. Not since I was little. Maybe fifteen years? Unless you went after I left home."

"Wait." Revka furrowed her brow. "Elves? Like, real, actual elves? I thought they all just...went away or something."

"Oh, no," said Anyala. "They came here and founded a great city where they could live. It's been here for quite a while, I believe. We've always gotten on rather well with them, you know. It will be good to see them again."

It was about this time that the group came across a long, wide trail leading through the grass. There were some other travelers as well, families mostly by the look of them. The road led straight to the city. In the distance, an opening could now be seen in the walls.

As they approached, the road widened so that several people could travel side by side. By this point, Revka could see that the entrance had not one but several gates, each with a line snaking back from it. Revka frowned. "I thought you guys said this place was lost."

Toth just smiled. "Well, it's more of a name than a description. You'll find out when we get there."

The herd fell into line before one of the gates and waited to get through. The line was moving fairly briskly, thank goodness, but there were still a lot of travelers in front of them. Revka noticed some other centaurs, a small group of green lizard-looking things, even a cluster of what appeared to be perfectly normal forest animals standing in the line, patiently waiting their turn.

Eventually, they made their way to the front. Toth waved a hand to the others. "I've got this." At the gate, a jowly, middle-aged elf pushed her glasses up, regarded the centaurs with a jaundiced eye, and took a deep breath. "Welcome to Malurria, the fabled lost city of the elves," she said. "Truly, a day of mystery and enchantment and childlike wonder awaits you and your entire family. No pets, no weapons, no pipeweed, no outside magic, no food, no booze. And no re-entry without hand stamp and no swearing stronger than 'poo.' How many in your party please?"

Toth smiled. "Yes, I think you can help me..." He pulled out an ancient, bedraggled bit of parchment board, which he handed over. "I think this will do."

The gate elf held up the card and regarded the writing suspiciously. She peered at it for several seconds, then cocked an eye at the centaur. "This is legit?"

Toth bowed. "Indeed it is, my lady."

The elf snorted. Not taking her eyes off Toth, she grabbed a lute. A quick strum brought a messenger elf panting to the gate. "Yes?"

"Run and get someone from upstairs, will you?" The gate elf flashed the card to the messenger, whose eyes bulged. He bowed and scurried off.

A moment later, a tall blonde elf was seen striding toward the gates. The elf's long, white robe was an elaborate affair, decorated in gold brocade. The glamourous elf was flanked by a small group of others, similarly attired. There was something about their walk that brought certain words to mind, such as boss. Also, 'sir and please and whatever you say.' They reached the gate, and the leading figure took the card, then looked up and saw Toth. The tall elf broke into a grin.

"Well, well, look who's here!" He nodded to the gate elf, who started to work the ticket machine. "Come through, come through! Everyone get your hand stamped!" He stepped back, sweeping his hand out. "Welcome, one and all!"

Toth came through and gave the elf one of his trademark, arm-pumper handshakes. "Good to see you, Lemuel!" he barked. "Been ages, it has!" He looked the leader up and down. "Nice gown. Got you out of bed, did we?"

Lemuel laughed. "This? Oh, ignore this. It's strictly for the tourists." He stepped back and gave Toth the once-over. "You look well, old friend."

Anyala joined her husband. "Very good to see you again, Lemuel." She held her hand out dutifully, as the gate elf stamped the back with a picture of a little cartoon elf.

"Enchanted, as always." Lemuel took Anyala's hand and graciously kissed the back. He smiled as Iyarra and Revka came through the gate. "And this, I am guessing, would be your daughter? Dear me, she *has* grown! Making an old man out of both of us, Toth!"

Iyarra waved shyly. "Hi."

Toth beamed. "Indeed she is, and don't I know it. Lem, this is my daughter's friend Revka. Revka, this is Lemuel, king of the elves. Knew him back in the old days, when we were both penniless adventurers."

"Enchanted, I'm sure." Lemuel bowed and smiled. "Toth here was a great traveling companion. Even helped us when we first started this place. I think it's changed since those days, eh?"

"I'll say!" Toth laughed. "Used to be just a dozen or so huts of 'authentic elven craftsmen,' a couple of rides, and a coach inn." He looked around. "It's definitely grown a bit," he said.

The city spread out before them like a picture out of the better class of fairy tale. A pleasant stream trickled through the city, with bridges crossing here and there, connected to widely spaced avenues flocked with visitors and elves alike. The alabaster white shops each bore a sign declaring its wares. Greenery was everywhere. Malurria was really more park than city. Fountains of clear water gave tourists a place to toss a coin for luck, then sit and watch the cascading spray. All of this, though, was mere background to the castle.

The castle was a dream. Revka had seen a fair few castles. Generally, they tended to be stern, no-nonsense kinds of places. Big stone fortresses said to the world there is an inside and an outside. As long as everyone stayed on their *side*, there wouldn't be any trouble, thank you very much.

Not this one. The pure white walls were scrubbed from top to bottom. Sky blue tiles covered the roofs and spires, and those flags... They were simply *everywhere*. That wasn't the half of it. Whatever stonemasons had put together the elf castle had resolved not to let a single stretch of wall go undecorated. Friezes, statue-laden alcoves, and stained glass windows in a rainbow of colors all fought for space until there was barely any left. The younger centaurs gaped.

"Wow," murmured Revka.

"Yeah," grinned Iyarra. "Wow."

Lemuel watched the rest of the herd file through the gate. "I hope you'll be staying for the evening. We'll have you for dinner at the castle."

"Oh, we'd love that," said Anyala graciously. "I think we could just set up camp outside your walls, if that's all right?"

"Won't hear of it. There's some space... Let's see, yes, over back of the saltwater taffy shoppe. Nice green area there, a little pond, you can set up camp there. Not a problem, people will just think it's another exhibit. Would you object if people took woodcuts? Never mind. Schlama here will show you the way." He stretched his arms out to the assembled herd. "My friends, the day is yours. Dinner's at eight. See you then." He bowed and swept away, carrying a half dozen others in his wake.

***

A little while later, after the group had set up camp in a patch of rolling lawn away from the main pathways, the herd broke up into groups and began to wander the park. Revka and Iyarra fell in together, promenading down the main avenue. Around them, tourists of all shapes and species milled about through the seamless run of stalls that lined each side of the avenue.

"So, you haven't been here in a while, I guess?" Revka bought a couple of snow cones and passed one up to Iyarra.

"Not since I was...oh, gosh. Four or five, maybe? I don't remember much about it. I remember the enchanted garden, because I got in trouble for trying to eat the exhibit."

Revka chortled. "Oh, no! Really? I'm guessing that didn't go over well." She looked down the avenue. "Is it just me," she said, "or are there an awful lot of shops along here?"

It was true. There were shops selling embroidered tunics and shops with glassware, and shops with large stuffed unicorns, manticores, and elves with big eyes. There was elf pottery, elf woodcuts, elven silverwork and beadwork. The elven made musical instruments were sold next door to the confectionary selling individually wrapped gourmet chocolates. There were elven flasks, elven short swords, elven roofing tiles and enchanted hernia trusses, all marked with the same mysterious sigil. Revka peered at the mark suspiciously. She'd noticed the same symbol over the gate when they came in. And all of the elves she'd seen so far had worn the token on a silver chain around their necks. She grabbed a tunic, on which the symbol had been rendered in multicolored glass beads, and held it up to Iyarra. "What *is* that, anyway?"

Iyarra peered at the design. "Oh, that? That's the sacred mark of the elves. It means it's from here. No one else can create something with that mark. If they do, they fall under a terrible curse."

"Let me guess, skin falling off?" Revka glanced down at her arm. The sleeve of her tunic covered the mark, but she tugged the fabric down a little anyway.

"No," said Iyarra. "Lawyers."

"Ah."

Revka put the tunic back, very, very carefully.

"Speaking of curses," she said as she moped along toward the next stall. "Should we really be spending the day kicking around like this?"

"I understand." Iyarra patted her on the shoulder. "Really, there's nothing much between here and the lake district. It would be better if we struck out for there in the morning. Besides, we're ahead of schedule. Taking the plains is a bit of a shortcut, you know. Also," she added, "Mom says there's someone here who might be able to help us."

"What, really?" Revka looked up at the mare.

"Oh, yes." Iyarra nodded. "Some old wise woman among the elves. Mom told me about it the other day, after looking at your...at your arm. She said it was beyond her to break that complex a curse, but apparently this woman is very good with that sort of thing."

"Good enough to crack a sealed one?"

Iyarra shrugged. "I certainly hope so. I didn't inherit Mom's knack for magic, so I really don't know much about it. But I figure anything is worth trying at this point. Besides, elves are supposed to be really good at magic stuff."

"I guess." Revka shrugged. "I just feel like we shouldn't be wandering around a fun park when we've got so much important stuff riding on our shoulders, you see? I mean, I understand we wouldn't be helping much by traveling more, and maybe this elf your mom knows will be able to help us and all that, it's just...frittering, right? Like we shouldn't be having fun."

Iyarra stopped. Gentle hands took Revka's arms and turned her toward a compassionate face. "Listen," Iyarra said. "I understand what you mean, but look at it this way. In a few days, we'll be back at the castle with a bunch of people who quite probably want to kill us. We've got to outwit them, steal back the book, and stop them from starting up an army or something. Right?"

"Well, yeah."

"So, the way I see it, we're very lucky to spend what might be one of our last days together with my family, just relaxing and enjoying ourselves. Just for a little while. We might be dead in a few days. We might as well have a little fun first, right?"

"Oh, *well*. Now I *really* feel like having fun."

Iyarra laughed and gave Revka's hand a squeeze. "Come on."

***

That evening in the castle, the group was treated to a feast that beat anything Revka or Iyarra had ever seen. Meats, fishes, roots, stews, several different kinds of bread, and a selection of drinks were spread out before them. They even had proper silver utensils and everything. Richly dressed elves sat or mingled, chatting amiably with the herd. At the head table, King Lemuel was holding forth with one of the great old elvish tales and just reaching the story's end.

"So, the old man looked down for a moment, then back up at her. He shrugged and said, 'Beats me, lady. It wasn't there yesterday.'" Lemuel beamed, as a wave of laughter washed over him. He smiled at Toth. "A good one, yes?"

Toth swallowed a bit of bread roll. "Should be," he said. "I'm the one told it to you."

"Oh! Right."

A few seats over, Revka munched a roast turkey leg with a puzzled frown. She and Iyarra wore matching felt beanies with papier-mâché elf ears and their names embroidered on the fronts. She leaned over to Iyarra and nudged her. "Listen," she said, "I still don't quite have a handle on this place. Is this really an elven city or what?"

"Oh, absolutely it is." Lemuel smiled down the table at her. "Everyone who lives and works here is an elf. We have the same things other cities do. It's just a little...different, here and there. That's all."

Revka cringed. "Sorry," she murmured.

The king laughed. "It's quite all right. These things aren't just for decoration, you know." He tapped an ear and smiled. "Would you like to hear the story?"

Revka looked at Iyarra, who shrugged. "Uhm, sure. If it's not too much trouble."

"None at all, dear ladies." Lemuel reclined a bit in his seat and slipped back into storytelling mode.

"You see us now," he said, "living high in our castle here, hundreds of visitors a day, doing amazing book, and that's not even getting into the merchandising. But friends, it was not that long ago that we were a poor people, wandering from place to place, our lands long gone.

"Once, we elves lived in high and secret places of lost forests and forgotten mountains. But even to these places, man did come with his civilization and his wars. And so, we moved from place to place. As those places got scarcer and smaller, so indeed did our number. We became nomads, sleeping rough every night. We traded what magics and arts were at our disposal for our survival.

"It came to pass, eventually, that even our magic was not sufficient. And therefore, I, a too-young king, was forced to take work in the mercenary armies to earn money for my people. Elven people are peaceful. Nevertheless we are swift, and our hand with a bow and arrow true. I was able to keep myself alive and provide for my people. It was during this time that I met my old friend, Toth here."

Toth leaned across to Iyarra and stage whispered, "This was before I met your mother."

"Quite. We were warring in...oh, one of the little local disputes out west. There were so many of them back then. Anyway, I was complaining to him about the problems of being an elf in modern society. Nobody really takes you seriously, you know. People half believe you don't really exist. And of course, even if they do meet you, they just assume you're a shoemaker or something. Used to be that was nearly the only work we could get."

"Which was bad," Toth interjected. "Because this guy here, he makes *terrible* shoes."

Lemuel threw his head back and laughed. "I don't deny it! I don't! But in all fairness, I should point out that my heart was really not in the job." He got up from the table and began to stroll back and forth, waving his wine goblet expansively. Little by little, the various conversations around the room petered out, and people listened to his tale.

"I told him all about how humans just think of us as, well, as stories. Everything they thought they knew about us came from some ridiculous fairytale their grandmother used to tell them. And that's all right. It's partly our fault for being so reclusive all those years, but it was just so frustrating! I mean, people generally got over that sort of foolishness once they got to know you. The brighter ones did, certainly. But you had to go through it *again* and *again* and it was just so *tedious*." There were murmurs of agreement from the elves in the room, and much nodding of heads.

"I seem to recall I was a bit, well, 'in my cups' that night." He held up his wine to a ripple of appreciative laughter. "So I was a little loose with my tongue when I said that I just wished I could make those people out there pay for their ignorance. Not a noble thought, I'll be the first to admit it, but that's what I said."

He moved over behind Toth and laid a hand on the centaur's shoulder. "And that is when this fellow right here, this brilliant centaur, said to me three little words which changed my life. 'So? *Charge* 'em.' Just like that. Charge 'em. He said to me, 'They want mystical elves, give them mystical elves. They want beautiful and mysterious, *give* them beautiful and mysterious. Hell, they want shoes, *give* 'em shoes! But do it on your own terms, and charge 'em out the flank for it!'"

There was applause from the elves in the room, and one or two cheers. "That night," Lemuel continued, "we sat down together over some mead and fleshed out the first inkling of what would become the thriving community-*cum*-industry you see today! And we owe it all to Toth of the Greatfoot. Take a bow, big fellow!"

Toth grinned and stood up, bowing to the applause that filled the room. "Thank you! Thank you. And I just want to say, I never would have believed, on that night, that your king here would have taken this thing and run with it as far as he's gone. I mean it. Look at this place! It's fantastic. You've all outdone yourselves. I say, good on all of ya!" There was another thunder of applause, and Toth sat back down.

The crowd, sensing that the show was over, settled back into its susurrating din of dinnertime conversations. Iyarra looked across at her parents. "You guys never told me Daddy fought alongside elves!"

Toth smiled. "Well, it was a long time ago. Don't really think about it these days."

"Your father was quite the warrior, once upon a time," said Anyala. "I remember when we met. He looked so handsome in his armor. Took my breath away, he did."

Revka gave Iyarra a playful nudge. "Awww, you hear that? Cute, huh?"

"Oh, hush."

Anyala leaned over to Lemuel. "Incidentally," she said. "is old Na the firekeeper still with you?"

"Oh, yes. They're still with us." Lemuel gestured toward a small table on the far side of the room. An old elf in a simple gray robe ate by themselves, not joining in the revels.

Iyarra peered over at them, then turned to her mother. "What's a firekeeper?"

"Well, it's sort of a shaman among the elves. Originally, they just looked after the fire, did general medicine, that sort of thing. Over the years, they became the principal healers and magic users. Na there has been firekeeper here for, well..." she trailed off, looking at Lemuel.

Lemuel smiled. "Oh, over a century by now. They were firekeeper when my father was king and we were still nomads. They have trained pretty much every other firekeeper out there by this point, I daresay. We're very proud of them. But you want to consult with them, perhaps?"

"If we could, yes. If it's not too much trouble." Anyala stole a glance at the two girls. "I feel their knowledge would be useful."

"Say no more." Lemuel nodded. "I'll have a word with them, and we'll get you in first thing in the morning. In the meantime, eat! Enjoy yourselves! Tonight, you are our honored guests. Let us show you the true extent of elven hospitality."

"Right," grinned Toth. "And don't worry about the bill, you can always pay it tomorrow, right?"

Anyala batted her husband on the arm. "Oh hush, you."

***

In the morning, Iyarra and Revka were summoned to the firekeeper's hut, escorted there by a young elf in a simple green robe, who chatted amicably as they went. "...and we built the funfair in just two months, you know. We mostly do new construction during the winter, off season. Not that the winters are that bad out here. It's mostly just wind, really. But Na is one of the greatest firekeepers ever. You're not the first non-elves to come seeking their counsel, I can tell you."

"No kidding." Revka loped along beside them. The elf was surprisingly young, basically a kid. Revka remembered what Lemuel had said the night before. "So," she said. "You a student of hers, or his, or, uhm...?"

"Theirs," the elf said. "A firekeeper is neither male nor female. Or more accurately, we hold aspects of both. It is part of where our power comes from."

Revka furrowed her brow. "Really? Huh." She shrugged it off. "Anyhow, I take it you're one of h—their students?"

The elf beamed proudly. "Indeed I am! My name is Paraman. I'm the apprentice. I'll be assisting today, though of course, Na will be doing most of the work. Don't worry. You're in very good hands. Here we are." Paraman beckoned the two into a hut that was slightly smaller than the others and back in a far corner of the city, out of the way of the tourist areas.

Iyarra had to duck and crouch to get through the opening, but inside the space was much more open. Furniture was sparse and lined around the wall, leaving the main area open except for the firepit in the middle. The pit was deep and clearly in constant use. A hole in the ceiling with a little roof over it allowed the smoke to escape without letting the rain in. Cloth sitting mats circled the pit, and just behind the fire sat Firekeeper Na, still concealed entirely in their gray cloak.

"Come in." The voice was a faint whisper, somewhat high and just a little rough with age. The firekeeper gestured to the mats. "Sit, please. Curse-marks facing the fire."

Iyarra and Revka shuffled into position. Revka tugged off her tunic into a half folded, half wadded rectangular heap. The fire was warm, but not uncomfortably so. Iyarra shifted a bit, getting properly settled. In the firelight, it was easy to see that the curse-marks had grown. Traces brushed along the crook of Revka's elbow, and several tendrils had wrapped all the way around her upper arm. It felt like they would contract at any moment, squeezing and eventually severing her arm right from her body. She had to look away.

The firekeeper rose and pushed their hood back, revealing old features lined with wrinkles, a little heavier than most elven faces. Their thin, white hair was cut to chin length. Ice gray eyes demanded attention, as colorless as their robe, save for that of the fire reflected in them. Far older than the face that held them, they held Revka locked in the firekeeper's gaze.

"Now, then..." Firekeeper Na knelt by Revka's side. Her arm was gently taken, and the curse-mark minutely examined. "Paraman," the keeper said quietly, "bring the showing glass." A glass disc passed between hands. Revka felt the cold against her for a moment, while the firekeeper grunted and muttered to themselves. "I see. Tell me, does it hurt when I do this?"

Revka felt a dull tingling sensation just below the surface of her skin. "Not really, no. Just feels a little funny."

"Very well. And this?"

There was a pause.

"Well?"

"Well what?"

"Ah. I see." Na turned back to Paraman. "Delving, please." The apprentice nodded and threw a handful of something into the fire. The flames flickered, then went bluish-green, bathing the room in an eerie light. Revka looked down and gasped. New lines had appeared on her arm. Thinner strands branched off at angles from each other like some sort of map. Revka got the impression that these lines were somehow *beneath* the layers of the mark visible on her skin. The old firekeeper traced a finger along several of them, their brow furrowed in concentration. "Paraman? Come and see."

The apprentice firekeeper knelt next to Revka and peered at the patterns. "My," they whispered. "Haven't seen one like this before."

Na shook their head. "No, and likely you will not again. But you see here? This bit all along here? What does that look like to you?"

Paraman narrowed their eyes. "It's some sort of...loop? Like, it keeps going over and over but not doing anything."

"Correct. The loop puts a delay on the mark. Right now, that loop will keep going until it degrades, at which point it will fall through to the next point. The actual curse, you see?"

"Dear me."

"Quite. I have used a similar technique before in delivering treatment over time. Sadly, it works for less wholesome purposes as well." The firekeeper looked up at Revka. "Do you know how long it is supposed to wait, child?"

"Oh uhm, about two months, they said. Maybe less."

Na frowned. "I see. And how long ago was this?"

"Well, let's see..." Revka furrowed her brow, counting off days. "Well, it's...almost a month, actually."

The elder firekeeper glanced down at the markings on the girl's arm. "Yes. A month. That seems correct."

Revka felt her stomach knot up again. Already a month? It sure didn't seem that long. Suddenly, she could feel the sands of time pouring away. Hadn't they had all that time ahead of them only a few days ago? Nearly a month had gone. Out in the wilderness, no artifact, no book, time closing in... She whimpered.

The old firekeeper moved to Iyarra and examined her in the glow of the blue-green light. "It is the same," they declared. "Very well. I cannot remove the actual curse without triggering its effects. They have sealed it against tampering. However, I might be able to reinforce the delay loop, keep it from expiring for a while. This would not change anything per se, and so should not trigger the seal, but I can make no promises. It might even make things worse, though I have examined the loop carefully and am satisfied this would not be the case. I will only proceed with your permission, of course."

Revka glanced at Iyarra. The centauress looked down for a moment, chewing on her lip. When she looked up, she gave a brief nod. Revka turned to Na. "Okay. We're in."

"Very well." The healer nodded to Paraman, who picked up a small bag and threw another handful into the fire. The flames changed again to a deeper blue, one that made Revka think of night. "Now then, both of you lie down and get comfortable. It will take a moment for us to prepare. Try to relax and clear your mind of unpleasant thoughts."

Revka nodded and lay back. She shifted, trying to get comfortable, then jumped up with a yelp.

The firekeeper looked up from their work. "What is the matter?"

Revka fidgeted in her belt pouch. "Sorry, laid down on my crystal." She fished out the blue gem and showed it to the elderly elf. "Found it the other day. Pretty, but I keep jabbing myself with it."

An odd sort of expression worked its way across the old firekeeper's face. They knelt next to Revka and took the crystal gently between two fingers. "Where...did you get this?" they asked quietly.

"On the plains. It was in some water. Why?"

"Do you know what this is?"

Revka and Iyarra exchanged glances. "Not us, no."

"It is a resonating crystal. A very old magic, and one you really do not see any more." They stood up quickly and started to rummage around in an old wooden trunk. "It takes two of them to be at all useful. But I do believe I...ah." They took out another blue crystal, extremely similar to Revka's.

"Now, watch as I do this. Paraman, you watch too." Na took the two crystals and touched them together, base to base. The healer began to tap one on the end, over and over again. "This is called tuning," the firekeeper explained. "It can take a few seconds, depending on...ah, here we are. Watch now." They moved the two crystals apart, then lifted one to their mouth. "Hello," they said.

"Hello," the other crystal echoed.

Iyarra cocked her head. "How did you do that?"

"They are attuned to each other now. Anything that causes a vibration in one will cause the other to vibrate as well, no matter how far away they are. By this way, sounds may be sent very long distances."

"That's amazing! How does it work?"

"Nobody is quite certain. When I was a girl, lovers would get them so that they could still speak to each other when they had to be apart. I fear they are mostly forgotten now." They sighed. "So many things lost to time."

Revka's eyes lit up. "Yeah, but think about it! If you could send messages like that all over the place, you could—well, I mean, you'd need a whole bunch, but—"

"No. Each crystal can only tune to one other, and after about a week, the tuning begins to degrade. The resonance weakens with time, you see. By the end of a month, it is gone entirely. You have to retune them. They're only good when you can tune them frequently. I think miners still use them, when they're down in the pits, but most prefer to send messages by scrye these days." The old elf sighed and set their crystal aside, handing the other one back to Revka. "In any case, let us proceed."

Revka nodded and lay back down again, tucking the crystal carefully into her belt pouch. "OK, so now what do we do?"

"Just gaze into the fire, breathe deep, and relax. Count to four as you breathe in, and eight as you breathe out. Feel your eyelids getting heavy..."

Chapter Nineteen

THE NEXT MORNING DAWNED bright, with a crispness in the air that hinted at fall on the way. The centaurs packed up their camp after breakfast and exchanged farewells with the elves, who had come out to see them off. Toth shook Lemuel's hand. "I think we're going to make camp at the north shore of Lake Peccaray, in case we're needed. Tell your people they can find us there."

"I will." The king nodded to Revka and Iyarra. "I wish you well on your quest. When you have settled this business, know that you are always welcome here." He handed them two pieces of elaborately engraved parchment, much like the one Toth presented when they arrived. "Lifetime passes," he explained. "Don't be strangers."

Revka tucked them away carefully. "Thanks," she said. "We won't."

"Very kind of you," added Iyarra.

Toth shook Lemuel's hand one more time, then looked up at the sky. "Well, if we get going now, we should be north of the lake well in time for the girls to get to Peccaray by sundown. Shall we, Mother?"

"There is yet one more thing." The crowd of elves parted, as Firekeeper Na hobbled forward, supported by Paraman. The firekeeper approached the two girls and looked up at them. "The work I did yesterday should buy you a few weeks, though I could not say how many. I will continue to research the curse, but it may take some time. If you cannot get them to remove it from you, come back quickly as you can. Do you understand?"

Revka nodded grimly. "Gotcha."

"All right." Toth nodded to the elves and raised his hand in the air. "Off we go, everyone! Lake district by sunset, yes?" There was an answering roar, a rumble of hooves, and a cloud of dust...then silence.

"Nice bunch of folks," said Lemuel to himself. He turned to the other elves. "What do you think? Should we diversify a bit? A centaur pavilion, maybe?"

"Possibly, sir."

"Well, we'll throw it up at the next board meeting. Anyway, opening time in two hours, everyone. To your places, and let's see those smiles."

***

The herd traveled quickly, veering sharply southwest until they began to come across the little lakes and ponds that marked the outlying areas of the lake district. They weaved their way around the various waterways until they came to the northernmost tip of Lake Peccaray. The area just to the north was a bit marshy, but firm enough for the herd to ease their way across to the opposite side, where they made camp. To the south, the lake stretched on as far as they could see.

"Now then," Anyala bustled about, making a late lunch. "We'll stay here for at least two weeks, all right? Send a message if you need help. If we don't hear from you, we'll just come along ourselves. You understand?"

Iyarra nodded. "Yes, Mom."

"Don't be afraid to send for help. They sound like a nasty bunch of folks you're dealing with, and I know your father wouldn't hesitate to go down there and give them a proper seeing to."

"Yes, Mom."

"In fact, I still don't see why you don't want us coming with you. It sounds like you could use the help."

"Well," said Revka, "it's like this. If we show up with a whole army at our backs, they'll probably just straight up kill us first thing. As long as they've got these stupid things on our arms, they've pretty much got all the cards. We have to play their game until we can find out what happened to the book and get it away from them. If we can't do that, then at the least, we need to buy time for the others. Those monks said they'd send down to the capital, but who knows how long they'll take to get there? It just makes sense to go in quietly, bide our time, and try to hold things off until everyone is ready."

"Right," said Iyarra. "*Then* you can come in and cream them."

Anyala laughed. "All right. You just... Well, you know I worry. In any case, we'll keep an eye out on the road for the gentlemen you talked about, the armies, I mean. We'll have scouts along the road, so if they go by, we'll see them."

"Thanks, Mom."

"Now, let's have a look at you." The older centauress turned and gave her daughter a close examination. "Yes, I think you'll be all right." She squeezed the girl's hands. "Yes. Yes, certainly all right."

Iyarra sighed and squeezed back. "It's all right, Mom. We'll get through this. I'm sure we will."

"I'm sure, too. But you're my girl, you know. I will always worry, and that's that."

"I understand."

"Good. Now, run and get your father. Let him know lunch is ready."

***

They ate in silence for the most part. Occasionally, someone would venture a question or comment, but nobody was really in a conversational mood. The meal was eaten quickly, final preparations and goodbyes were made, and the two girls headed south, following the lake shore.

It was just a little before sunset, when they found their way down to the town. Peccaray was crowded as ever, though things were beginning to quiet down for the evening. The last ferries had already left, and the market was beginning to close up. They found room at one of the inns and settled in for the night.

After dinner, the two sat outside, passing a bottle of ale back and forth and looking up at the stars.

"Nice folks."

Iyarra tilted her head. "Hm?"

"Your parents. Nice folks."

"Oh. Yes, they are."

"You uh, you think they're okay about...?" Revka waved the bottle back and forth between them.

Iyarra shrugged. "Maybe. Mom, definitely. Dunno about Dad."

"Oh. Well, she certainly seemed to pick up on it pretty quickly. I'll give her that."

"Yeah, Mom's always been very good at noticing things about people. She's very observant."

"That's nice." Revka leaned against Iyarra's back and stared at the sky for a while.

"Revka?"

"Mm?"

"What are we going to do?"

Revka rubbed her nose for a moment. "Well," she said. "I honestly don't know. They've got the book, the wizards, those thieves, and their own private army. We've got... Well, we've got curses on our arms and backup that may or may not be on the way. We're going to be hash unless we can outwit them. So, I guess we're going to have to come up with something. The way I see it, we've got about three days of travel in front of us to put together some kind of plan."

"Well, you've always managed to come up with something before. I have faith in you." Iyarra smiled.

"Thanks." Revka looked up at the centauress. "I don't suppose you've got any tricks up your sleeve?"

Iyarra shrugged. "Not me, sorry."

"Well, think it over. I will too." Revka sighed and stretched. "Probably time we hit the sack."

"OK." Iyarra gave Revka a squeeze. "See you in the morning."

Revka leaned up and gave Iyarra a good night kiss. "Sleep well." She watched Iyarra mosey off to the stables, then picked up the bottle and headed for her room. Time to think.

She sat alone in the darkness, staring up at the ceiling. Round and round went her mind, trying to find a way forward and getting nowhere. How the hell did you win when they literally had you by the arm? Iyarra was right about one thing. Revka was good at coming up with ideas on the spot, way better than trying to plan ahead. It just seemed to be one of those things. Well, in a few days, they would be back at the castle. She just hoped an idea would present itself then. It certainly wasn't now.

Eventually, the empty bottle slipped from her hand and rolled across the floor to the accompaniment of her snores.

Chapter Twenty

THE CASTLE WAS JUST visible through the trees from the hill where Revka and Iyarra lurked. They'd spent three days traveling and the last few hours watching the castle. There was barely any activity at all. Normally, a castle should be full of people running around, seeing to the family, the laundry, the cooking, all the daily business of running a self-contained village. If Revka was any judge, there were only the barest minimum of people around. Even the security was woefully inadequate. Revka watched a lone guard plod his patrol around the courtyard. What were they playing at?

"I don't get it," she said. "We know they have it, and yet this place is just about shut down. You'd think they'd be busier than ever, wouldn't you? I would."

Iyarra shrugged. "Unless they went somewhere else," she said.

Revka turned. "What?"

"Well, it seems to me that they probably wouldn't want to do their magic army raising around here, would they?" Iyarra shuffled a hoof. "I mean, probably they would do it off somewhere private, where no one could see."

Revka pursed her lips. "Hmm," she said. "That is definitely a possibility." She thought it over for a minute. "You know, I think you're right."

Iyarra brightened. "You think so?"

"Probably."

Iyarra preened and Revka gave her a pat.

"So, any ideas about where they went to? Because I have no idea."

Iyarra thought it over. "Well, somewhere with a lot of space, I guess. But not open, like a field. Uhm, maybe in the mountains? Only there's hardly any mountains here. I suppose you could clear a space in the middle of a forest, or... Oh!"

"What?"

"I bet *he* knows." Iyarra pointed to the south road.

Revka looked. Sure enough, three horses were approaching the castle. Two carried guards, but the one in the middle...

"All right," Revka nodded to herself. "I think it's time. Iyarra, hon, I'm going to need you to do something for me."

Iyarra cocked her head. "You have a plan, then?"

"Yeah," she said. "But you're not going to like it."

***

Down in the heart of Castle Lonngren, Mister Treadwell sat back in his office and rubbed his eyes. The life of a clerk was filled, end to end, with drudgery and mental labor in service to even the least ambitious of lords. With the new project and the constant travel back and forth, his days were getting progressively longer, changing of the seasons be damned.

Anyway, time for a break.

Treadwell set aside the latest in a seemingly never-ending pile of supply lists and strode out of his office and down the corridor to the water closet. No one was using it. Good. He shut the door behind him, then took a seat and let his mind go blank.

After a moment or two, he glanced furtively around and pulled a slim volume from the confines of his robe. Printed on the cheap chapboard cover could just be seen *The Disgusting Disclosures of Anais Nun, Special Illustrated Edition for the Connoisseur.* He flipped through to the bookmarked page and began to read.

The next morning found myself most tired and vexed, and somewhat hard of hearing, which last did not go away for some few days. During morning prayers, Mother Superior announced that the bishop had directed we take part in a new devotional practice, effective immediately. To that effect, a trampoline was being installed in the inner courtyard, and we would all be receiving a set of rubber—

Suddenly, there was a knife by his throat. "Hello, *Mister* Treadwell," a voice hissed. "Remember me?"

Treadwell froze, barely willing even to shift his eyes toward the voice. A shadow moved, and there was a figure covered in a dark cloak before him. The knife still pointed at his neck. The shape shook its head, causing the hood to fall away. Treadwell gasped. "Y-you!"

"Yeah," grinned Revka. "Me." She leaned in close, her eyes gleaming. "Miss us?"

Treadwell did his best to recover. "Well, er, I see you made it back. I trust you retrieved the relic?"

"Stop it." Revka jabbed at him with the knife. "We know all about the other two, and the book. You sent us as a distraction. We were *supposed* to be caught."

Treadwell shut his eyes. "It wasn't my idea!" he whimpered. "It was His Grace! He wanted someone to attract attention away, while his people got the book and brought it back. You just seemed likely enough candidates. It's not my fault!"

The blade pushed in closer. "Where did they take the book? Got it here, have you?"

Treadwell tried to shake his head, but the knife was making this difficult. "No, we don't have it here. His Grace wanted to use it at..." he stopped, then looked at Revka. "Why should I tell you?" he sneered. "I think you are in no position to be intimidating me. Remember your curse-marks!"

"Ohhh, that's right! Our curse-marks!" Revka leaned in closer. "Funny thing about those." She shifted a bit, and for the first time, he noticed the other sleeve of her cloak hung empty.

"By the seven gods...!"

Revka grinned. "Didn't expect that, did you? Now, be a good boy, and tell Auntie Revka what you did with the book."

The clerk sagged. "All right. All right. There's an old quartz mine to the south of here, along the coach road to Duneaden. The duke has set up operations there. It's a few hours' ride to the abandoned town from when the mine was operating. There's signs and things. Not that it will do you any good." His voice gained back a trace of hauteur. "The duke has it well guarded. But listen, if you promise not to hurt me, I may be persuaded to forget I ever saw you. You might as well know he was minded to have you killed in any case. His Grace does not like loose ends."

Revka pursed her lips in thought. "Mmm, no, no, I don't think I can go along with that. Thank you all the same." She gave him a rueful smile. "No, I think I'm just going to tie you up and gag you, so that I can get out of here in one piece."

"Oh, really?" The clerk snorted. "And how do you expect to do that with only one arm, pray?"

"Good point." Revka smiled. The cloak flipped back, revealing her other arm, still very much intact.

"Oh."

Her fist came sailing out at him, too fast to block. Everything went black.

When the guards finally battered down the door and released him, he wasn't sure what was worse; the humiliation of having to explain, or the fact that she had stolen his book.

***

"Oh, man, listen to *this!*" Revka cackled. She began to read aloud. "It was about that time that Sister Bernadette offered to help me in becoming a more disciplined acolyte. She said the key was regular and vigilant flagellation. She then offered to school me in this most holy art, vouchsafing that she had a not inconsiderable collection of—"

"Uhm, do I really want to hear this?" Iyarra made a face. It had been a good couple hours on the trot, and Revka's constant gleeful excerpts were not making the time go by any faster. Not for Iyarra, at any rate.

"Aw, come on. This is hilarious." Revka flipped back a page or two and chortled to herself. "Wow, somebody has a real imagination."

"It's a very weird book."

"Yeah well, he's a really weird person."

A little while later, they came upon the remains of the mining town. It was obvious the place hadn't been touched in ages. Old weeds grew everywhere. A few of the cottages had fallen in on themselves. Most of all, the whole area had that feel a place gets when people abandon it. There's a sort of melancholy emptiness, a feeling of stories acted out again and again, then ended, and finally forgotten. You could almost hear the echoes of the lives that played out there so long ago. Iyarra stopped in what had once been the town square and sniffed around. "Oh, yes," she said. "People have been through here recently. Let's see…" She turned her head back and forth a few times and honed in on a road leading off to the west. "That way."

They abandoned what was left of the town and followed a dirt road that led toward a set of hills in the distance. The road was straight and broad, and in its time must have carried large groups of miners and pit ponies hauling cartloads of precious quartz. On either side of the road, rough stone walls stood about waist high, behind which trees grew out and canopied the road, almost creating a tunnel. Unlike the rest of the area, the road showed definite signs of recent use. Very recent, by the look of it.

They kept along the road for an hour, neither of them talking much beyond the occasional lone comment. There was something about the place that did not invite conversation. Once in a while, Iyarra would point out rough tracks in the dirt where a cart had recently come, or hoofmarks heading along the road.

"Drafts," she said. "Big ones."

After a while, the dirt began to give way to occasional slabs of stone. The walls were higher there, almost shoulder height. The trees hung heavy over the road, making it darker than it ought to have been.

A large hill was beginning to loom up in the distance, barely visible through the trees, where there seemed to be a little bit of activity going on. Iyarra moved to the shadow of the wall and slowed their pace.

"Revka?"

"Mm?"

"The walls. They're up past our heads, now."

"I know."

"And there's hardly any dirt on the road anymore. It's—"

"I know."

"—all stone, and I can't see the sky anymore. It's like we went from outside to inside without even..."

"Yeah. Just keep going."

Iyarra shivered and moved even closer to the wall.

After a while, the road widened out to reveal a sort of courtyard. This place was far from empty, with carts and drivers and people and centaurs hauling things in every direction and arguing at cross purposes. There were a few guards scattered around, but they didn't look especially alert. Revka and Iyarra moved behind a cart loaded with hay and watched for a while.

"What do we do?" whispered Iyarra.

Revka scanned the area. Off to one side, a largish man held a clipboard. He seemed to be directing a small group of men and centaurs to haul things down into the cave. Revka pursed her lips a moment, then stood up. "Okay. Follow my lead."

The duo strode out from behind the cart and headed for the man. Revka carried herself with an insouciant swagger. Iyarra tried to follow suit as best she could. The foreman looked up as they approached and grunted. "Yeah? What do you want?"

Revka spoke with a voice that had gone down about an octave and several IQ points. "Uh yeah, mister. They said there was work here. Back at the castle. Like, hauling and stuff. Said we was to report to the guy in charge."

Iyarra nodded. "Yeah."

The man looked them over. "All right," he snorted. "We can use more loaders and haulers. You'll be hauling stuff down into the mine. There may be some building stuff, too. Either of you can swing a hammer?"

"Sure, no problem."

"Yeah."

"Great. Terrific. It's three gold a day, hours are from when I tell you to start to when I tell you to stop. No lazing, no stealing stuff off the job site, no going where you weren't sent, no asking questions, and no even *thinking* about not doing what you're told. Clear?"

"Got it."

"Yeah."

"All right." He jerked his head toward a queue of other workers. "Fall in line over there. We're carrying some provisions down. Just follow the others." He immediately went back to his clipboard and muttering.

Revka and Iyarra made their way to the queue. "Are you sure this is a good idea?" Iyarra whispered.

"Sure." Revka nodded. "Think about it. We need to get in, right? What better way? And whatshisface at the castle can't have alerted them already. Way I see it, we got a couple hours at the very least to sneak around. We'll find the book, sneak out, and get the hell out of here. What could go wrong?"

"Well, for a start we—"

"All right, all right. But can you think of a better plan?"

Iyarra glanced over at the entranceway. There weren't many guards, but it would have been a real trick to get by them without their noticing. She sighed. "Not really, no."

"All right, then. Let's just get this over with as fast as possible."

Chapter Twenty-one

THE MINE HAD EVIDENTLY lain empty for quite some time, and things were just starting to ramp up again. As they were led through the tunnels they spotted picks and helmets, relics of old mining equipment. Chalked arrows on the walls directed the way to various seams. They were taking the stuff to a large gallery a good way down, a sort of natural oval area with tunnels branching off in several directions. The place had a makeshift feel about it. Tents had been hauled down and set up, tables served as desks, and supplies were stacked in odd corners. It was obvious the activity was only very recent.

They spent the afternoon hauling down rice and wheat, then timber for propping and shoring. It was nightfall by the time the foreman said they could knock off. There was another large room off the main gallery, which the workers were using for a makeshift camp. Their tents and sleeping rolls surrounded a central fire. There were benches scattered around, and some other makeshift furnishings, but overall, it was strictly no frills.

Iyarra looked around and wrinkled her nose. "Cozy."

Revka shrugged. "Not like we'll be here long. Okay." She dug Treadwell's book from a pocket and held it up to Iyarra. "Can you get his scent from this?"

Iyarra took the book and sniffed delicately. She stepped out into the main gallery, closed her eyes, and sniffed around. "Oh, yeah," she said. "He's only been gone a little while, and the scent kind of lingers. No wind, you know. There's something..." she took a deep, slow breath and concentrated for a moment. Iyarra gasped and narrowed her eyes.

"What? What?"

"The magicians," Iyarra whispered. "The ones who cursed us, they've been here too."

"What? You sure?"

"I remember their smell." Iyarra nodded. "Sulfur and ammonia. I think they must use that for their magic work." She looked around. "Hmmm. Yes. They've been here recently." She looked around and pointed. "That way. Both trails."

"All right." Revka grabbed a bag of rice, which she loaded onto Iyarra's back. There were some papers on a nearby table. She grabbed one at random and nodded to the centauress. "Ready?"

"I guess."

They headed toward the opening. The guard was picking his nails with the end of his pike and paying only desultory interest in the goings on around the cavern. Revka waved the paper at him as they went by. "More stuff," she said. "We know the way." The guard looked like he was about to say something but didn't. They hurried down the corridor.

"OK," Revka whispered. "Where to now?"

Iyarra moved forward, letting her nose do the heavy work. This place felt emptier, like only a few people came down this way. The scents were more prominent and hung clear and strong in the still air. She could practically follow them blindfolded.

A few cross paths down, she stopped, swiveling her head back and forth a couple of times. "Hmm," she said.

Revka looked up. "What's wrong?"

"The scents, they split off here. Treadwell seems to have gone in several different directions, but the others only go left."

"Hmm. Well, our good friend Mister Treadwell would have been all over this place, that makes sense. But the magic guys... Probably, they are the ones dealing with the book. Let's follow them, all right?"

They worked their way down a tunnel to a small doorway, which had been covered with a rough tarpaulin. A series of nasty looking glyphs was scrawled on the surface. Iyarra wrinkled her nose and took a deep sniff. "No one in there," she said. "But this is probably it. What's that on the door?"

Revka took a torch off the wall and moved it closer. "Let's see... Oh, it's a curse. Whoever removes anything from this room will have their skin burned off once they pass the threshold." She winced. "What is it with these people and taking your skin off?"

Iyarra shrugged. "Don't know. Anyway, it couldn't hurt to peek. It doesn't say anything about no entry, does it?"

"No, no. Nothing about that. All right. You stand guard. I'll see what I can find." She pushed the tarp aside and slipped in.

***

The smallish gallery had been set up as a makeshift laboratory. There were tables covered in alchemical glass, old books, and a bunch of other nasty looking things she didn't like to look too hard at or speculate about. There were lanterns here and there, hanging from the ceiling and on the wall. She carried the torch around the room, looking for the book.

The problem… Well, the problem wasn't finding *a* book. There were stacks of them, easily a few dozen. For Revka, who had never seen more than a handful together in one place, it was practically a library. Rather belatedly, she realized it would have helped if the monks had given her some idea of what the thing looked like.

She began to work her way around the room, poking at the various old books lying around. Most of them were creepy looking things, dealing in curses and alchemy and gods alone knew what. Nothing really seemed like what she was looking for. What was that guy's name again? Alakazam? Ashkente? Dammit. She should have written it down. She was going to have to check every one of…oh. Wait. That was it. Ashkahn. Now, if only she—

Revka stopped dead in her tracks. Where did she just see that name?

She swept her eyes back over the nearest table. Notebooks, a few loose scraps of paper. Quills, inkwell, graphite stick. A lantern, some loose bits of string and bent wire… There, right in the middle…

"Oh, my gods."

There. It. Was.

There should have been more to it. There should have been gargoyles, sinister creatures engraved on the cover and leering out a warning to the would-be reader. There should have been an aged leather cover made from the skin of some long forgotten creature. There should have been an aura of menace radiating outward from the book, with the title written in strange and mysterious letters that squirmed when you tried to read them, written in the blood of a thousand bats or something.

But this? This was a perfectly ordinary, cheap pasteboard binder with the title written rather badly with a pen that blotted too much. She flipped it open carefully. This wasn't even a proper book, really. Someone had just impaled the pages with a couple of wires threaded through the spine. If she untwisted the wires, she could pull out the pages and everything.

She flipped through the book, shaking her head in disbelief. The thing was a mess. Scribblings, crossings-out, no titles on the page, half-baked instructions like *Mixxe an quantity of Alum with ye Precipitate of*

Amber, and distill in the Usual Way until ye result is somewat Redder than normal. What the heck did that even mean? She flipped back to the front of the book. There wasn't even a table of contents, for pity's sake. How did they—?

Something on a sheet of paper caught her eye. It seems there *was* a table of contents after all. Judging from the relatively new condition of the paper, it wasn't part of the book but the work of the duke's sorcerers. Still very much under construction, too, by the looks of it. She dragged her finger down the list.

Never-Tire Servants Page 2
Hypnotic Owls Page 13
Pocket Sized People Page 29

There were also a good number of variations on the theme of talking animals. Ah, there.

Soldiers Page 73.

The entry was even circled. She looked back at the book and noticed for the first time that someone had been going through and penciling in page numbers in the corner. This was a different hand than whoever wrote the book. Must be the work of the sorcerers again. She flipped along until she found page seventy-three. It looked pretty much like every other page, filled with closely written script and obscure instructions. There wasn't even a title. Clearly, this book was meant only as a personal reference. Ashkahn probably never expected anyone else to come along and try and make sense of it. She suspected that, even if you did know your magic, these spells were probably a major headache to try and understand.

She drummed her fingers on the table, trying to decide what to do next. She couldn't take the book out of there, not with that stupid curse on the threshold. For two bits, she'd burn it. After all, Father Eliot said he'd square it with the other abbot, hadn't he? Definitely an option, but maybe there was another, less drastic way. Maybe she could just burn that one page. Of course, they'd notice it was missing. She'd have to go through and renumber all of the...

A light went on in her head. Hadn't somebody said something about...?

She turned back to the table of contents, muttering to herself as she scanned the page. She found what she was looking for on the back, noted the number, and flipped the pages of the book.

Oh, *yes*.

She put the torch in a nearby wall sconce and turned her attention back to the book...

***

Five minutes later, she and Iyarra were making their way back along the hallway. Revka was humming.

"So," said Iyarra. "Did you find the book?"

"I did, yes."

"They really have it?"

"They sure do."

"And we can't take it away because of that stupid curse?"

"Afraid not."

"Well, what do we do?"

"We wait. I don't know about you, but I don't see any army of magic soldiers standing around. They must not have tried it yet. So, we've got time."

"And what if they use it before we can take it?"

Revka just smiled. "Don't worry. The Great Revka has already taken care of things. All we have to do is bide our time."

"The Great Revka?" Iyarra harrumphed.

Revka didn't even rise to it. "No, really. Already taken care of. Right now, all we have to do is to head back up to the surface, get ourselves good and lost, and wait for reinforcements. Heck, they'll probably even get here before these clowns try to make their 'invincible army.'" Her fingers made quotation marks in the air. "Now, let's just get out of here and wait for the fireworks."

"I wish I had your confidence." Iyarra sighed as they stepped into the main gallery. Her nose twitched. Something...

"Don't worry about it, sugar. It's gonna be fine. These guys don't know who they're messing with."

"YOU!"

Revka froze mid-step. Iyarra gulped as the memory of that scent flooded back. *Oh, no...*

Chapter Twenty-two

HEADS TURNED ALL AROUND the cavern as Treadwell emerged from a small cluster of men near the tunnel entrance and headed straight for the girls. He pointed at them, nearly shaking with rage. "It's them, Your Grace! These are the ones, right here! They're the ones who tied me up! Guards! Arrest them at once!"

A dozen or so guards ran to surround them. A well-dressed man followed, with the unconcerned demeanor of someone who knew the show wouldn't start without him. He glided smoothly up to the group and waved a languid arm at some other guards, who hurried over with torches.

Treadwell turned to the new arrival and bowed. "Your Grace, these are the ones I told you about. The ones we sent to Kalazad. They tricked me into—I mean, they somehow found out the location of this place." He fumbled a second, then rallied. "I believe they are here to steal the book, probably to use it for themselves."

The duke stepped forward into the light. He was...well, he was quite good looking, actually. Younger than Revka had expected, certainly. Tall, slim, and fair skinned. Tousled light brown hair just framed his boyish face. He was rather charming, really...until you got to his eyes. There was something...not evil, no, nothing like that. Not angry, or cunning, or glowing red. No. There was...emptiness. No emotion, no humanity, nothing at all. The blankness put Revka in mind of the dolls she had played with as a child, crude things with painted on eyes. That was it. It was like looking at a doll, a perfect porcelain replica of a person, with no life shining from within. She shivered.

The duke tilted his head, looking back and forth between the two of them. "I see. Interesting. And they are the ones we sent?"

Treadwell bobbed his head. "The very same, Your Grace. As you will recall, you wanted a team to—"

The duke waved a hand. "Yes, yes of course." He looked Revka over for a moment. "Tell me," he asked pleasantly. "Did you manage to secure the...whatever it was we sent you after? I'm afraid I don't recall."

Revka glowered. "No. Not that you really wanted it, anyway."

The duke *tch'd* and shook his head. "Pity. Well, I suppose there's no denying it. My men tell me you were quite effective. After your payment now, I suppose?"

"Look, we don't care about the money, okay? We just want these things off our arms. We played your little game, right? So why not just let us go? I mean, what can we do to you?"

Iyarra looked puzzled. She opened her mouth as if to speak but caught herself. Revka willed Iyarra to hear her thoughts. *Please...they don't know we know where the book is...*

The duke just smirked and shook his head. "Now, I really don't think so. As I recall, you are still very much on the hook for...horse thieving, wasn't it? It rather seems to me that you'll do what I say or be hanged." He stopped and tilted his head at them. "Actually," he said. "We might just have some further use for you." He walked slowly around the two, never taking his eyes away from them. "Yes, I think I will allow you two to do me one more little favor. I'll even make it nice and easy for you. How does that sound?"

Revka and Iyarra looked at each other and shrugged. "I guess," said Revka. "Not like we have a choice, right?"

Iyarra nodded. "Yes. Thank you."

"Not at all, dear ladies. Not at all." He turned to the guards. "Take them down to the cage and lock them in."

"Wait."

"What?"

The duke turned back to them, his face impassive, his tone as even and friendly as ever. "You see, we'll be creating the first batch of soldiers tomorrow. Naturally, I'm itching to see just how effective they are. We'll be wanting to make sure they have something to practice on. You, in fact. We were going to drag some cows down here, but I think you two will be rather more entertaining. More hygienic, too, I fancy. Guards?"

"Now, hang on—" Suddenly, they were surrounded by guards, swords and spears hovering centimeters away. Revka sighed and put her hands up slowly. Well, *this* felt familiar.

"Just a moment." Treadwell stepped forward. He patted Revka down, then rooted through her belt pouches until he found what he was looking for. "*My* book," he said, tucking it away. "And now, gentlemen, take them to the cage."

***

The cage, it turned out, was exactly that. The old supply cage had been dragged down, piece by piece, during the mining days and assembled in an isolated gallery. Their luxurious accommodation was furnished with an old desk and a chair, and even some rusty old shelves in the back. Revka rummaged through the contents of these and tried to work out what clever plans she could concoct with a few dirt clods, several old documents, a couple of cans of dried up whitewash, and a box of candles. There weren't as many as one would think.

"Okay. I take the candles and set fire to the...right. No flint. All right, then...The torches here are"—She looked up. "Too far away on the wall to reach. Farg." She went back to inspect the door. It was a simple setup: metal door, metal bars, and large metal padlock connecting A to B. Still, the bars weren't too close together. If she flattened her hand out and wriggled it around then... Yes, she could flail helplessly at the lock and bat it around a bit. Terrific.

"Any luck?" Iyarra had found a relatively comfortable spot to sit down and was watching quietly. Revka thought longingly of all the useful little tools and things she kept in her belt pouches, which had been removed and spirited off somewhere. She slumped against the door and shook her head.

"I've got nothing." She looked back around the cage, hunting for something, anything that could be used. Maybe if she did something with the shelves... She gave them an experimental tug. All welded together into one piece. Great. She slumped over to the chair and flopped back onto it. "We are so dead."

Iyarra nodded. "Well, maybe their soldier spell won't work. It's possible, after all. Or we might be able to fight them. We've had to fight our way out of things before, you know?"

"Yeah, but generally we had weapons. I kind of doubt they're going to let us have any tomorrow." She picked idly at a loose bit on the stone floor. "Besides, it's not the army I'm worried about. It's after."

"You're not worried about the army?"

Revka shook her head. "No. There won't be an army. Or rather, there will be, but not exactly the one they're counting on."

"All right." Iyarra sighed. "What did you do?"

Revka told her.

"You did what?"

"Yup."

"Seriously?"

"Oh, yeah."

"Wow." Iyarra blew out a big breath. "They're really not going to be happy."

"No. No they're not."

The future played itself out in two different minds. Neither of them much liked the result.

"You think they'll realize it was you?"

"Oh, sure. Eventually." Revka shrugged.

"I'd almost rather take my chances with the soldiers."

"I don't know about that." Revka got up and wandered over to Iyarra. She lay out against the centaur girl and hugged her upper back. "I'm sorry."

Iyarra reached behind and patted Revka's shoulder. "Don't be. It was all worth it."

"Was it?"

Iyarra thought about it. "Well. Up until this part, anyway."

Revka made a noise that might have been a laugh. "Yeah, it's definitely been...interesting, hasn't it?"

Iyarra tugged at Revka's arms, pulling her up and around to face her. Revka found herself looking Iyarra right in the eye, her hands held with a reassuring squeeze.

"I wouldn't have missed it for anything."

Chapter Twenty-three

MORNING CAME. IT MUST have been morning, not that you could tell down there. Iyarra and Revka were awoken by a guard, who slid in a plate of bacon and eggs and a large bowl of mush. Revka blinked at the portions. "Wow," she said. "Are you sure this is for us?"

The guard grinned. "Special instructions from the duke. Said to eat up. You two are going to need it." He laughed nastily and left them to it.

"Well," said Revka. "that just did wonders for my appetite." She passed the oatmeal over to Iyarra and began to poke at her eggs.

"Oh well," said Iyarra. "At least we won't die hungry, you know?" She tilted the bowl to her nose and sniffed. "Hm. Not bad."

Revka mechanically forked eggs into her mouth. She had to admit, they were pretty good. Odd. Still, when she thought about it, it kind of made sense. The duke was clearly a guy who fancied himself Mister Clever. Probably got off on being extra nice to people he was about to be *really* nasty to. The kind of guy who would have you chained to the rack but put a pillow under your head and send someone down after an hour to see if you wanted a glass of water. You had to be really inventive to turn kindness into a different form of cruelty.

A little after breakfast, a phalanx of guards led them, bound and hobbled, down a series of passages to another gallery not too far from the main area. This room was massive, almost a perfect circle and lit by torches that went all the way around the walls. There was also a lake taking up most of the space. Iyarra and Revka gawked.

"It is rather impressive, isn't it?" The duke entered, flanked by guards and assorted lackeys. He was dressed somewhat more formally, in what looked like a military uniform covered in webbing and sashes and epaulettes and all the usual candy floss of the upper ranks. It was the kind of uniform worn by someone who never went near a battlefield themselves, just stayed at the back and gave themselves medals for sending other people. Several gray faced, soberly dressed men stood on either side of the duke. They were similarly attired but with the look of those who had personally seen more than their share of battlefields. A few regarded the two young women, their expressions unreadable.

Revka looked out at the water, then back to the duke. "It's...it's a lake. What's a lake doing down here?"

"Well, it's more of a pool." He stepped to the shore and swept an arm out over the water. "As I understand it, the water leaks through the stone and down those, er..." he gestured vaguely towards the roof. "Treadwell?"

"Stalactites, sir."

"Ah, yes. Never can remember which ones they are. Thank you. But it comes down and just collects, drop by drop. Must have taken centuries. One of nature's little miracles, and of course, very useful for us." He nodded to a couple of guards, who tethered Revka and Iyarra to a thick iron post anchored into the ground.

Revka snorted. "What are you gonna do? Wait a few thousand years and drown us?"

The duke laughed. It was an odd little laugh, almost mechanical. "You know old Ashkahn would create his creatures one at a time? He would pour the ingredients together into a cauldron, apply the proper magics, and the creature would form up out of the water, just like that. Amazing stuff. Alas, rather too slow. But this!" His gaze took in the pool again. "Like a thousand cauldrons all in one place! We shall raise up our army overnight and sweep across the continent before anyone can even react. This army will be quick. It will be efficient. And it will be *mine*. All of it.

"And you lucky two get to be their first conquest. A little aperitif, if you will, before the main course."

Treadwell coughed. "Begging your pardon, Your Grace, but I do feel I must, once again, recommend, in the strongest possible terms, that we just do one or two to begin with. Just to make sure what we get is what we expect to get."

The duke turned. "Oh really, Treadwell. You have no confidence."

"No, Your Grace. I'm paid not to have confidence. It is part of my job."

"Well I, for one, am entirely certain our sorcerous friends know exactly what they are doing. Besides, I hear from my scouts that there are rumblings from the capital. There's talk of an army marching in this direction. Almost as if some foolish person had tipped them off." He turned his gaze on Revka, but she gave nothing away. "In any case, it seems we are best served by moving forward at all speed."

"As you say, sir."

"Quite. In any case, we're only doing a hundred to start with." He turned to another clerk. "Have the spell components been added?"

The clerk nodded. "Indeed, sir. We have put in enough for a thousand, easily." He nodded to a cluster of casks and empty cloth sacks piled up in one corner. "The servants have been mixing it around all night, so it should be more than ready."

"Excellent. Now, where are my magicians?"

The two sorcerers were off to one side, poring over the book. There seemed to be some sort of discussion going on. The duke watched for a moment, then nodded to Treadwell. "Just run over there, will you? Let them know we are ready whenever they are."

Treadwell bowed and scurried over. There was more discussion and quite a bit of hand waving. In the end, the sorcerers collected their things and moved to the water's edge. Treadwell rejoined his master. "It will just take them a few minutes, Your Grace," he said. "As I understand it, one will create an enormous channel of power, which the other will split into one hundred separate streams. Each of these will strike the pool in a separate place. In theory, this should start the creation process at one hundred individual points inside the vat. Er, the pool. Then, we just wait for them to emerge."

The duke clapped his hands, rubbing them together. "Excellent. Can't wait."

It took several minutes to prepare, what with moving the magicians' equipment to the shore of the pool, sampling the water to ensure everything had been mixed properly, and triple checking the book. There seemed to be some sort of discussion going on about the book. Revka pretended not to notice, but inside she was screaming. Any minute now, they were going to realize what was up and call the whole thing off. Any minute now...

The discussion between the magicians finally ended with one of them making the vocal equivalent of a shrug and moving over to the very edge of the water. He raised his arms into the air, muttering something under his breath. A blue-white glow began to emanate from his fingers. The glow brightened and grew to engulf his hands. Suddenly, the light shot upward. Two beams helixed around each other, up and up, then joined in a giant circle of light. An intricate pattern like a dream catcher throbbed within the circle, the pattern dividing into dozens of sinister shapes.

Behind him, the other magician began to chant. The book floated in front of him, supported on a puff of luminous green cloud. The words...

Well, they weren't really words, as far as Revka could tell. They were more shaped sounds, magic carved into raw syllables. He raised one hand, which began to glow just like the first magician's. The light grew brighter as the chant went on. Revka fancied she could see the words on the page glowing with their own light, but it was probably her imagination.

With the final sonant, a bolt of magic flew from the second magician's hand to the great circle. The light spread out, filling the patterned space completely. A beat later, beams of raw magic shot out across the length and breadth of the pool. A hundred blue-white lances of energy stung the water, causing not even the tiniest ripple. The uniform, algae-green water began to glow so that the entire chamber was filled with bright illumination. After a moment, the water began to bubble and churn. The blue of the magic and green of the waters combined, casting a sickly pallor over everyone and everything. The bolts of magic snapped and roared, echoing and rebounding through the chamber, until the senses were overwhelmed with it all.

And then... silence.

The magic stopped. The glow of the water faded. Only the sparse torchlight held back the darkness. Revka strained her eyes. It would be a good minute or two before she could see properly. The cave was quiet, save for a sickly bubbling noise coming from the pool.

Revka tugged at her bonds. The rope was new and in very good shape. There weren't any sharp objects on the post, so no way to do anything about that. Besides, what if she did get free? How were they going to get past the duke and all of his guards and so on? She slumped back against Iyarra and waited to see what would happen next.

At first, nothing seemed to be happening at all. Then the bubbling of the water increased, followed by a sizzling sound. Revka's eyes were drawn toward the lake. Little hillocks of green water seemed to rise, then settle down again. Then they stopped receding and just kept growing. Even distant ones on the other side of the pool were becoming visible. If she squinted, she could almost tell herself that she was beginning to see shapes.

The water was churning hard and had taken on an odd, thick consistency, like some sort of primordial ooze. Waves rippled slowly over the mounds that were now rising up above the surface of the water. Revka could just see the beginnings of a head on some of the nearby shapes. There were other details, slight suggestions of legs...and tails. Revka let out a breath. It *had* worked.

The duke was not going to be happy.

One of the shapes nearest the shore began to bob its way closer. The green sludge began to slide away, revealing the form underneath. There were murmurs of consternation as the... the *thing* stepped ashore and shook itself dry.

There was a long, dangerous silence. Without taking his eyes off of the creature, the duke coughed. "Treadwell," he said calmly, quietly. "What exactly am I looking at?"

Treadwell sighed. "It appears to be a small horse, Your Grace. Er, a pony. A pink one, in fact."

The pony bounded up to the duke, eyes shining bright. "Hi there!" it chirped. "Would you like to be friends?" By this time, several more were splashing happily through the water, headed for the shore. There were blue ones, green ones, even a couple of purple ones. They called out to each other, cheering and laughing as they made their way to the duke's retinue. A couple had wandered over to Iyarra and were enthusiastically conversing with her.

Some of the senior officers stepped forward, swords sliding from their sheaths. The ponies hopped and skipped out of the way of the slashing blades, laughing as they went. A few had wandered over to the magicians' equipment, poking around and making "Ooo" noises.

Revka managed to flag down a lime green pony as it skipped by. "Excuse me?"

"Hi!" The cheerful thing cantered over to her. "Are you playing a game?"

Revka thought fast. "Why uh, yes." She smiled. "Me and my friend here are playing a game called, 'See Who Can Free Us from This Pole the Fastest.' Would you like to play?"

"Would I!?" The pony capered in its excitement. Soon there were a half dozen of them, all tugging at the knots and shackles. Off to one side, a ring of dancing ponies circled a clerk, singing about how nice it was to be in a cave. He kept trying to slip out, but the circle traveled right along with him. All the while, there were more and more ponies splashing up to the surface and getting absolutely everywhere. The noise was tremendous.

In the middle of the chaos, the duke stood fuming. Not that you could tell by looking. If anything, his facial expression was more placid than ever. The slightest ripple of heat distortion rose from the top of his head, but it may have just been a trick of the light. He strode his way through the multicolored din to the magicians, who were flipping frantically through the book and shooing away ponies. They paled as he approached.

The duke folded his arms and raised an eyebrow at them. "Well?"

One of them shuffled forward. "Er, it seems apparent that the pages in the book have gotten shuffled around, er, Your Grace. We've done the best we can trying to get it organized, but frankly..."

"Yes, yes. I see." He rubbed his temples for a moment. "Fine. Fine. Just figure out where you went wrong and fix it. In the meantime," he turned to his guards. "Kill these things. Somebody drag them outside and, I don't know, use them for target practice or something." He glared at Revka and Iyarra. "Looks like we'll have a few extra test subjects after all. I suppose you don't have— Yes, what is it?" he snapped at the lackey who had been trying to get his attention for several seconds.

"Er, Your Grace? There's an army outside here to see you. Well, several armies actually. They say it's urgent."

Chapter Twenty-four

THERE WAS A BATTLE, if you could call it that. Actually, in the official report, the skirmish that ensued was referred to as "a temporary failure to surrender." The armies swarmed through the mines. There was no chance of the duke's scant forces resisting.

Revka and Iyarra watched the aftermath from a shady spot outside the mine. They had been freed and helped back up to the surface. The duke and his generals had already been hauled away in chains, and everyone else was being led out of the mine as well. Off to one side, several of the ponies were putting on an impromptu musical number about sharing. The song was rather catchy, actually.

"It was nice of the magicians to take the curse-marks off of us," Iyarra said.

Revka shrugged. "Well, it just goes to show what you get if you ask nice."

Iyarra snorted. "You call 'Take these things off of us right now, or so help me these guys will chop your lips off'' asking nicely?"

Revka smirked. "Well, *comparatively* nice, all things considered. Anyway, it worked." She rolled up her sleeve for what must have been the tenth time in an hour. Yup, still gone. She grinned. The future was definitely looking up.

"One of you by the name of Revka?" A large, bearded man covered in armor approached the two women, looking from one to the other. Revka recognized the crest on his shoulders and raised an eyebrow. Well, this certainly *was* getting attention from high places. She waved a hand at the soldier. "Right here."

The soldier strode over and held out an oblong object wrapped in cloth. "Father Eliot said you'd probably be here and that you would know about the book." He unwrapped the cloth and let it fall away. "This it?"

Revka looked. "Yup." She grinned. Such a ratty old thing, and yet it managed to cause so much trouble. *Kind of like us, really.*

"Okay. Only he said he'd like you to take the book back to Kalazad yourselves. He said you know the way as well as anyone. We'd go ourselves, but we've got to drag these clowns down to the capital for trial. You think you can handle it?"

Revka took the book and turned it over a couple of times. She looked up at Iyarra, who smiled. "Not a problem."

"Good." He grunted and turned away to yell at some soldiers. Another troop was leading a line of prisoners out of the mine. Iyarra brightened as she saw the procession. She hopped up to her hooves and galloped over. "Daddy!"

"Hello, *Puya*." Toth gave his girl a one armed hug. He and several other centaurs had emerged, all dressed in full armor and packing some serious weaponry. "You're all right, I see?"

"Daddy, what are you doing here?"

"Oh, the elves picked us up as they came through." He smiled. "What do you think, eh? My old armor, and it still fits!" He laughed, then patted her. "I think we're going to drop these prisoners off, then head back up toward the plains. I'll let your mother know you're all right, yes?"

Iyarra nodded and gave him a quick peck on the cheek. "Thank you, Daddy." There were some amused chuckles from behind. Toth waved a hand at them irritably. "All right, all right. Let's get going, eh?"

Next to emerge were the elves. The gaily embroidered gowns were gone, replaced by armor, lots of armor. The sun glinted off of chain, plate, and some exquisitely sharp swords. The one in charge wore a full-face helmet. The tall thing shaped a portrait of elegant menace. The leader seemed to notice Revka and Iyarra, and the elf army moved toward them.

There was a moment as the helmet came off, then King Lemuel smiled down at them. "Hello, you two. I'm glad to see you made it out intact. Oh, and without your curse-marks, I notice."

"Yep, all taken care of." Revka cast an eye over the battalion of elves standing behind the king. "This your army?"

Lemuel coughed. "Actually, they're my legal team. We're very *vigorous* about defending our business interests." He leaned forward. "By the way," he added. "Na wanted me to tell you it was very clever of you, sending them that message via the resonating crystal. We were able to muster up and get onto the main road in no time. Once we got near the castle, we ran into the capital's army. Seems they were heading the same way. We told them what we knew, and we all headed down here together."

Revka waved a hand. "I can't take credit for that. It was Iyarra's idea. I just sent the message while we were on the road to the mine."

Iyarra shrugged. "Well, I remembered what they said about sending messages. Figured it might work."

"Fantastic." He hesitated a moment, looking away. There appeared to be something on his mind. "Listen, while I have you here..." He gestured toward the ponies. Most of them had wandered off and were now resting in the sun. "The ponies. Where in the world did they come from?"

"Oh, that was us. We uh, swapped a couple pages around in the magic book." She held it up by way of explanation.

"So the ponies...have no owner?"

Revka shrugged. "I guess they own themselves."

Lemuel looked back over at the colorful herd, pursing his lips in thought. "Interesting..."

Just then, one of the ponies noticed him looking at them and wandered over. "Hiya, mister! Would you like to be friends?"

Lemuel's face broke into a deeply sincere smile. "Why yes, yes I think I would." He knelt down face to face with the pony. "My name is Lemuel. And what is yours?"

"My name is Amber Rose."

"Well now, Amber Rose, do you and your friends like making people happy?"

"Do we ever!"

"Really? Well, that is good news." He beamed. "You see, we have a city where people come to be happy, hundreds of visitors a day. I just bet they would adore getting to visit you and have a good time learning your songs. Tell me, do you have an agent?"

The pony tilted its head. "What's an agent?"

"An agent. A manager. Professional representation."

"Pro-fess...uhm..."

"Never mind. It doesn't matter." He rose. "Shall we go talk to your other pony friends?"

"Okay!"

"Wonderful. And do call me Uncle Lem."

Revka watched them wander off toward the other ponies. She looked up at Iyarra. "You think we should say something?"

"They'll probably be fine. But I'll take some of them aside later and give them a little advice, if you think it would be a good idea."

"Tell them the magic words are 'percentage of the gross'."

211

"Those are magic words?"

"Trust me."

***

The soldiers had carted the duke's men off to face justice. The centaurs and elves were headed back to their homes, the latter with a procession of singing ponies in their wake. The next day, Revka and Iyarra headed east again, just the two of them. Back on the road to Kalazad.

"You know," said Revka as they trotted along. "I believe this is about where those bandits got to us. I bet we could find their camp again. Probably even see if they have a treasure hoard. We've got time to look, now."

"Well yeah, but...those bodies. The bandits, I mean. They've been there about, what, a month now?"

"Ooo. Good point."

"Yeah."

They walked on.

"You know, when we've got the book back to the monks, maybe we could go back to the elf city, hang out there a while."

"All right. But let's not take any shortcuts this time. Drakul mating season is coming up."

"I hear ya." Revka sighed and hugged Iyarra. "I hope the monks won't be too mad at us that we switched the pages around."

"I think it was a good idea. Certainly bought everyone some time and made it easier to round everyone up. Besides, we can always swap it back."

"Oh, I dunno." Revka grinned. "I think it works better this way. You know, in case anybody ever tries that again."

Iyarra giggled. "That's terrible! But I see your point."

"Oh, sure. The minute I saw that duke guy, I said to myself, 'There's a guy who needs some pretty ponies in his life.'"

"Oh you did, did you?"

"Well, it worked for me." Revka gave Iyarra a squeeze.

Iyarra blushed, her ears flicking. "Silly."

"You!"

The shout startled the women. Suddenly, there was the sound of a cart skidding to a halt. A weather-beaten old man in a farmer's smock leaped off the front of his hay cart and brandished an accusatory finger at Iyarra. "Two months! Two months you owe me! And you took off just before the harvest too. Damn your eyes! Bill! Carl! Jessie! Get over here now!"

Three burly young men jumped off the back of the cart. They were carrying hay forks and seriously grim expressions.

Revka leaned forward to Iyarra. "Uhm, is that..."

"Farmer Green," Iyarra whispered. "Wasn't expecting to see him again."

"You took off owing me two months of labor," he snarled. "Nobody gets the best of me, you hear? Nobody." The four men surrounded the centaur and her rider, watching them like hawks, waiting for them to make a move.

Revka glanced back and forth between them, then at the road. There was no one else visible, no guards around. Oh, well...she leaned forward again and whispered in Iyarra's ear.

"Okay," she said. "Here's my plan..."

Villians of Kalazad

(Kalazad – Book 2)

Chapter One

LISTEN!

THIS IS THE Hell of Unfinished Stories.

In this place are the crippled tales: sagas with no end, two-part trilogies. Victims of time, writer's block, and circumstance. All the stories once begun but never ended.

Here, in a Victorian drawing room, a detective stands over a dead body and waits for an insight which never, never comes.

Here, in a dungeon in an ogre's cave, two princes await rescue from their brother who, having suddenly found his older siblings missing and the throne all to himself, decided to give up adventuring and take up politics instead.

Here, in a windowless brick house, a lone pig chokes down another energy drink, rubs his eyes, and goes back to scanning a wall of security monitors in search of a wolf long since dead of trichinosis.

They all float here, nebulous in the never-never land between the pages. Fantasy, tragedy, drama, romance: all frozen in time, spinning in eternal limbo, groping blindly to unlistening ears, and all desiring one thing:

An Ending.

And just lately, there seems to be a lot more of them.

***

Once upon a time, there was a little girl who lived with her mother in a cabin by the woods. And she had a lovely red riding cloak which she wore all the time, and for this reason she was known as Little Red Riding Hood.

One day when she was five, her mother sent her through the woods to deliver a basket of goodies to her grandmother, who was feeling poorly. "Be careful," said the mother, "For there is a big, bad wolf in the forest, and he eats little girls. So never stray from the trail, and hurry back as quickly as you can."

Little Red Riding Hood did as she was told, skipping through the woods and never giving a moment's thought to the big bad wolf, or to wandering off the narrow trail which snaked through the heart of the forest. Nor did she give a thought to the fact that her mother, being fully aware that a man-eating wolf was on the prowl, nevertheless sent her five-year-old child into the woods alone while she stayed at home. Little Red Riding Hood didn't think about a lot of things.

While she was strolling along through the woods, she heard a curious sound. It was rather like a windstorm, but it came on suddenly and stopped almost as soon as it had started. There had been a hollow sort of quality to it, and what might have been a muffled yip at the end. Little Red Riding Hood waited for a moment by the edge of the trail, to see if more was forthcoming, but after a moment it was clear that there wasn't. So, she went hoppity-skip down the trail to Grandma's house which smelled like feet and came back as quickly as she politely could and never gave it another thought ever.

Little Red Riding Hood grew up and settled down with an itinerant woodcutter some twenty years her senior. Grandma choked on a bone in her gruel and was discovered a few weeks later. The riding hood, once outgrown by its owner, got demoted to dust cloths.

And nobody ever saw the big bad wolf again.

***

The rains of the morning had moved away west, and the sun was drying out the road as the centaur Iyarra loped unhurriedly along. On her back, her girlfriend Revka munched a mid-morning apple and fussed with her hair.

Iyarra glanced back. "How's it going back there?"

Revka worked another burr free, and flicked it away into the woods. "Think I've almost got 'em out of my hair, at least. Pretty sure there's one in my boot, plus a couple of other places I won't get into. I swear those things, they get everywhere."

Iyarra reached back a chestnut brown hand, and patted her girlfriend. "Sorry about that. Guess we missed 'em because it was so dark when we made camp."

Revka grumped. "Mm, well, we wouldn't have had that problem at an inn, that's all. I know you prefer sleeping outdoors but I kinda got used to having a bed, you know?"

That was true, at least. After they'd trekked halfway across the continent and back again to stop a mad duke from building an army of magic soldiers, Revka had definitely needed a week or two to clear her head. The monks who guarded the magic book stolen by the duke were very grateful, of course. But, as monks were notoriously short on material wealth, the girls'd had to settle for some provisions and a promise of shelter any time they felt like climbing up the mountain trail to the monastery again.

Revka frowned at the memory. "You'd think that that would have at least been good for some kind of reward, though, wouldn't you? I mean, I'm not asking for a knighthood, but maybe a medal or two, royal commendation. Sack of cash. You know."

"Oh, me too," Iyarra maneuvered around a dead badger in the road. "But you know what they said."

"Yeah, yeah." Revka rolled her eyes. "Them and their 'Delicate political situation'." Her voice took on a sarcastic lilt. "'The general feeling is that everyone is better off just pretending nothing happened'. Real convenient. Means they don't have to reward us or anything."

Iyarra shrugged. "Well, you can kind of see what they mean. I'm sure the king has got enough to worry about without word getting out about how close things came."

"Eh, maybe. But I bet the king didn't wake up this morning with burrs on his butt."

Iyarra stifled a laugh. "Revka!"

"Not that he'd have to pick them off himself," Revka added. "I bet he's got someone for that. It's probably a special job with a title and everything."

Iyarra covered her mouth, desperately trying to suppress a giggle.

Revka sat up, her old leather armor creaking as she did so. "Oh, Lord, can't you just see it? The king ringing a little bell for a servant. 'What is it, your majesty?' 'A great crisis has come upon our land,'" now Revka was sitting bolt upright, one hand draped over her chest while she spoke in a high nasal tone. "'A burr has been visited upon Our posterior. Send for the Royal Burr Picker at once!'

"Suddenly, a flourish of trumpets! And there he is, the Pluckmaster General! Resplendent in his spiky jodhpurs, holding high his ceremonial golden tongs—"

"Uhm, Revka?"

"The king bends over, somewhere a drum begins to roll–"

"Revka..."

"The Archbishop douses the afflicted area with holy water just as the–"

"Revka!"

"What?"

"Royal guards."

Revka blinked. "What? What about them?"

Iyarra tilted her head forward. "Royal guards. Coming this way."

Indeed they were. There were four of them, heading the opposite way down the road from the two girls. Revka & Iyarra kept quiet as the guards went by, their faces carefully blank. It wasn't until the guards were around the corner and out of sight that the girls dared look each other in the eye. Almost immediately they began to laugh, and kept it up until other travelers on the road began to look at them strangely.

Iyarra smiled back at her girlfriend. "Feeling better, I take it?"

Revka grinned. "Yeah, I suppose." She leaned forward, giving Iyarra a quick pat. "So, what now?"

The centaur shrugged. "I don't know. I thought maybe we'd head south ahead of the winter, maybe find somewhere warm this year if you like."

Revka pursed her lips. "Okay, we can do that. I know you're no fan of the snow and cold. Maybe we can hit a beach somewhere. Or..." She trailed off

Iyarra waited a moment, but nothing was forthcoming. "Or what?" Revka didn't reply. She just nudged the centaur, and pointed. A family was passing them in a farm cart. One of the children was wearing a rough, cheaply made tunic upon which was emblazoned the legend: I Hath Bene To Ye Enchanted Foreste, As May Be Vouchfafed By These Words Upon My Shyrte.

Revka turned to Iyarra. She smiled.

"Fancy a vacation?"

***

Opinions differ as to the exact nature of the Enchanted Forest. There are some who say it is the site of an ancient magical accident. There are others who claim the area is under a curse of some kind. There are some who say that there is nothing unusual at all at work: it is

217

simply the brain's natural predilection for seeing patterns where none exist, like buying a blue cart and then suddenly seeing them everywhere. There are even those who staunchly believe that the whole thing is a put-on, cooked up to bring in the tourist money.

But the fact of the matter is, the Enchanted Forest has earned a reputation over the years for generating more stories, yarns, tales, sagas and fables per acre than any other spot in the world. Animals walk and talk, there's magic swords and rings all over the place, wishes are granted in the most ironic way possible as a matter of course. When, a few years previous, a boy traded the family cow for a bag of beans which turned out to be perfectly ordinary and not magic in any way, it was the talk of the forest for months afterward.

Unsurprisingly, once word of the forest got around, it became a popular tourist destination. People of all sorts flocked there: wandering troubadours in search of fresh material, fair (or at least reasonable in a good light) maidens with an interest in handsome princes or vice versa. There was also a steady stream of swineherds, woodcutters, and would-be adventurers, all hoping to get caught up in some of that fairy tale magic.

There were also families, and lots of them. And this was odd because, when you get right down to it, most fairy tales weren't really what anyone would call family-friendly. Oh, they often involved children. And usually there was an important lesson to be learned. But they were never really *nice*. Get past the bowdlerized versions and later editions with tacked-on happy endings, down to the bone where the oldest stories live, and they are filled with blood and teeth and gore. Lessons learned are brutal, and even the good guys can be pretty sketchy. Even when the woodchopper *does* come, you can expect to spend a little time in a wolf's stomach.

Fairy tales aren't nice.

Fairy tales are *nasty*.

Available Fall 2021

About K.L Mitchell

K.L. Mitchell was raised all over the south in a series of increasingly tiny towns until she finally joined the Air Force out of a desire for some Culture. She's spent most of her professional life working on computers in one capacity or another, and occasionally manages to get them to actually work.

She's been writing for fun most of her life, and for publication since about 2011. She's written for multiple websites and local publications, and in 2013 was a recurring columnist for the Kansas City Star. She lives with a gray cat named Molly and would like to be an astronaut when she grows up.

Connect with ...

Email: k_l_mitchell@mail.com
Facebook: https://www.facebook.com/KLMitchellHere/

Cover Design By : Rachel George
www.rachelgeorgeillustration.com

Note to Readers:

Thank you for reading a book from Desert Palm Press. We appreciate you as a reader and want to ensure you enjoy the reading process. We would like you to consider posting a review on your preferred media sites and/or your blog or website.

For more information on upcoming releases, author interviews, contests, giveaways and more, please sign up for our newsletter and visit us at Desert Palm Press: www.desertpalmpress.com and "Like" us on Facebook: Desert Palm Press.

Bright Blessings

www.ingramcontent.com/pod-product-compliance
Lightning Source LLC
Chambersburg PA
CBHW051130020726
47501CB00005B/1438